For Jamie, Jackson, and Leah, who inspire me to be a better man, and bring joy and purpose to my life.

Acknowledgements

There is a common phrase that says, "No man is an island." In no endeavor have I found this to be more accurate than in the completion of this book. There are many people who deserve credit for the development and refinement of this work, so I would like to take a few moments to recognize them.

First and foremost, I would like to thank my loving wife, who encouraged me, even when this seemed like another one of my temporary hobbies. Not only did she provide a steady source of encouragement, but she also sacrificed her very limited leisure time to help me in the editing process.

Next, I would like to say a special "thank you" to Jim "American Grouch" Dellinger. Jim is a very well-known and well-respected member of the Bushcraft USA community, and is the author of the popular "American Grouch Blog." I have never been to the Brooks Range/North Slope region, and had a great many questions about the climate, geography, and topography of this area. Jim, who had recently been on a caribou hunting trip to this region, took the time to patiently and informatively answer my questions. The descriptions that are true to the region are based mostly on the helpful explanations that I received from Jim (most of the trees in the area were my own imagining).

Ben and Allyson Potter also deserve mention. Allyson was the first person to whom I showed the very, very rough beginnings of my story. She encouraged me to continue with my efforts, despite my misgivings that my talents as a writer were severely limited. Equally as impactful was her husband, Ben. While it took me a while to work up the courage to show him a sample of the story, we occasionally talked about my endeavor to write a fiction novel. Every time we spoke, he always encouraged me to finish this book, even if I could only work on it little at a time. I'm not entirely sure that Allyson and Ben are aware of the great effect that their words had on me, but I truly believe that if it wasn't for their influence, I would have given up this attempt at writing long ago.

Terry Barney also deserves a hearty thanks. Terry is the developer of the Bushclass USA courses on the Bushcraft USA forums. These free courses teach individuals how to become more confident in the outdoors, by instilling them with the skills that they need to be a well-rounded outdoorsman. Many of the skills that are described in this book are skills that I have learned through participating in Bushclass USA. The lessons in the Bushclass series are worth hundreds of dollars, in my opinion (and in reality, if you take bushcraft classes from any number of schools), yet Terry graciously offers them to the bushcraft community for free. Several other notable members of the Bushcraft USA forums also donated their time and talents to make Bushclass a reality, so, from the bottom of my heart, thank you.

I would also like to thank Dan Barry and Brendan Berkley for all of their work designing the cover for this book. I couldn't be more pleased with the finished product!

Last, but certainly not least, I would like to thank those who read my manuscripts, both early and late, and offered helpful suggestions about how I could make this story better. I truly value your input, and more especially, your gesture of friendship and support. It is a big commitment to serve as a reader, and I truly appreciate the investment that you made in me and in this story.

Michael and Casey,

It has been great getting
to know you. I hope
you guys enjoy the story.
If you ever need anything,
don't hesitate to let me
know.

Brian Ady

Contents

Author's Note

This story came about quite unintentionally. It started back in the summer of 2014, as a simple discussion among friends about what 10 items we would take with us if we knew we would be stranded in the wilderness for an extended period of time. Each of us made the case for the items we would bring, and tried to convince the others why our particular list was the best. Even weeks after the conversation had ended, I found myself thinking about what items would be the most versatile, and allow me to survive in the wilderness.

This mental exercise slowly began to take on a life of its own. I found myself thinking through various scenarios of wilderness survival in which my items would need to be used. Over the course of a couple of time, the scenarios began to take on the form of a story, which ultimately became *this* story.

The main male character, Ryan, is by no means an expert. He makes mistakes, and lacks some skills that would make his experience in the wild much easier. However, I made him fallible for a two main reasons. First, to make the story more realistic; we all have varying levels of skill and confidence in the wild, but few people possess the skills and mental acuity to excel under the conditions described in this book. So, I wanted Ryan's level of skill to be on par with, that of the average person who has an interest in bushcraft. Second, I wanted to allow for you, the reader, to put yourself in Ryan's shoes, and theorize about what you might have done differently.

The Character of Paul

The boss in the story, Paul, was a difficult character for me to develop. I have the privilege of working at an institution where the administration is top-notch. Unlike the character of Paul, my bosses are sensitive to the needs of their staff, and go out of their way to ensure that we have what we need to do our jobs, and that we are happy in our employment.

Because of this, it was hard for me to develop the character of a boss who was insensitive, and even, at times, vindictive. If I have done a poor job of developing this character to his fullest potential, it is because I am blessed to work in a very positive and encouraging environment.

Gear in the story

The kit that Ryan takes with him is, with one or two minor exceptions, based entirely on the kit that I, the author, use in the outdoors. I own, and have used every piece of gear that is listed, and find that it works well for me. Your kit may be very different, and that is great, since that is what works best for you. However, I tried only to speak from experience, to make the story more realistic. Furthermore, the brand names listed in my book are not advertisements; I was just listing the gear that I use and that works for me – the gear that I would really take on such a trip, and currently take on most of my outings.

Wildlife

There are several encounters with wildlife in this story. I tried to approach descriptions of wildlife from the perspective of someone who was unacquainted with specific species in the Brooks Range area. So, names of animals used in this story may not belong to those that are native to the North Slope, but the main character is approaching them out of ignorance. I did a great deal of research before writing this, and am aware of which animals are native to this area, and which are not. There is a correlation between the descriptions of the wildlife in this story and wildlife that is actually native to the North Slope, however, the main character may misidentify some creatures.

Landscape

The Brooks Range/North Slope region was chosen as the setting of the story for one main reason. Despite notions to the contrary, it is very difficult to find an area in America that is more than a dozen miles from civilization. Had I used any other region for the story, it would have been a three or four day wilderness adventure, and not the challenging fight for survival that I wished to portray.

However, choosing this region presented me with a major challenge. This region is all tundra and grassland. The trees that do exist in this region are small and stunted, and are generally only found along the banks of rivers, streams and lakes. In all reality, survival in this setting would be particularly challenging, especially since the main character (and the author) is mostly familiar with the northeastern woodlands. In order to provide variety in the storyline, I inserted a few bands of forest that do not exist; I hope the readers will not hold this against me... this is fiction after all.

Chapter 1

The Adventure of a Lifetime?

"You need to decide what is more important…. And, Ryan, for *your* sake, make the right decision." My boss's words rang freshly in my mind as I closed the door to his office. This meeting hadn't been a friendly chat about the company picnic. I was in trouble, big trouble. I had the audacity to do something that no one in our small company had done for years – request an extended vacation.

On paper, we all had two weeks of vacation time, but no one ever used more than a day or two at a time, and even that was frowned upon. There was, however, one person who was the exception to this rule – Paul, my boss. "Time off makes someone else have to pick up your slack" and "be a team player" were some of the many words of wisdom he had on the subject of vacation time. No one ever dared to point out the hypocrisy of his position.

"What was that about?" asked Dean. He had apparently witnessed the whole ordeal from the relative safety of his cubicle.

"Just rocking the boat as usual," I said with a mischievous smile.

"What did you do this time?" Dean inquired, shaking his head slowly in disapproval.

"I asked for a raise."

"You didn't!" he gasped, unable to hide his shock.

"No, it's actually a little worse than that," I confessed. "I put in a formal request for a two-week vacation."

"Dude," he said, lowering his voice as the congenial grin vanished from his face. "What's up with you lately? You're going to get yourself fired."

I just shrugged my shoulders as I walked back toward my cubical.

What was up with me lately? Why was I feeling like this? Little did Dean know, but I had been asking myself the very same question for the past several days, but I just couldn't seem to figure out why a sudden change had come over me lately.

As I sat down in my well-worn chair, I noticed the empty seat in the cubical across from me. It was Kyle's cube. *Poor Kyle,* I thought. *I really don't think this was part of his five-year plan.*

It was Kyle, that's what was *really* bothering me. I didn't even know the guy all that well. He had been a permanent fixture across the aisle from me for as long as I could remember.

Kyle was a workaholic – always stayed late, always arrived early, and always volunteered to work weekends. He capitalized on every opportunity to chat with the boss at the water cooler and went to every office get-together after work. Rumor had it that his efforts were finally paying off. He would have been up for a big promotion next month, but now he was dead.

When I heard the news about Kyle's death last week, it felt like someone had punched me in the stomach. I kept thinking about how futile this rat race we call "life" seemed. Kyle had been working so hard to "get ahead" in life, whatever that meant. Anytime I would see him in the break room and ask him if he had any plans for the weekend, he would always shake his head and reply, "Nope. Just too busy right now. I'll have plenty of time for stuff like that later, once I'm established in life." Well, later never came for Kyle. Now here I was in the same pointless quest for success, trying to "get ahead," and for what? What did it get me in the end? Did it make me any happier? Did it add any years to my life? Did it give me any tangible benefit, other than a paycheck?

Kyle's death somehow haunted me. I kept thinking, *What if "later" never comes for me? Why am I doing this? Why am I here?*

Last night I had what I can only describe as a crisis moment. As I lay awake, plagued by a flood of existential questions, I decided that I wasn't going to make the same mistakes that Kyle had made. No, I was going to live my life while I could. I would do all the things that *I* wanted to do instead of putting them off for a day that may never come. At least this was what I told myself last night, in the comfort of my own bed, where I had no bosses to face, no fears of losing my job, and no condescending looks of scrutiny from my coworkers. But, the next morning, as I placed the ominous vacation request form on my boss's desk, I couldn't help but wonder if I was doing the right thing. There was so much at stake. On one hand lay my long-term financial security and, on the other, my personal happiness. Who could say which was more essential? And, more importantly, did they have to be mutually exclusive?

Now, after my ill-fated meeting in my boss's office, one thing had been made very clear to me – I had a decision to make. My boss had all but said that, if I took this two-week vacation, I wouldn't have a job when I got back. However, if I gave in to his ultimatum now, I knew that I would be stuck in a cycle of subservience. It would be the death knell of my chances of happiness, at least while I was trapped in a loathsome job with a tyrant for a boss.

As I sat in my cubicle, staring off into space, weighing my options, my mind began to wander.

I had always liked the outdoors, even as a small child. I couldn't count the hours I had spent exploring the forests around my childhood home. As I grew older, my interest in the outdoors continued to increase. This passion had made me somewhat of an anomaly in the business world. I had always felt like I didn't fit in, probably because, in all reality, I didn't. All of my coworkers were more concerned with keeping up with the Joneses, and even the Kardashians, than with staying in touch with nature. While I took pleasure in the great outdoors – backpacking, camping, hunting, and fishing – they took pleasure in the "great indoors." They talked about their 401(k)s and their most recent stock purchases, while I talked about my most recent hike. It was almost as if they were so worried about getting ahead in life that they weren't bothering to live it. And, the thing that bothered me the most was, I had recently felt myself beginning to be pulled into their style of living.

Sitting there in my cubicle, carefully weighing these thoughts against the words my boss had just spoken to me, I felt like I needed to do something frivolous, something crazy, something adventurous.

Ever since I was in middle school, I had fostered this half-baked idea of going to Alaska and living in the wilderness. I dreamed of building a cabin in the middle of nowhere and living a quiet, simple life. Now, as I sat in a high-rise office building of a prestigious accounting firm, I realized that I was living anything but the simple life. At 28, I was a junior partner making six figures a year. Sure, it sounded good when someone asked what I did for a living, but, in reality, I felt like the cost of my success was too great. It seemed like I was losing my identity in the process of gaining wealth. It was almost like I was selling out, sacrificing my true self in order to live the kind of life that society told me I should want to live.

As I processed these thoughts, I began to wish that there was some undiscovered frontier that I could explore or some remote jungle that I could lose myself in. Deep down, even though I may have wanted to, I knew that I couldn't actually just leave everything and move to the wilderness. However, if I had the courage to stand up to my boss, I could experience a short reprieve from the life that I was beginning to dread.

For two glorious weeks, I could escape to the wild, to Alaska, just like I had always dreamed of doing. For two weeks, I could forget all the troubles that came with the financial success that I had been seeking. However, there was a very real possibility that my two-week vacation would really be a permanent vacation, unless I could somehow find a way to smooth things over with Paul. All of these thoughts swirled around in my mind in a dizzying vortex of thought.

Slowly, my mind came back to the present moment and I realized that, for quite some time, I had been staring blankly at my computer screen. I had opened a window to start an email to Paul, but I had been too consumed by my thoughts to actually type anything. Now, almost reluctantly, and with great deliberation, I began to compose an email to my boss.

"Upon considering your suggestion," it began, "I have taken the time to decide what, as you put it, 'is more important.' Therefore, I ask that my vacation request form be processed in its current state and that my vacation days be reserved on the company calendar. I appreciate your guidance in this matter. Thank you for helping me to reach the proper conclusion. Sincere Regards, Ryan."

I cringed as I moved my cursor over the "send" button and clicked. It was too late to call back those words now. I had made my decision, and, whether or not I had just lost my job, one thing was certain – I was going to Alaska!

****

This was going to be the adventure of a lifetime, that's what I kept telling myself. I couldn't believe that I was actually doing this. I was preparing for 10 days of hiking, canoeing, camping, and fishing in the Alaskan wilderness. It was going to be great! Just me, my gear, and a guide. No cell phone reception, no TV, no internet, no crowds. No emails to answer, no clients to pacify, no traffic to sit in, no office gossip, no troubling news stories to hear, no worries.

Instead of hearing car horns blaring as I sit in a gridlock of traffic, I would hear geese honking while I watched the sun sink below the pristine horizon. Instead of the grating sounds of road construction, I would be lulled by the soothing ripples as my canoe drifted lazily along a winding stream. I felt like I was going to be just like the trappers and longhunters of old, like Jedidiah Smith or Daniel Boone. It was a boyhood dream come true, and it was really happening... the adventure of a lifetime.

I spent every free moment over the next few weeks feverishly searching for a guide who wasn't already booked for the season. Had I planned this vacation a year in advance, I would have had no problem, but I was flying by the seat of my pants with this whole "spur of the moment trip" thing. After desperately searching, and nearly giving up on finding a guide, I received a phone call from a well-respected outfitter who had just had a cancellation.

"I like your style," Jake said as I explained that I wanted to "rough it" as much as possible. I could tell right away that we would get along famously.

"I'm not coming out there to stay at the Hilton," I replied. "I want this wilderness adventure to be just that, a *wilderness* adventure." Looking back, I wonder if I wouldn't have been better off staying at the Hilton.

After a little more small talk, Jake said he would send me a recommended packing list. His company, Wandering Bear Outfitters, would take care of the gear for fishing, canoeing, and camping, and the food. I was on my own for everything else.

After I hung up the phone, I was struck by the realization that I had a lot of packing to do and not very much time to do it in. I glanced across my bedroom to look at the calendar hanging on the wall. It was July 27, and the tentative start date for my 10-day trip was August 5. That left me only nine days to finish my preparations and get out to Fort Yukon, Alaska. I cursed myself for not allowing enough time to properly plan this trip, but, deep down, I was just glad to be getting away from it all, even if I did have to run around like a madman to get myself ready in time.

After reviewing Jake's recommended packing list, and making some alterations, I finally settled on a loadout. Aside from the clothing I would be wearing, I decided to bring:

LA Police Gear Operator Pack, containing:

-1 32 oz. Nalgene bottle
-1 Sawyer Mini Water Filter
-1 Bottle of water purification tabs (25 count)
-1 Handheld LED flashlight
-1 LED headlamp
-1 Glock 20, with extra magazine and holster
-25 Rounds 10mm ammo
-1 Mossberg 500 Persuader (recommended by Jake for bear protection)
-15 3" mag rifled slugs
-1 Swedish Military Poncho
-2 Pairs of wool socks
-1 2-person emergency blanket

-1 Silky Gomboy 270 folding saw

-1 Gransfors Bruks Small Forest Axe

-1 Survive! Knives GSO 5.1 in leather sheath

-1 Stilwell Knives Model Five in leather sheath

-1 Spyderco Endura

-1 Leatherman multi-tool

-1 Small sharpening stone

-1 Small leather strop

-2 4 Mil 55-gallon drum liners

-1 Pair of work gloves

-1 Wool cap

-1 Box UCO Stormproof matches (25 matches)

-1 3/8"x3" ferro rod

-1 Handkerchief

-1 Safety razor

-1 50' roll duct tape

-2 Rolls camp toilet paper

-1 Sleeping bag (rated to 0 degrees)

-1 Bed roll

-1 Small first aid kit

-1 Field Notes booklet

-1 Ballpoint pen

-1 Map of Alaska

After considering all of my travel options, I decided that it would be best to head to Alaska a couple of days early, just to give myself a buffer against flight cancellations or any other unforeseen delays. Besides, adding some extra time to my trip wasn't much of an issue at this point. After receiving my email, Paul, called me into his office and unceremoniously fired me on the spot, explaining that "the company had to do what it had to do to make it through these tough economic times." He and I both knew the real reason he was firing me, though. So, at this point, I had all the time in the world, and I intended to make the most of it.

The night before I left, I nervously checked and rechecked my list, making sure that I had everything I thought I would need. I had read plenty of horror stories of people who had gotten themselves into some pretty rough situations in the wild by overlooking one or two seemingly trivial items when packing, and I definitely did *not* want to be one of them.

The morning of my flight was something of a blur. With my excitement and apprehension about this trip, security checks, the hassle of checking my firearms, navigating to the correct terminal, and boarding my flight, I never really had much of a chance to reflect on the fact that this was the start of a journey that had been a lifetime in the making. However, there would be plenty of time for me to revel in my excitement later.

Before I knew it, I was 30,000 feet above the ground, traveling toward the West Coast at close to the speed of sound. Now, all I had to do was catch a connecting flight in Seattle, and I would be safely on my way to Fairbanks, Alaska. After that, things would get a little more interesting; I would have to charter a single-engine plane to fly me to Fort Yukon, Alaska, where I would then embark with my guide on a journey into the great, untouched wilderness of Alaska.

I was not looking forward to the single-engine flight, but I figured that it would probably be a pretty cool experience once I got used to being in such a small plane. At least, that's what I told myself.

With layovers, baggage collection, the connecting flight and, finally, the chartered flight, I arrived in Fort Yukon nearly 18 hours after I had left my hometown. I was worn out, but I was also extremely excited that I was this much closer to starting my once-in-a-lifetime adventure.

I found it hard to sleep in the tiny shack that would serve as my "hotel" for the next couple of days, until my adventure began. This cabin was part of the package that had come with my adventure. It was where all of Wandering Bear Outfitter's clients stayed until their trip began.

As I surveyed the interior of the little cabin, the room was comfortable enough and had a quaint hominess about it, but I was restless and wanted to get out and start exploring as soon as it was light outside.

I woke suddenly to the sound of my alarm going off, forgetting that I had set it the night before. I immediately got up and started a pot of coffee while taking in the delightful sight of this rustic cabin as it began to fill with the first rays of the morning sun. It seemed like the beginning of the perfect day for an adventure. The only problem was, I still had two days to wait until my wilderness excursion actually started. I would have to find something to do to occupy my time while I impatiently waited for the 5th of August to arrive.

On a whim, I decided I would ask around this little village to see if it was possible to charter a flight to Point Barrow, the northernmost point in America. I had always considered it a pipe dream to visit Point Barrow, but now that I was actually here in Alaska and had a couple of days to kill, I figured that it wouldn't hurt to try to turn that dream into a reality. The worst that could happen would be that I wouldn't be able to charter a flight, and I would just have to spend the day exploring the majestic countryside around this village.

After I had finished my coffee and a hastily consumed breakfast of cold Pop-Tarts, I eagerly made my way outside of my little cabin and into the village. It didn't take long for the villagers to recognize me as an outsider. After all, in a town of only 600 residents, everybody knows everybody.

The people that I met were very friendly, and, as I was soon informed, several of the residents of Fort Yukon had their own airplanes (a common thing in much of Alaska). However, try as I would, I wasn't able to convince anybody to fly me as far north as Point Barrow. I was growing discouraged and considered giving the whole thing up when one of the villagers approached me on the street and said, "You the guy that wants to go to Point Barrow? Try Harold, he's probably crazy enough to do it." He pointed to a rather nondescript house a few hundred yards away.

Despite my initial misgivings about his appearance, Harold turned out to be a nice guy. By my best guess, he looked to be in his mid-to-late fifties, with wavy grey hair that had just a hint of black sprinkled in and a thick, bushy grey beard. I was actually surprised by the strength of his grip as he shook my hand. For a relatively thin guy he was a lot stronger than he looked. He lit a cigarette as we talked over the trip.

"Might as well see some of the countryside on the way up," he said, the smoke pouring lazily out of his mouth as he spoke. "Some pretty country out by Lookout Ridge. You might want to see Liberator Lake and Birthday Pass too."

"Is it going to add a lot of time onto the flight?" I asked, anxious to conclude negotiations and get on our way to Point Barrow.

"About an hour," he replied, with no further comment on the issue.

"How much do you charge?" I asked, finally getting to the issue of money.

"How much you got?" he shot back with a good-natured chuckle. "I'm just joshin' you kid. Thousand sounds 'bout right." He looked me in the eye with as good of a poker face as I had ever seen. I knew very little about chartering flights, having only done it once before, so, for all I knew, I could be getting a steal or he could be ripping me off.

"Well, this is a once-in-a-lifetime trip, so I might as well go all out," I reasoned. We shook hands again to seal the deal, then I counted out ten crisp $100 bills into Harold's upturned, grease-stained palm.

"You don't mind if my daughter comes along for the ride, do ya?" he asked, almost as an afterthought. "She's up here visiting me during her summer break from college. Says she's bored. She ain't used to living in a small town like this. I think she could use a little adventure."

So, here I was, loading my gear into his tiny plane and wondering if even I would fit inside, let alone Harold, and now he wanted to try to squeeze a third person inside? I didn't want to seem unreasonable. After all, he was doing me a favor just by agreeing to fly me to Point Barrow, so, I reluctantly acquiesced.

"This here's my daughter, Bailey," said Harold, making the introduction as Bailey walked out of the front door of Harold's little house.

As I shook her hand, I was struck by the fact that the father and daughter were so dissimilar, yet, at the same time, so alike. She was thin, just like Harold, and of average height, and had similar facial features, but there the similarities ended. He was dressed in Carhartt pants and a flannel shirt and she was in trendy jeans, a designer long-sleeved t-shirt, and a chic jacket. His hair, somewhat disheveled, was short and greying, while her hair was long, well-kempt, and chestnut brown. His eyes were such a deep brown that they were nearly black, while her eyes were a strikingly vibrant hazel.

I must have gotten lost in these thoughts for a moment, because both Harold and Bailey were exchanging sidelong glances at one another as I ended my musings.

"You guys get inside while I give the plane a once over." Harold suggested, breaking the awkward silence.

Bailey and I squeezed aboard and began making small talk while Harold gave the plane a thorough preflight check. Apparently she was just visiting her dad for a little while and was getting ready to go back to the University of California, Berkeley, where she was majoring in journalism. She also informed me that she was minoring in liberal studies, whatever that meant, and was very active in her campus's chapter of Animal Activists for Animal Rights.

How do I get myself into these kinds of situations? I wondered. *Let's just hope she doesn't bring up politics, otherwise this is going to feel like the longest flight in the history of mankind.*

Call me paranoid if you like, but I've never liked the idea of being unprepared. So, before we loaded up the plane, I asked Harold if he would mind me taking my backpack and shotgun along, giving the excuse that I didn't want to leave all of my gear unattended back in town. However, the real reason was that I had probably watched too many movies about people getting stranded in the wilderness. There was a one-in-a-billion chance that something like that would happen in real life, but I felt better knowing that I would at least have a little "insurance" if I needed it.

The takeoff and initial stages of the flight went by without incident. Bailey and I had been talking for most of the flight, occasionally being interrupted by Harold pointing out various landmarks and points of reference along the way.

While Bailey and I came from two entirely different worlds and probably had very little, if anything, in common, there was an instantaneous rapport between us that I had never experienced before. As much as I wanted to dislike her at first, I now found myself strangely drawn to her effervescent personality. Even though I was normally reflective and introspective, I found myself being coaxed into a steady stream of conversation, encouraged by her pleasant smile.

We were a little over an hour and a half into the flight when Harold's expression began to change from carefree to a look of deep concern. He had just gotten done pointing out the eastern edge of Lookout Ridge when he became silent and contemplative. This may have been normal for some people, but, despite the short time I had known him, it seemed distinctly out of character for Harold. There was a tangible sense of uneasiness emanating from him, which quickly spread to Bailey and me. Soon the cockpit was filled with a palpable silence, in spite of the noise of the steadily droning engine. Finally, after what seemed to be hours, but was likely less than a minute, the voice of Harold broke the dreadful silence.

"Electrical fire," he said, in a half-shouting kind of way. "Guess that was what I smelled."

"What? What does that mean?" asked Bailey, with a slight quiver in her voice.

What does that mean? It means we're screwed, I said to myself, but managed to ask instead, "Is there anything we can do, Harold?"

A thick, acrid smoke was pouring into the cockpit as he yelled, "Help me look for a place to land! I've got to lose some altitude fast, before it's too late."

Bailey's eyes went wide with terror as she heard her father's words. "Are we going to die?" she asked pleadingly.

All I could manage to say was, "I don't know," as I asked myself the very same question.

We were diving fast, and the dreadful smoke was starting to fill the cabin, making my eyes water from the pungent smell.

"How can I tell a good place to land?" I shouted to Harold. I wasn't a pilot and didn't know the first thing about normal landings, let alone emergency landings.

"Look for a gap in the…" Harold stopped midsentence. We were all immediately aware of a deafening silence. The engine had just stopped.

"I can't see anywhere to land!" I yelled to Harold.

"Look harder!" he shouted. "We're going down one way or another, so help me find a place where we can do it without dying!"

Bailey was clutching at her father's shoulders from her position in the back seat of the plane. "Daddy," she pleaded, "Daddy, I'm scared. I don't want to die…" she trailed off as she started to sob.

The ground seemed to be racing upward to meet us as we plunged desperately toward the earth. I've heard that people think the strangest things when they are about to die. I found it odd that in that moment, I wasn't thinking about death, I wasn't thinking about family, or past girlfriends, or even an afterlife… I wasn't even sure that I was thinking about anything. It was almost as if I was completely enmeshed in the present moment, unaffected by the constraints of time. I was shaken from this reflection by a deafening whoop from Harold.

"Think I see a space I can squeeze into!" he shouted as the plane banked violently. "Coming in hot!" he screamed.

The plane leveled off to reveal a small, open space just below us. We were so close to the ground now that the wall of trees was almost touching the wings on either side as we continued our rapid descent.

I can say with no shame that I have absolutely no idea what happened during the next few seconds. My adrenaline surged as I saw the treetops rise above our heads. Then, looking through the clearing smoke inside the cabin, I noticed a solid wall of trees, directly in our path, a few hundred feet ahead. Things didn't look very hopeful in that moment. I knew that, with as fast as we were going, that wall of trees was going to turn this plane into a pile of rubble. With this realization, I closed my eyes, ducked my head, and gripped my knees, praying that we would somehow make it through.

I could hear a steady hiss as Harold let some breath out from between his pursed lips. Then I felt a thunderous jolt as the plane's wheels slammed into the uneven ground. I felt weightless as the plane rebounded from this impact, rising into the air again. I had just started to think that we were safely on the ground when I felt another jarring jolt, sending my body violently into the side of the plane.

I heard another sharp hiss as Harold sucked a quick breath in. The wheels pounded into the ground again, more violently than before, and the plane began to veer sharply to the right.

"This is it," I said to myself, as I prepared for the plane to spin out of control and mercilessly dash us into pieces against the unforgiving ground.

Suddenly, the plane lurched violently back to the left, and I felt another jolt, much softer than any of the others. This time I could hear the tires running steadily over the uneven ground below. We had finally touched down, but this perilous ride was far from over.

"Too fast, too fast, too fast," Harold chanted to himself in quick, staccato tones.

We were rolling along the bumpy ground for what seemed like an eternity. Unable to take the suspense any longer, I quickly sat upright and looked out the windscreen, only to wish I had stayed hunched over in the "crash position." To my horror, just ahead and rapidly approaching, was a staggered wall of ominous pine trees, standing like a row of hungry teeth about to devour their prey.

"Hold on tight!" shouted Harold.

A second later, we slammed into this solid wall of trees. There was a deafening bang, and then it seemed as if I was thrown in all different directions at once. Sound and motion all melded into an agonizing cacophony. I held my breath, waiting for the end, and then, as quickly as it had all begun, it was over.

So this is what death feels like, I reasoned. *It isn't as bad as I thought.*

"Harold?" Bailey's voice brought me back to reality. "Dad!"

"I'm here," Harold struggled to reply as he breathed heavily.

Cautiously, I opened my eyes to survey the damage. It took me a few moments to make sense of our current situation. I was now sitting next to Harold, the yoke of the plane slightly pushed into his chest. He was staring down at his left hand, which was covered in gashes, scrapes, and bruises. The windscreen was cracked and splintered into a thousand intertwining lines of broken glass. Much of the right wing was missing, and the left wing was totally gone. In the back, Bailey looked disheveled. Her hair was hanging in thin, haphazard strands across her face, and she was sprawled across both of the seats in the rear of the plane. She had a nasty bump on her forehead, and blood was running down her cheek.

"Dad?" Bailey asked again, full of concern and attempting to sit up as she spoke.

"Try your door." Harold said to me as he vainly attempted to open his.

This all seems so surreal, I thought as I reached for the door handle.

I pulled on the handle as thousands of thoughts raced through my bewildered mind. At first, the door seemed as if it would never open, but, after applying the full weight of my body against it, it slowly began to give way.

After I managed to push my door open far enough that I could squeeze out of the plane, I glanced back over at Harold as he struggled with his door. His left hand was too badly injured to be of any use, and he couldn't manage to get enough force from his right hand to push the mangled door open.

"Can you jump out and help me get my door open?" asked Harold.

"Sure," I said as I lowered myself to the ground, still unable to fully process what was happening.

As I reached the ground, I surveyed the scene around me. Even though I knew we had crashed, I was shocked by the sight of the propeller buried deep into the trunk of a massive pine. Looking behind me, I realized that we were well within the staggered wall of trees I had seen just before we plowed into them.

As I carefully picked my way around the plane, I tried to mentally trace the route that the plane must have come through to get to where it currently was. Try as I could, I was unable to figure out how we made it through all of these trees in one piece. Harold had to be an excellent pilot just to get the plane on the ground without killing us, but navigating through the wall of pines we were now within was beyond anyone's skill. It was nothing short of miraculous.

My legs felt rubbery as I made my way around to Harold, and I had to fight to steady myself as I walked around the back of the plane. Grabbing ahold of the badly-damaged door, I quickly realized that there was no knob on it. It must have been ripped off during our harrowing landing. Opening Harold's door was going to be harder than either of us had anticipated.

Harold looked out of an empty space where the window used to be and said, "I'm gonna push. You pull on the door anywhere you can get a grip. Be careful not to cut yourself on any exposed metal."

"On three," I said. "One... Two... Three!"

With both of us working together, we were able to force his door open just enough for him to squeeze out. He pushed himself free from the yoke, then half slid, half fell out of the plane and onto the ground below. I helped him over to a nearby tree, and he grimaced as he leaned back against the trunk, sliding down into a seated position.

He's in pretty bad shape, I thought to myself as I looked at him, sitting there against the pine. He seemed to be having some trouble breathing and was only partially coherent, at best. His left hand was covered in cuts, scrapes, and bruises. It was pretty clear that at least two of his fingers were broken.

"Go check on Bailey," he instructed as he took some labored breaths.

I rushed back to the plane and poked my head inside the fuselage. "You OK in there?" I asked.

I was surprised to see that Bailey was still sitting in the exact same position she was in when I had gotten out of the plane. She was conscious, but seemed totally unaware of my presence, or anything else that was occurring around her.

"Bailey?" I asked. "You need help getting out?"

She still didn't seem to hear me.

I climbed up into the cockpit, struggling to make my way into the back, where she was seated.

"We need to get out of here," I said, gently touching her shoulder to get her attention. She looked up at me vacantly, unbuckled her seatbelt, and, without saying a word, followed me out of the plane.

The adrenaline rush I had just experienced was beginning to wear off, and my mind was finally beginning to process our current situation. My first thought was that I needed to get some essentials out of the plane now, in case it caught fire. I had no idea if there was much risk of this happening, but, with the kind of luck we had been having today, I didn't want to take that chance.

I guided Bailey over to where Harold was sitting and let both of them know that I was going back to the plane to get some things that we might need. Bailey was still dazed and didn't seem to notice her father sitting there, bleeding and breathing heavily.

"Do you have anything else in the plane we can use?" I inquired, as I returned with my backpack, Bailey's small backpack, and my shotgun case.

"Got my pack, a .22 rifle in the back of the plane, some rope, a tarp, and an emergency pack with a few more things we might want," replied Harold.

He seemed like he had caught his breath a little more, but now he was starting to sweat profusely. I bent down beside him as I opened the small first aid kit from my backpack.

"When are they coming to get us?" I asked, as I dressed the cuts on his hand.

"Who?" replied Harold.

"You know, the rescue crews," I answered.

I'll never forget the coldness in his eyes as he said, "Kid, ain't nobody comin' to get us."

Chapter 2

Ain't Nobody Comin' to get Us

"What! What do you mean nobody is coming to get us? You have a radio don't you? Didn't you call out an S.O.S., or something? Don't you have one of those emergency beacons somewhere in your plane?" The questions spewed out of my mouth in rapid succession.

He shook his head slowly, and said in a defensive tone, "All I was thinkin' about while we were going down was keepin' us alive, which I did." He paused to let this point sink in. "Once we got down, the radio was dead."

"Why would it be dead? It's not like *it* was burnt in the electrical fire," I reasoned.

"Well," he replied, "battery could be dead." He winced in pain, and his labored breaths came a little more rapidly. "Wires connecting it to the battery could have been fried... or, it could be just plain old broke."

As he finished, I began to suspect that Harold's internal injuries were very serious, possibly even life-threatening. My mind raced, thinking of how I could help, when I realized that I hadn't checked myself or Bailey for injuries. I chastised myself for being so careless, then I gave my full attention to helping Harold. The matter of being rescued could wait.

"How are you feeling?" I asked him.

"Like a herd of caribou is... sittin' on my chest."

I unbuttoned his flannel shirt to see the extent of his injuries. He had some minor bruising on his chest and stomach, probably from the yoke of the airplane, but these bumps and bruises didn't seem serious enough to cause the pain that he was experiencing. Upon further examination, I also noticed that his skin was cold and clammy, as if he had just burst into a nervous sweat.

Not good, I thought, reflecting back on the first aid courses I had taken in the past. There were several things that could be causing Harold's distress, and none of them were good.

Harold was still taking short, deep breaths, as I finished checking him over.

He fixed a concerned look upon me as I stood up. I was an accountant, not a doctor, but two dreadful words seemed to be pressing themselves to the forefront of my mind, heart attack.

"Harold, can you describe your pain?"

"Feels… like… my chest… is being crushed… from the inside," he explained, his struggle to breathe interrupting his sentence.

I looked over my shoulder at Bailey. "You might want to get over here," I called with a sense of great urgency in my voice.

Harold looked up, his eyes acknowledging what I was beginning to fear. "You think so too," he said, more as a statement than a question.

"Heart attack," I nodded, feeling helpless. "But," I added, "I'm not a doctor by any means."

"No…." he shook his head. "I can feel it… I'm dying," he said, his voice choked by a sudden flood of emotion.

"Dad?" Bailey said, finally coming out of her near-catatonic state. She rushed over to his side, as the tears began to stream down her pallid cheeks.

"It's OK, honey," Harold replied in comforting tones.

He looked up at me, then over at Bailey, as if there was something he wanted to say, but he wasn't sure that he should actually speak the words that were in his troubled mind.

Finally, his decision made, he began to speak, still struggling in vain to catch his breath. "Ryan... I need you to get... Bailey home. Don't know you well... but, you seem like a good kid. Seem to have your... head on straight. Gonna be hard... but do your best."

I nodded, not sure what to say at such a moment.

After a moment of silent understanding passed between us, I spoke. "Is there anything, *anything*, we can use to contact *anyone* in the outside world? We still might be able to get you some help... before it's too late."

"Could try your phone... but I doubt it'll work. I don't have one of them... fancy emergency beacons. Don't even have... a transponder in the plane. That means... nobody knows... and... there ain't no way... to make them know."

Bailey knelt there, bent over her dying father, her tears falling freely in a steady stream. "Daddy, you can't die," she pleaded.

Harold was becoming pale, and his lips had taken on a bluish tint as he struggled to keep the life from ebbing out of his body.

"Want you guys... to leave me alone... for a little," Harold said, casting a resolute look in my direction.

"I'll give you and Bailey some time together." I said feebly, trying to fight back the tears as I witnessed this scene unfold before me. This was really happening. I was watching a man die while his daughter looked on helplessly. It would be bad enough under the best of circumstances, when an ambulance would come to take him away, but, here, now, in the middle of God-knows-where, with no one to help, it just seemed so wrong, so cruel.

"No. Want you both to go," Harold replied, giving me a look that said as plainly as words could have, "Please! I don't want her to see this... to see me die."

I walked over to Bailey, and, helping her up, I guided her toward what was left of the plane.

"I love you, Bailey.... Wish we had... more time.... Sorry for everything.... Hope you... can forgive me... someday," Harold stoically said as we walked away.

Bailey began to sob uncontrollably as I ushered her toward the aircraft.

"Take good care of her!" Harold called. "Ryan!" He shouted with a sense of urgency, still fighting to catch his breath. "Take care of me... after I'm gone... if you can. Don't... don't let... the critters get me."

As we walked toward the plane, my head was reeling. A flood of questions came to my mind in rapid succession. Where exactly are we? Did anyone in Fort Yukon know where we were headed? Did Harold file a flight plan? If he did file one, did he follow it? How long will it be until someone realizes we are missing? When they do, how big will the search area be? What are our chances of being rescued?

"Let's sit here for a little bit," I said, as I pointed to a pine tree a few yard from the plane.

Bailey sat down and continued to cry, taking no notice of me.

My mind continued to spiral as I pondered our situation.

This can't be real, I thought. *This is something that only happens in movies, or in books, or in people's imaginations. Is this a dream? Maybe I'm really dead, and this is hell,* I reasoned, as I desperately tried to grasp the gravity of our current situation.

No, this is reality, I eventually had to admit. *This is really happening.*

A fresh surge of adrenaline coursed through my veins as the seriousness of our situation hit me. Feeling the sense of panic beginning to take hold, I realized that I needed to get ahold of myself before my mind spiraled completely out of control. Now was not the time to allow myself to be overcome by fear.

Evaluate the situation. What do you have? What do you know? And, what can you do? I coached myself.

Taking a deep breath, I thought through the list of items that we had at our disposal, hoping that they might be able to, at the very least, help us, and, at best, give us a way to contact the outside world.

My mind seemed to be struggling to come up with a single asset, let alone something of immediate value. It was almost as if, even though I knew most of the supplies that we had, I was too overwhelmed to think of even a basic use for any of them. I was experiencing a mental block, and I needed to fight through it.

I took another deep breath and tried to calm myself and very deliberately began to consider our resources.

Cell phone! I have a cell phone. Why didn't I think of that before? I chided myself for not considering this sooner, even after Harold had suggested that I try making a call.

I hurriedly pulled it out of my pocket; however, I didn't hold out much hope as I illuminated the screen to check for a signal. Even in Fort Yukon, the cell phone service was spotty, at best. Out here in the arctic, miles from civilization, it would be next to impossible to have reception. As I gazed intently at my phone, my misgivings were soon confirmed: no signal.

As my feeling of disappointment began to grow, a new thought entered my mind. What about Bailey's cell phone? Maybe she might have reception.

Back in civilization, I had, in times past, seen instances where, even in remote areas, one person would have no reception, while someone else's cell phone would work excellently. Maybe this could be the case now. At least, that was what I hoped.

"Bailey, give me your cell phone!" I exclaimed. She looked up vacantly, as if she either hadn't heard or didn't understand what I was saying. "Your cell phone," I repeated. "Can you give it to me for a minute?"

Bailey, still racked by her recent fit of sobbing, slowly removed her phone from a pocket and handed it to me, then wiped her tear-stained eyes. I hesitated for a moment, as if delaying the inevitable and preserving a false hope might somehow, in some way be better than being certain of the dreadful reality that we had no way of contacting the outside world. Reluctantly, as my body struggled against my mind, I slowly raised her phone to my line of sight and illuminated the screen. For some reason, even though I was almost certain of the outcome, I felt a sense of dread as I looked down at the screen. My stomach tightened as I discovered that there was no signal on her phone either.

I stood for a moment, silently willing the phone to work, like a child might wish for a cherished, broken toy to suddenly be reanimated, but to no avail. After several minutes of fruitless wishing, a new thought entered my mind. What if I tried to make a call anyway? What would that hurt?

First, I tried to make a call from my phone, dialing 9-1-1 and, with a sense of apprehension, I pushed the send button. After a long silence, during which I hoped and prayed that I would hear the familiar sound of ringing, showing that my call had gone through and we could be rescued, I was greeted by the ominous beeping tones that told me that trying to call the outside world was futile.

Frustrated, I moved on to Bailey's phone and dialed the same three numbers. Even more reluctantly this time, I pushed the send button and hoped and prayed again, only to be greeted by the same disheartening tones.

Defeated, I slumped down against a nearby tree, and gave in to self-pity. After several moments had passed, I felt a sudden and unexpected stab of hope.

Harold! He had a phone, didn't he? Maybe his cell phone would work. I started to get up and make my way over to him, but then thought better of it. There would be plenty of time to check, after…. I should leave him in peace for his last few minutes on earth.

"Think! What else can I do?" I coached myself aloud. I knew I was starting to lose my composure, and, deep down, I knew that once I lost it, I probably would never regain it. I didn't want to consider what that would mean. The stakes were too high right now, and I needed to get my mind focused on the task of getting us help… of finding a way to be rescued.

Relax, I told myself. *Think. What do you know? Start there this time.*

I knew that I was alive; that was a good start. I knew we were in Alaska. I knew we were on our way to Point Barrow when the plane went down, which meant that we were flying northwest. I knew we had crossed a mighty range of mountains, the Brooks Range, and that we went down shortly after Harold had pointed out Lookout

Ridge, ahead in the distance. I knew that we didn't have any way to contact the outside world.

Wait, did I know that? What about the radio? Harold had said it wasn't working, but what if I could find a way to get it to work?

I rushed over to the plane and quickly pulled myself inside. As I settled into the cockpit, I searched around the cabin, hoping to find Harold's headset and praying that it was still in one piece. After a moment, I found the headset and swiftly put it on. Initially, I didn't hear anything, not even static, but that wasn't very surprising. Maybe the radio was off, or maybe Harold had shut the plane off at some point after we landed, cutting the power to the radio. Looking around the cabin, I soon found that the plane's ignition was in the "on" position. So much for that theory…. I tried turning the radio off and on. Nothing.

"Think," I muttered to myself. "Think! There's got to be something I can do."

Looking down, I examined the wiring coming out of the back of the radio. I had been interested in CB radios when I was in my teens, so I knew a little bit about how these kinds of radios worked.

As far as I could tell, the wiring looked fine. While that might sound like a good thing, I was beginning to run out of easily-addressed issues that could cause the radio to malfunction. Next, I unscrewed the antenna's coaxial connection and reconnected it again, fairly certain that it would do nothing to help, but unwilling to admit defeat, at least not yet. Then, I disconnected the power cord from the back of the radio and plugged it back in. Nothing.

As I sat alone in the cockpit, I began to rack my brain, desperate for a solution to our communication problem. Aside from Harold's cell phone, which was almost certain to be useless, the radio was our only hope of reaching the outside world. I had to find a way to make it work.

The battery! I thought. *What if I can hook the radio up directly to the battery? That should get it to work.*

Assuming some component in the radio wasn't broken in the crash, connecting directly to the battery terminals would allow the radio to work, giving us a chance to call for help. Hopping back out of the cockpit, I made my way toward the engine compartment, oblivious to everything else around me. The seemingly distant sound of a voice broke my single-minded focus, making me suddenly aware of my surroundings again.

"What are you doing?" asked Bailey.

"Trying to see if I can get the radio working," I said over my shoulder as I tried to figure out how to open the engine compartment. This compartment housed the plane's battery and would need to be accessed if we were going to have any hope of being rescued.

Bailey stood up and walked over toward me. As I watched her, I noticed that her eyes were red and swollen from crying for what had to have been a very long time, much longer than the couple of minutes that I thought had passed while I had been trying to get the radio to work.

How long had we been here? I suddenly thought as I instinctively pulled out my cell phone to check the clock. It was 12:49 p.m., and we had taken off at almost exactly 10:00 a.m. We had only been here, stranded in this group of trees, for a little over an hour, as far as I could remember, yet it felt like we had been here forever.

"When, exactly, did we go down?" I asked aloud, to no one in particular.

"I'm not sure," Bailey responded.

"Well, I guess it doesn't really matter right now, does it?" I replied. "Do you know how to open this thing?" I said, pointing to the cover over the airplane's engine compartment.

"Yeah, you pull up on this latch, and turn it like this." She paused her motion and opened her mouth to speak, then hesitated. "When do you think we should…" she began, but a stream of tears stopped her from finishing.

I was pretty sure that I knew what she meant, but wasn't really sure what to do. However, one thing was certain – Bailey needed to feel like something was being done to ascertain the condition of her father. Harold had asked for his space, wanting to spend his final moments in peace. I didn't want to disturb him if he was still hanging on, and I also didn't want to be the one to find his body, but I knew it wasn't right to let Bailey do it.

"I'll go check on him," I replied. "You stay here."

I slowly walked around the plane, hoping to catch a glimpse of Harold without disturbing him, in the event that he was still alive. After a moment's observation, it was apparent that he wasn't moving, but I couldn't be sure he was gone. I quietly approached where he was seated, hoping that I was wrong in my suspicions, and that he was just resting as he recuperated from his injuries – hoping that we had both been wrong about the heart attack.

Once I came within a few feet of him, I knew he was gone. He looked somewhat peaceful, as peaceful as he could look under such circumstances, but there was a hint of worry fixed on his cold brow as he sat there, slumped against the trunk of the pine tree. I couldn't help but wonder if that worry wasn't for himself, as he crossed into the Great Unknown, but rather for us, for Bailey. We didn't have much of a chance, not if we couldn't find a way to contact the outside world, and Harold knew that. As I stood there looking down at the vacant, fleshly shell that used to be Harold, I couldn't help but think, knowing what Bailey and I were left to face, that maybe he was the lucky one.

I broke out of my dark broodings, afraid of where the thoughts might take me, and took a couple steps closer to Harold's body. Reaching down, I respectfully pulled his eyelids down, to close his vacant eyes.

"I'll do my best, Harold," I promised. "You laid a heavy burden on me with your last words. You knew the odds. This land is desolate and unforgiving; you had to have known that. I don't know what hope Bailey and I have if we can't call for help, but I'll do my best… I swear it."

I found it strange how connected I felt, there in that moment, to someone I had just met hours before. Maybe it was the fact that we had just gone through such a harrowing ordeal together. Maybe it was the fact that I was lonely and desperate for hope. Maybe it was the fact that he had felt me worthy of the charge that he laid upon me, the charge to lead his daughter out of this wilderness, against all hope, and bring her back to civilization again. To this day, I'm not really sure how to describe it; it is beyond my skill to put into words, but it was almost like he became a part of me in that moment.

I felt the hot tears forming in my eyes as my vision began to blur. "I'll find a way," I vowed, feeling my resolve harden within me. I hoped that he heard me from somewhere beyond this world, but I didn't have the luxury of being philosophical in that moment. Bailey and I were on our own, and if we didn't think of something soon, we were going to die out here.

Slowly, I made my way back to the plane, back to Bailey. It was just a short walk, but my legs felt leaden as I struggled with the thought of bringing the devastating news to Bailey that her father was dead.

"Is he...?" she asked as I appeared around the corner of the plane.

I just slowly nodded in assent, not having the heart to put into words so cruel a fact.

She began to violently sob, and sank to the ground, stricken with grief.

I didn't know what to do. Here was a girl whom I hardly knew, who had just lost her father, and now we were thrust together in a perilous situation, in the middle of one of the largest and most daunting wildernesses left on this planet.

How long I stood watching her cry, I don't know. Surely I couldn't comfort her, but it would be inhumane to leave her there all alone, consumed with pain and sorrow. All I could do was look on helplessly. Slowly, almost imperceptibly, her sobbing slowed until eventually she was able to look up at me, with cheeks stained and glistening from a flood of tears.

"Can we try the radio?" she implored as she rose from the ground.

"Absolutely." I didn't have the heart to tell her it was probably hopeless.

Opening the engine compartment was much harder than either of us had anticipated. The damage it had sustained from the crash and the fact that it was firmly lodged against a formidable pine tree, turned a usually simple task into a nearly impossible endeavor. However, we eventually got it open after many aggravating and fruitless attempts.

Now, with the cover open, I stood on tiptoe and tried to peer inside the engine compartment. Even in the daylight, the cover of the pine trees blocked out so much light that it made it difficult for me to discern one part from another.

Flashlight, I thought to myself, and dashed off toward my backpack.

"Where are you going?" Bailey asked, startled by my sudden retreat.

"To get my flashlight out of my pack. I need it to be able to see inside the engine compartment."

"Why don't you bring all of the stuff over," she suggested. "I don't want you disturbing Harold. I know it's weird, but..." Bailey trailed off.

While I felt like the delay that this would cause was unnecessary, I also recognized the need to respect her feelings. She had, after all, been through more trauma in the past few hours than many people go through in a lifetime. So, delaying our efforts to connect the radio to the battery, I honored her request. After a couple of trips, I brought all of our packs and my shotgun case over to what had become "our side" of the plane.

After a moment, I was able to fish the flashlight out of my backpack. Anxiously, I looked inside the engine compartment, hoping that the battery would be in an easily accessible area. I must have let out an audible gasp, because Bailey suddenly asked, "What's wrong?"

I was unsure of the cause, but one thing was abundantly clear – we were screwed. Inside, the engine compartment was a sticky mess of melted plastic and charred wiring. Most of the parts were fused to one another by a solid mass of something I could only describe as "gunk." Even if the wires had been useable, our plight still would have been hopeless. The battery, the main source of power for both the engine and the radio, was reduced to a flattened, formless lump of plastic.

Looking down at the remains of the battery, most likely our last hope for reaching the outside world, I heard the ominous sound of Harold's voice in my head saying, "Kid, ain't nobody comin' to get us."

Chapter 3

Middle of Nowhere

Hit with the full weight of this realization, I staggered back, slumping against a tree for support, until I half sat, half fell into a seated position.

"That bad?" Bailey asked, her eyes widening with fear.

That bad? I thought to myself. *It couldn't get much worse.*

Unable to suppress my pessimism, I looked up at her and launched into an angry tirade. "Everything is fried. That means no radio. With no radio, we have no way to tell anyone where we are, not that it matters, since we don't even know."

"So, basically, we're screwed," she replied matter-of-factly.

"It's not as bad as that," I said, trying to muster up some confidence that I didn't have.

"Well, then, how bad is it?" she inquired.

It was bad, really bad, bad beyond description, but I couldn't tell her that.

"How bad is it?" I asked myself aloud, falling into silent thought for a moment.

We have no way to contact anyone... wait. We didn't try Harold's cell phone yet.

I knew that digging through her dead father's pockets would probably not sit well with her, so I had to tread carefully as I broached the subject. Sure, I could just march over there in spite of her protests and take the phone, but, if it didn't work (which was almost certain), she would be livid, and we needed to get along right now. Causing a serious division between us now could have some deadly consequences later.

"I don't know how bad it really is," I replied cautiously, "but there is a long-shot that just might make our situation a whole lot better."

She just looked at me, waiting for me to finish my thought.

"Your dad's phone," I stated. "We haven't tried *his* phone yet to see if we can reach someone that might be able to help us."

She didn't say anything in response, but the look she gave me said that she understood what had to be done, even if she didn't like it.

Reluctant to disturb his body, I walked back over to where Harold was sitting against the tree. As gently as I could, I reached into the left front pocket of his flannel shirt, where I could see the outline of a phone. His body was already cool and stiff, which only served to augment the vile feeling I had rummaging through his pocket. I retrieved the phone, which was an old flip-phone, and opened it to check for a signal. The phone was a mass of cracked plastic and wouldn't even power up. Apparently it had been so badly damaged in the crash that it was now completely inoperable, despite my repeated efforts to turn it on.

"Well," I thought, "there went our one last chance of being rescued."

Putting the phone in my pocket, I walked back to where I had left Bailey. I shook my head somberly in answer to her questioning look. Taking a seat next to her, I tried to figure out what our next course of action should be. Soon, my mind began to wander from finding a solution to our problem, to simply considering the position I was in. The more I thought, the more depressed I became. The ironic thing was, when I was younger, I used to fantasize about being in a situation like this: stranded in the wilderness with a beautiful girl and tasked with tackling problems that would destroy most mortal men. In these fantasies, I would always know what to do, no matter how dire the problem, and would emerge as the hero, against all odds. However, this was no fantasy, and now that I was actually in such a situation, I felt anything but heroic. In fact, I could sum up my feelings in two humble words: helpless and alone. I must have been sitting there for quite some time, lost in my thoughts.

"Did you hear me?" Bailey said. "What are we going to do?"

"We're going to survive."

"But, how?" she asked plaintively.

"By doing what we have to do to stay alive," I answered evasively, mostly because I wasn't really sure that we even could survive out here long-term, let alone how we would.

I began thinking out loud, speaking more to myself than to her. "We need to assess the situation. We need to consider what we have, what we know, and what we can do. Let's start with what we know. We know we're in Alaska, and we know we're somewhere between Fort Yukon and Point Barrow. We know that we crossed that big mountain range, so we must be north of it." I got up and fumbled through my pack, looking for the map of Alaska that I had brought with me. Having found it, I asked, "How long do you think we were flying?"

"I don't know. More than an hour."

"Do you have any idea how fast the plane was going?"

"I don't know! I wasn't the pilot, you know!" she snapped.

"Whoa. Let's not overreact. If we don't at least try to figure out where we are, we're not going to have any clue how far we are from civilization."

"I'm not sure," she replied, seeming a little embarrassed about her outburst as she took some time to consider the question. "The number 150 seems to come to mind, but I'm just not certain."

"It seems that flying in straight lines would make the most sense," I said, guessing at the route we had taken before we crashed.

Going over to my pack again, I pulled out a pen. Based on what I knew so far, I figured we had flown at least 150 miles, possibly more. I knew that I was just guessing on the distance, but at this point that was the best I could do.

Needing something to illustrate a straight line on the map, I improvised, uncoiling a few feet from my hank of paracord. A rough estimation of 150 miles placed us south of the Brooks Range mountains. That wouldn't do, since we already knew we were north of the range. Bailey and I tried to match the landscape we had flown over just before the crash with areas that corresponded on the map. After some deliberation, the best guess that we could come up with was that we were somewhere within a 20-mile radius north of the Brooks Range, possibly east of Liberator Lake. Had Lookout Ridge been marked on my map, we would have had a much easier time of finding our location, since we had been flying toward it just before the crash. However, we had no such luck.

This wasn't much to go on, but it at least gave us a very rough idea of where we were. Now that we had a location to work with, we could see how far we were from civilization. The view on the map wasn't very encouraging. There weren't any villages, cities, or any otherwise populated areas for nearly 60 miles in any direction. Sure, there may have been a village or active mine that was out there, but without it being marked on the map, we were totally in the dark.

"Ok," I said, looking up from the map, "now that we have a general idea of where we are, let's figure out what we have."

"What do you mean?" she asked.

"I mean, let's take an inventory of literally anything and everything that could possibly be of use to us. Nothing gets overlooked, including parts from the plane."

Bailey and I took the next 20 or 30 minutes to scour the areas inside and outside the plane for anything that we could use. We avoided going near Harold's body, but when Bailey walked on that side of the plane, I could tell that she was anxious to give him a proper burial, or, at the very least, to cover his body. However, for now, that would have to wait.

After scavenging, aside from the clothes we were wearing, here is what we had:

-3 Cell phones
-4 Packs (Mine, Bailey's, Harold's, and the emergency pack in the plane)
-2 Sleeping bags (mine and one that was in Harold's emergency pack)
-1 2-person emergency Mylar blanket
-1 Sawyer Mini water filter
-1 Bottle water purification tabs
-2 16 oz. bottles of water, full

-1 32 oz. Nalgene bottle, half full

-1 Can of soda, mostly full

-5 Protein bars

-1 10'x10' Bushcraft Outfitters tarp

-100' Paracord

-50' Nylon cordage

-50' Synthetic rope (larger diameter than the nylon cordage)

-1 Gransfors Bruks Small Forest Axe

-1 Survive! Knives GSO 5.1 in leather sheath

-1 Stilwell Knives Model Five

-1 Spyderco Endura folding knife

-1 Leatherman multi-tool

-1 Silky Gomboy 270 Folding Saw

-1 Small sharpening stone

-1 Small strop

-1 Handheld LED flashlight

-1 LED headlamp

-2 4 Mil 55 gallon drum liners

-1 Pair work gloves

-1 Swedish military poncho

-1 Wool cap

-2 Pairs wool socks

-1 Box UCO Stormproof matches

-1 Ferro rod

-1 Handkerchief

-1 Safety razor

-2 Rolls camp toilet paper

-1 Bed roll

-1 50' roll duct tape

-1 Mossberg 500 Persuader

-15 3" mag slugs

-1 Glock 20, with extra magazine, and OWB holster

-25 Rounds of 10mm HP

-1 AR-7 .22 rifle

-50 Rounds .22lr

-1 Hair brush

-1 Small make-up pouch with assorted beauty products

-2 Tampons

-1 Copy of *Rogue States*, by Noam Chomsky (Bailey's; definitely not mine)

-1 Set of earbuds

-2 hair ties

-2 Small first aid kits

-Assorted credit cards

-$457 in cash

-My and Bailey's driver's licenses

-1 Rubber band (which held all of my credit cards together)

-1 Field Notes booklet

-1 Ball point pen

-1 Map of Alaska

"So, now we know what we have," I said as Bailey looked down at the assorted items that we had spread out on the tarp.

"How does this help?" she asked, looking doubtful.

"Knowing what we have realistically allows us to know what we can and cannot do. So..." I stopped, noticing the crimson streaks of blood on Bailey's face. So much had happened since the crash and my mind had been preoccupied by so many other things that I had completely neglected her.

"Here, sit down for a minute," I said. "Let me take a look at your head."

The cut on her head had stopped bleeding awhile ago, and the stream of blood, running from the top of her forehead down past the base of her neck, was completely dry. By now, it had been hours since the crash, and I had left Bailey unattended with an open wound. I chided myself for making such a major mistake. While we were back in civilization, this might have been inconsequential, but out here, it could be fatal.

Fatal... the word terrified me. It wasn't so much the thought of dying, but the thought that if something happened to Bailey, I would be stuck out here in the wilderness alone. I tried to push the thought out of my mind, but the idea of being left out here completely by myself, without another living soul for over 60 miles in any direction, terrified me. I knew I was letting the adrenaline rush from today's events get the better of me, so, taking a couple of deep breaths, I tried my best to focus completely on tending to Bailey's injury.

The sharp intake of Bailey's breath as I lightly touched her forehead clearly told me that her wound was causing considerable pain. She had a large lump by her left temple, which was bruised, and there was a superficial cut on her scalp, right in the center of the lump. Thankfully, it was only this minor cut that had caused all of her bleeding.

"I'm sorry. I'm trying to be gentle," I said in response to her obvious discomfort.

"It's OK," she replied, looking up into my eyes.

Taking the handkerchief out of my pack, I dipped the end of it into my Nalgene bottle. While this wasn't the most sanitary practice, water was a precious commodity that we were running very short on, and I was hesitant to open either of the other bottles. While I was certainly no doctor, I knew enough about head trauma to be concerned that her injuries were more serious than just the superficial wound on her head. Gingerly wiping the blood from her face, I asked her some questions to try to determine if she was suffering from any internal trauma.

"Well, the good news is, I don't think you have any serious trauma," I opined after my examination was completed.

"What's the bad news?"

"Two things," I responded. "First, I'm going to have to clean the actual wound, which is going to be painful."

"What's the second?" she winced.

"I'm a lousy cook," I replied, trying to add some levity to the situation.

"What?" she asked, seeming perplexed.

"It's true." I returned, with a chuckle. "Here, see for yourself." I said, as I opened a protein bar and handed her a piece.

Food. It was almost as much of a problem as water. We had about 1,400 calories worth, which, even if used sparingly, would only last another day or two. I tried not to show my concern as we shared our frugal meal.

"You're right," Bailey said with a smile. "You are a lousy cook."

As we sat, chewing in silence, I looked myself over for injuries. Somehow, almost miraculously, other than some muscle soreness and a couple of bumps and bruises, I emerged from the crash unscathed.

"Here," I handed my water bottle over to Bailey, "just take a little drink. We need to be very careful with our water."

After taking a couple of small sips, she handed the bottle back to me. I also drank a small mouthful of water, then we checked our remaining supply again. We had 48 ounces of water left, and, as far as we knew, there was no foreseeable way to replenish it in the immediate future. What we had was barely enough to last the rest of the day, let alone the rest of the time we might be stranded out here.

Don't dwell on it, I thought. *One thing at a time.*

We decided to repack most of the gear after eating our meager meal. All of the gear that had come from my pack went right back where it came from. Since Bailey's and Harold's packs were mostly empty, she was able to fit much of the remaining gear into her small pack. However, this still left us with three packs for two people (mine, Bailey's, and the emergency pack from the plane). If we ended up having to try to walk to civilization, we were going to have to figure out how to solve this dilemma, but for now we were content to let the matter rest.

Ever since we had crashed, the thought that we were in "bear country" had been looming in my mind. Earlier, we had been so consumed with all of the more pressing problems we had encountered, that I hadn't been able to do anything to mitigate this potential threat. However, now that we had a moment of downtime, I thought it might be prudent to do so. So, opening the shotgun case, I loaded the Mossberg Persuader with seven rifled slugs, chambered a round, and then inserted another slug into the tubular magazine, topping it off. After checking to make sure the safety was engaged, I slung the shotgun across my back. Then, I started loading the magazines for the Glock 20.

"Why are you doing that?" asked Bailey. She was visibly uncomfortable with the sight of my firearms.

"Doing what?" I responded shortly.

I was pretty sure I knew what she was really asking. She was a college girl going to an extremely liberal school, reading an extremely liberal book, and was studying what many considered to be a liberal major. I figured I knew where she stood on the issue of firearms. However, she was in Alaska, and her father seemed to have lived here for a while, and he had a gun of his own in the plane, so maybe I was wrong.

"Loading those guns," she asked, with a hint of disdain.

"Where are we?" I inquired.

"What does that have to do with anything?" she quipped.

"It has everything to do with what I am doing," I replied. "So, where are we?"

"Alaska."

"Who is at the top of the food chain out here?"

She didn't respond.

I looked up from the task of loading my handgun's magazines long enough to see that my point was definitely not having the desired effect. If anything, it only served to further aggravate her.

"There are things out here that want to eat us," I said, not content to let the issue go, "and we are dangerously low on food ourselves. One way or another these guns can help to keep us alive, either by keeping things from eating us, or allowing us to eat by hunting for food."

"I don't want to talk about it anymore," she said dismissively, obviously startled as much by the thought of being eaten as by the sight of my guns.

I finished loading the Glock in awkward silence and was beginning to turn my attention to Harold's .22 rifle, which I recognized as a Henry Arms AR-7, when I was interrupted yet again.

"What are we going to do about my dad?" she asked.

I looked up at her with an expression of dread on my face. I had been thinking of this very thing for a while now, and I was pretty sure I knew the answer. However, now that it was time to explain my position to Bailey, I was afraid to say what I thought we should do. It was cold and callous, but we couldn't afford to be anything but cold and callous if we were going to survive.

As I struggled to formulate the sentence, I moved closer to Bailey. "You're not going to like this," I stammered, "but... we're not going to do anything with him."

I watched Bailey's face tighten as she processed my words. She clenched her teeth as I waited for the inevitable stream of invectives to burst from her mouth. Suddenly, my vision blurred as my head was rocked by an unexpected blow. I wondered what was happening as I felt myself losing control of my senses. The world around me faded to black.

Chapter 4

Harsh Reality

A split second later, everything came back into focus. Bailey was standing right in front of me, her arms flailing as she shouted incoherently. My mind was struggling to catch up as she did her best to beat my body into oblivion. Finally, my ears were able to catch portions of the string of epithets that was pouring from her mouth.

"You heartless, little..." she half yelled, half growled.

"Hey!" I shouted, grabbing her arms. "Stop it! Stop! Stop. Listen!" I said as I looked into her rage-filled eyes.

She stopped, panting for breath, still shaking with pent up violence as we stood face to face.

"Listen," I said more softly this time. "What can we do? We're in the middle of nowhere. We don't even have a shovel. What are we going to dig with?"

Her body was still tense with rage as she stared icily into my eyes.

I continued, "Even if we could dig, just think of how long that would take. We only have enough food and water to last us a day, and that's if we're really careful not to overexert ourselves. If we bury your father, we might as well dig our own graves while we're at it, because we'll be writing our own death sentence."

A look of helpless pleading began to replace her angry stare, as fresh tears streamed down her flushed cheeks.

Encouraged by this change in her demeanor, I resumed, "What did your dad ask me to do? He asked me to take care of you, to get you home. Do you really think he would want us to kill ourselves, *literally*, just to bury the empty shell of his body?"

"But we have to do something." She emphasized the last word as she struggled to speak through her tears.

"Well... there is the plane. What better place for a pilot to take his final rest?"

She nodded, the tears coming too quickly for her to speak. Relaxing my hold on her arms, I walked slowly over toward Harold. The sound of Bailey's sobbing faded as I went.

Getting Harold to the plane proved to be a much more grueling task than I had originally thought. Harold wasn't a big man, but then again, neither was I. I was 6'0", 165 pounds. I was in relatively good shape; however, I was drained from the day. The lack of food and water, combined with the tiring effect of the several adrenaline rushes I had experienced, had left me feeling utterly exhausted. So, whatever strength I did possess was already sapped, and lugging a man of similar size over to the plane was no easy feat.

Once I got him beside the plane, it was apparent that there was no way I was going to be able to get him inside by myself. I stood for a while, hesitant to ask Bailey for help.

She's been traumatized enough, I reasoned, unsure of how she would react to such a request. However, soon my thoughts were interrupted by the sight of Bailey timidly walking into view.

"Thanks for doing this," she said meekly as she approached.

I nodded solemnly.

"I'm... I'm sorry for how I acted earlier," she confessed.

"It's OK. He's your dad. It's only natural for you to want to make sure he's laid to rest in peace.... I hate to do this," I continued, "but I don't think I can get him in here all by myself."

We got Harold into the plane within a couple of minutes, but the ordeal was both physically and emotionally draining. Afterward, Bailey and I sat against a tree near the plane, exhausted, and lost in thought.

"You know, I didn't even know his last name," I said aloud, to myself.

"It's Wallace," she replied, looking over at me.

"So that makes you Bailey Wallace?" I asked, realizing that I didn't know her last name either.

"No, my last name is Reynolds. It's complicated," she offered in response to my look of surprise.

I nodded in assent, thinking it best to let the matter drop.

"What's your last name?"

"McQuaid."

We sat in silence for a few moments, collecting our thoughts. The sun was beginning its descent toward the horizon when a new and troubling fact presented itself: we had no shelter, and it was going to be dark soon. We certainly couldn't sleep in the plane, even if Harold wasn't entombed there. For one thing, the metal fuselage might easily be blown around by any sudden wind gust. Also, since metal is a conductor, there was a very good chance that we would lose more body heat by staying inside of the plane than by sleeping outside. So, setting up a tarp shelter seemed to be the most expedient and sensible thing.

I contemplated just sleeping under the stars, but if it rained, even under the cover of all of these pine trees, we would get soaked. That would be bad enough under normal circumstances, even in a warmer climate. But with the average daily temperature in this region peaking in the low 50s, getting soaked presented a very serious hypothermia risk.

"It's getting late. We should probably start setting up our shelter for the night," I said.

Finding an appropriate place to set up the shelter was the first and most important task. We needed an open space at least the size of the tarp on level ground and far away from any standing trees that looked like they were dead, leaning precariously, or rotting. Such trees are called widow-makers for a reason, having occasionally claimed the lives of unwary outdoorsmen.

After a few minutes of searching, we found a suitable spot a couple hundred yards away from the plane. We immediately focused all of our efforts on rigging up the tarp. Tying one end of the nylon cordage about chest high around a sturdy pine, I proceeded to feed the line through the tabs on the side of the tarp. Had we just been camping or backpacking, I probably would have cut several lengths of cordage and tied them individually to trees or tent pegs, but cutting any of our cordage in this scenario was a very bad idea. So, I was going to have to find a way to finish hanging the tarp while keeping the line intact.

Using my folding saw, I cut two small branches off of a nearby pine and quickly carved them into tent pegs. Pounding one of these into the ground with the poll of my Small Forest Axe, I left about eight inches sticking up to secure the bottom corner of the tarp against. Next, I tied a clove hitch around the peg and, feeding the rest of the cordage through the back of the tarp, I secured the other bottom corner in the same way. Having fed the nylon line through the tabs on the far side, I tied the line off, using a double half hitch.

Now that the right side, back, and left side of the tarp were secure, all I had left to do was secure the front of the tarp. Having fed the line through the tabs on the front of the tarp, we encountered our first minor problem. The nylon cord wasn't long enough to wrap around the trunk of the pine. After a moment's reflection, though, I thought it best to simply tie the cordage around the original loop we had made when first starting to build the shelter.

Now we had a shelter, and we had managed to keep our 50 feet of nylon cord intact, something that we might be very thankful for down the road.

"How do you know how to do all of this?" Bailey asked after we had finished putting up the tarp.

"How to do all of what?" I replied, unsure if she was asking about making the shelter or just generally knowing how to survive in the wilderness.

"What you're doing now," she responded. "Making this shelter, and those pegs, and stuff like that."

"Experience. I like the outdoors, and I go backpacking and camping regularly. Although, even with all of that experience, I never really learned many useful outdoors skills until I started taking some courses through something called Bushclass USA."

"Oh. I've been camping before, but I don't know how to do any of this. But, I've only gone twice... and we stayed in a cabin," she said as an afterthought.

I chuckled to myself. "You sound like my coworkers."

"Where do you work?" she asked. The thought that I had a job seemed not to have crossed her mind up to this point.

"An accounting firm," I replied evasively. It wasn't entirely true, since I had recently been fired, but I really didn't feel like discussing any personal drama at the moment. Plus, I didn't want her to think that I was some kind of loafer who lived in my mom's basement and played video games all day.

"Oh." Seeing that I didn't offer any further explanation, she let the matter drop.

It had become noticeably darker by the time we finished setting up our shelter, and we still had more work to do before night set in. However, completing even the most basic tasks was becoming increasingly difficult as our muscles were growing stiff and sore from the combination of exertion and being jostled during the crash. Fighting through the pain and exhaustion with as much speed as we could muster, we carried all of our gear over to the shelter.

"Now what?" Bailey asked as we set our packs on the ground beside the shelter.

"Now we get our sleeping areas ready."

We quickly encountered another hindrance to our progress. We only had one bed roll, but both of us needed some kind of barrier between us and the ground. While I wasn't sure how cold it was going to get at night, I did know that hypothermia was a constant danger and the ground would literally suck the life out of anyone who laid on it without sufficient insulation. And, even though we each had a sleeping bag, that was hardly enough of a barrier between us and the ground.

Time was running short, and we were in a race to set up our shelter before darkness overtook us. Sure, we could use our flashlights to illuminate the area around us, but working in the dark in unfamiliar territory presented its own separate set of risks, especially in the condition we were in. We needed to solve this dilemma quickly if we were going to finish our preparations before dark.

Quickly, I decided to lay my bedroll out for Bailey, and then I racked my brain about what to do for myself. After a couple of moments of deliberation, I decided to make a natural insulation bed. It was getting too dark to safely use my axe to cut some small branches, so I opted to make it out of the pine needles that were abundantly scattered on the ground. Hurriedly, I filled one of the 55-gallon drum liners from my pack with a generous pile of these pine needles, hoping the bag wouldn't be punctured in the process.

It was now so dark that it was difficult to see anything other than the vague outline of even the closest objects as Bailey and I finally rolled out our sleeping bags. I thought it would be prudent to retrieve my headlamp and handheld flashlight now, while I could still see the outline of my pack. I had learned from previous experience that locating a flashlight in total darkness was extremely difficult, if not impossible, and was likely to result in spilled gear, twisted ankles, or worse.

Turning on my headlamp, I walked over to where I had set the AR-7, hoping to finally assemble and load it.

"Where are you going?" Bailey asked, her voice shaking as if she was afraid of me straying too far. She had reacted like this once already, so I gathered that she was extremely uncomfortable with the idea of being alone, even if I was still nearby.

"To get the AR-7... the other gun," I corrected myself. Judging from our previous conversation, she didn't know much about firearms.

"Shouldn't we start a fire or something?" she called out after me.

This was something that I had been considering as we set up our shelter. I knew that it was going to be cold tonight. In fact, it was already cold. Both Bailey and I were shivering as we set up our sleeping bags. However, to get enough wood to make a fire that would last, I was going to have to use my saw, axe, and knife in the dark. This was something I had done before; however, in the past, there was always the possibility of seeking medical attention if something went wrong. Now, if I cut myself it could have deadly consequences. Furthermore, both Bailey and I had decent sleeping bags, which should be able to keep us warm enough throughout the night. And, even if they didn't, I could always decide to make a fire late, if the choice was truly between freezing or risking injury.

Bailey's voice brought me out of my musings. "You do know how, don't you?" she asked with a hint of fear.

Reentering the shelter with the rifle, I was in no mood for such a comment. I was hungry, sore, battered, and downright exhausted. After all I had done that day, and all I had been through, my patience was completely gone.

"For both our sakes, you'd better hope I do," I snapped, and, sitting down, I extinguished my head lamp, leaving us both in total darkness.

Chapter 5

Difficult Decisions

I doubt that either of us slept much that first night. Although I was exhausted beyond anything I had experienced before, the darkness of the night was ominous and foreboding. As strange as it sounds, it was almost as if out of the darkness itself, there came a negative energy that filled my mind with wild imaginations and dark, troubling fears.

What was out there lurking under the cloak of darkness? Wolves, bears, or maybe even hideous, nameless creatures that are the source of myth and legend? Then, there was Harold. While I had seen my fair share of death, the thought of sleeping so close to a corpse was discomforting. Scoff if you like, but there, in the remote wilderness, with no way to contact the outside world, these thoughts troubled my already weary mind.

Relax, I told myself. But, try as I might, I couldn't think of a reason why I should. Taking some slow, deep breaths, I tried to clear my head, only to be assailed by a new set of worries.

How long would our food last, and how could we replenish our supply? What if we didn't find water tomorrow? What if we really did have to try to walk all the way back to civilization? How long would that take? What chance did we actually have of surviving out here anyway?

A sudden sound jarred my mind back into the present moment. My heart racing, I strained my ears to figure out where this sound was coming from, and what was making it.

After a moment, I heard it again. It was Bailey. She was crying. To say that she had been through a lot would have been an understatement. She had lost her father, been in a plane crash, and was stranded out in the wilderness with someone she had just met. How would I feel if I were in her shoes? As I pondered this, there came an ugly, disquieting thought, and, slowly, as it took root, it began to haunt me.

How much of this situation was my fault? I had set events into motion that led to Harold's death and to Bailey and me being lost in the wilderness. If I hadn't chartered the plane at the last minute to take me on an unplanned trip to Point Barrow, Harold would surely still be alive and Bailey would still be safe, back in Fort Yukon.

Bailey had to be thinking the very same thing. She had to have realized all of this by now. She must have thought that it would have been better if she had never met me, if I had never come into her life and Harold's life. She had to blame me. But, should she blame me? Did *she* blame *me*?

The crying continued.

As the night wore on, I wrestled with the feeling of guilt, punctuated occasionally by Bailey's sobs, until the faintest hints of grey light growing in the forest showed the coming of the dawn. Somehow, knowing that day was near brought a renewed sense of hope, however slight it might be.

As the forest slowly began to fill with the light of day, a feeling of awkwardness began to accompany my feeling of guilt.

How would I be able to face Bailey today? I thought. *She had to hate me, to view me as some kind of monster. That's how I would feel in her place, wasn't it? Or, would I realize that no one could really be blamed for what happened, for what was an unforeseen set of circumstances beyond anyone's control?* I had no way to know for sure how I would feel, so, for now, I gave up the attempt at guessing.

Thinking it best to occupy my mind with more immediate matters, I began to sit up, hoping that the day's activities would keep my thoughts in check. However, my body immediately rebelled against the attempt. I was much more stiff and sore than I had expected.

"How do you feel?" I asked Bailey, who looked over in response to my groans.

"Terrible."

"Are you sore?" I inquired more specifically this time.

As she tried to sit up, a groan escaped from her mouth.

"I'll take that as a yes," I quipped.

After a moment's struggle, which verged on comical, she finally succeeded in getting herself into an upright position. She brushed some of her long, chestnut brown hair away from her face, and, looking over at me, asked embarrassedly, "What do I do about going to the bathroom?"

That was the last thing I was expecting her to say. Now, it was my turn to be embarrassed.

After rooting around in my pack for a moment, I handed her a roll of camping toilet paper. "Here, this one is yours. When it's gone it's gone. Hopefully we'll be back to civilization before that happens." I didn't have the heart to tell her that it would probably be gone long before we were anywhere near a populated area.

Standing, I tried to take in our surroundings while I stretched my aching muscles. As I surveyed the forest around us, despite our current trials, I was impressed by its simple, rugged beauty. It was filled with pine trees of many different shapes and sizes. Their resinous smell, which had escaped my notice on the previous day, now filled my senses. The birds singing cheerfully at the sight of the dawn added to the majesty of this old and regal wood. This was an amazing spot, but the weight of our current plight robbed me of the full appreciation I would normally experience in such a place.

Bailey came back to the shelter a few minutes later. I was struggling to tie my boots, still unable to bend or move freely. Grabbing a protein bar out of my pack, I asked cheerlessly, "Want some breakfast?"

"Sure."

"We need to decide what our game plan is." I counseled as we ate. I knew that the longer we put off this discussion, the easier it would be to just languish where we were – a potentially deadly mistake.

"Okay?" she replied, seeming unsure where this conversation was headed.

"The way I see it, we have three options," I stated, handing her my water bottle. "Just drink half, and I'll drink the other half," I instructed, and then continued. "First, we could stay here and hope that someone comes to get us. There are bound to be planes and helicopters searching for us at some point, but, even if they are, that doesn't mean they will find us. I'm not even sure that anyone knows the route we were taking. So, theoretically, no one knows where we are.

"Also, there is a major strike against staying here – water. After I finish off what's left in my water bottle, we'll have 36 ounces remaining. That will last us the rest of the day, at best. Then, if we finally do decide to move a day or two from now, we won't have any water, just when we need it most.

"Now, we could find water nearby, but, even if we do, there is another problem with staying here and waiting to be rescued. If no one comes, even with a steady supply of water and food (which is yet another problem), it is going to start getting a lot colder in the next couple of weeks, and we aren't equipped to survive out here in the cold. In short, if we stay here and no one comes to rescue us, if we don't die from dehydration or starvation, we're going to eventually freeze to death."

It was clear that the reality of our situation was making Bailey very uncomfortable. I was beginning to wonder if I should have been so blunt, but she needed to know the truth if she was going to give any input into our decision.

"The second option is to wait here for a few days to see if we are spotted by a search and rescue crew. If we choose this option, we still have the issue of a lack of water and food. Also, the longer we wait, the more likely it is that we are going to encounter harsh temperatures when we finally do decide to make our way to civilization. So, if we end up choosing this option, I think we should limit our stay to two days maximum."

I paused, giving her time to process everything I had said thus far before continuing.

"Then, there is the third option: we start walking toward civilization immediately. In my opinion, this option offers us the most flexibility. First, we still have a chance of being spotted by search and rescue crews while we are on the move. Not necessarily a good chance, but maybe just as good as we have if we stay here.

Second, we have a better chance of finding water if we are moving, and right now, that is a priority. Third, it is the *only* way we are going to get home if we aren't rescued."

Pausing for a moment, I debated whether or not to add my final thought on the issue. Shifting my glance toward the shattered fuselage of the plane, where Harold's body was entombed, I said, "Your dad didn't seem to think anyone was going to find us. In fact, he seemed almost sure of it. That alone makes me hesitant to try the other two options."

Bailey sat silently, pondering for several minutes while I savored the remaining water in my bottle, trying my best to be patient. I was sure that this decision was as daunting to her as it was to me. However, I wasn't certain that she would arrive at the same conclusion that I had come to. I didn't know what I would do if she wanted to stay and I wanted to go, but I was hoping it didn't come to that.

"What would you do if I wasn't here?" she finally asked, breaking the contemplative silence.

"You *are* here," I replied.

"I know. But, I mean, if I hadn't come, and it was just you left now, what choice would you make?"

"I would start walking toward civilization as soon as possible."

The expression on her face showed that she thought this was the best answer. However, she also seemed very unsure about taking such a drastic step. It was risky, but so were the other two options. We had no way of knowing the outcome of our choice, whatever it was, until we tried it, and then it would be too late to go back. A wrong choice now meant certain death, but, in all actuality, so might the "right" decision.

"Do you think we can make it?" she asked, wanting to hear that I thought that it was possible, whether or not it actually was.

"I'm not saying it's going to be easy, but, yes, I think we've got a chance," I replied.

Sure, we had a chance, but I wasn't willing to consider the actual odds, since I was certain they weren't in our favor.

"Ok… but how do we know where to go?" prodded Bailey.

How do we know where to go? I asked myself.

We had several options as far as the directions in which we could walk, but none of them seemed reasonable. The nearest inhabited area, according to the map, was Atqasuk, about 60 miles north of where we thought we were. However, the map showed that much of the land in that direction was an intricate series of interconnected bogs. The wet terrain, while great for keeping us supplied with water, would make it extremely difficult to stay warm and dry. We might not be able to find a dry place to camp along the way, or, worse, we could even get stuck in the middle a bog, which would mean succumbing to a slow death from exposure. No, north definitely wasn't the way to go, despite the fact that it was the shortest route.

We could try going south, but to get to civilization we would have to cross the Brooks Range mountains. Even if I was an experienced mountaineer, which I wasn't, we would need a ton of specialized gear help us successfully navigate the range. People take entire crews with them just to climb one mountain, and we would be encountering dozens of them. So, we couldn't go south either. This left us with the decision between going east or going west.

East or west? The choice we made might literally mean the difference between life and death.

Poring over the map, I tried my best to objectively weigh the options. It looked like we were almost equidistant from two areas of civilization. To the west, Point Hope lay about 150 miles away. To the east, State Route 11, the only road running from north to south in this region, was also about 150 miles from where we guessed we were. That meant that whichever way we chose, we would have to walk 150 miles through rugged, unfamiliar, pathless terrain, with limited gear, limited food, and limited water. Either way seemed hopeless.

Agonizing over the decision, I analyzed every minute detail of the map, going both east and west. Eventually, one direction began to emerge as the clear choice. Looking up at Bailey, I explained my thought process.

"I think that it makes the most sense to head east. Route 11 is a much bigger target to hit than Point Hope, since it runs from north to south for hundreds of miles. If, when we finally make it to the west coast, we miss Point Hope by a few miles to the north or to the south, we could waste days trying to find it. Furthermore, the next closest town to the north of Point Hope is at least 60 miles away, and the next closest town to the south is about 30 miles. That means our 150-mile journey could end up being closer to a 200-mile journey if we don't navigate precisely. We have no GPS, and, even if we had a compass, we're so far north, it wouldn't work properly anyway, so we have no way of being sure we'll get to Point Hope. No, I don't like our odds with going west.

"I'm not saying east is much better," I continued, "but at least we can't miss the road. Like I said, it runs from north to south through most of the state, so, even if we are a few miles north or south of where we are aiming, we're eventually still going to come to the road. And, once we get there, it is only a matter of time until someone comes along and finds us so that we can go home."

Home. The thought seemed almost foreign. Yesterday morning, before the crash, before Harold's death, before I was stranded in the wilderness with a girl I hardly knew, home was just a plane ride away. Now, the only plane that could have taken me home lay in a shattered heap and was now the final resting place of the only pilot within thousands of square miles.

These thoughts proved to be too much for me. Feverishly pulling my cell phone out of my pocket, I dialed 9-1-1 again.

Someone had to find us! Didn't they know we were going to die out here?

"Work!" I screamed, as if my rage contained some unknown power that could make the phone connect to the outside world. "Work!" The merciless beeping of an unconnected call was the only response. In impotent rage, I turned, dashing my phone against a nearby tree, then, collapsing, I wept.

After several minutes, I slowly regained control of myself. Looking up, my eyes met Bailey's. She seemed to be genuinely concerned for me, but it was obvious that my actions had terrified her.

"I'm sorry," I began, "but this seems so pointless. How can this be happening? I mean, how can we be stranded out here with no way to get ahold of anybody who can help? We live in the digital age, where we have Wi-Fi everywhere, even on airplanes and tour buses. Even people in third world countries, who don't have enough to eat and have no clean water to drink, have cell phones that work. And here were are, stranded, and our only lifeline to the outside world is absolutely worthless! It just makes me feel so insignificant, so helpless."

Bailey simply nodded in response.

An awkward silence began to set in.

The woods were now clearly alight, showing that the morning was quickly passing us by, and we still had done nothing about our present situation. Realizing that we had a lot to do if we were going to get started today, we began the necessary preparations.

As morning progressed, we took down the tarp shelter and stowed both it and the cordage in my pack. We also repacked the remaining items into the larger emergency pack from Harold's plane, leaving both Bailey's and Harold's packs behind.

As much as we hated to do it, being hesitant to disturb Harold's body, we also scavenged the seatbelts from the plane to use as pack straps and for a sling for the AR-7.

"Best be off then," I said after all of the preparations were complete.

"Are you sure about this?" Bailey asked, filled with concern.

In reality, I was not, but I didn't want to admit it. So, I said nothing in response.

Hoisting our packs, after we had checked and rechecked the area to make sure we weren't leaving anything important behind, we began walking, but, to what end, neither of us could tell.

Chapter 6

On the Move

We each said a few words over Harold's makeshift grave before we left. I recited the 23rd Psalm, as best as I could remember. Bailey said a few words mixed with grief, anger, and regret.

"You weren't much of a father to me for most of my life," she confessed, "but that was just starting to change. Just when we were starting to patch things up and finally have a real relationship, this had to happen and take you away forever. I know you were changing, and maybe I was too. Now neither of us will ever know how things could have turned out…" She trailed off as the tears pooled in her eyes.

After that, we began our journey in silence, neither of us feeling much like talking.

We had been walking due east, as best as I could judge, for about a half an hour. I was replaying Bailey's words to Harold over and over in my mind, trying to piece together a picture of her seemingly broken life, when, suddenly, the dense forest we had been walking through came to an end.

Bailey and I both gasped in wonder at the savage beauty of the landscape before us. As far as we could see, to the north and the east, rolling, rock-strewn grasslands, punctuated by occasional mountains and thin bands of trees, stretched to the horizon. The plain before us was a mix of red, brown, and green plants, all stunted and gnarled from growing in inhospitable, rocky ground. To the south, the tundra grassland rolled away, coming to a sudden stop against a solid wall of majestic mountains. The large patch of forest behind us seemed to be an anomaly in this landscape, at least for as far as we could see at this present moment.

At some other time, under different circumstances, I would have been thrilled to hike through this rocky sea of tundra grass, beautifully interspersed with vibrant wild flowers. Even now, I couldn't help but be affected by this striking scene.

"It's beautiful!" I exclaimed, glancing over at Bailey.

"It is. But, it's so desolate," she replied.

Desolate wasn't quite the word that I would have chosen; "untouched" would have been nearer the mark. Raising my hand to my forehead to shield my eyes, I searched the landscape for some sign of water nearby.

"I think I see a stream out there," I said, pointing to a shimmering, silvery thread on the eastern landscape, a little more than a mile away.

Taking a moment to reevaluate our current course, I tried to ascertain if I needed to adjust our bearing at all. We had no way of knowing our current direction, other than an educated guess based on where I had seen the sun rise earlier in the day. I knew there was some method I could use that involved sticks and marking the motion of the sun which would enable me to know the true direction, but, if I had ever learned this skill, I had long since forgotten it. Neither of us had a wristwatch to serve as a makeshift, nonmagnetic compass either, so an educated guess at where true east lay was the best that I could do. As I viewed the landscape, I wished, to no avail, that I had taken the time to learn the skill of orienteering.

Steadily, we made our way eastward, toward what we both hoped was a source of water, since all three of our bottles were now almost empty. Within another half of an hour, we came to the small creek that we had seen from the forest's edge.

"Let's drink as much as we can now, then refill the bottles before we move on," I instructed. "Worst-case scenario, we can always come back here if we don't find any water ahead."

I was amazed by the profound emotional impact something so simple as finding water had on both Bailey and myself. I had gone from being grim and disconsolate to being almost jovial, and Bailey's downtrodden demeanor gave way to a tentative lightheartedness as we slaked our thirst.

After we drank our fill, a smile came to my lips as I asked, "What is the first thing you are going to do when you get home?"

She thought for a moment, then answered, "Take a hot shower."

It occurred to me that it must have been hard for any girl, but especially for one her age, not having running water, soap, conditioner, or any of the other things that we take for granted in our daily lives.

"What would you do?" she asked.

I pondered the question, running through an ever-growing list in my mind. Finally, I answered, "I'm going to order the biggest bacon cheeseburger I can find."

I was hungry. Actually, I was more than hungry; I was ravenous, and I was sure Bailey was just as famished as I was. Somehow, after the mental image of a steaming, juicy cheeseburger, the concept of having half of a protein bar for lunch seemed anything but appetizing. "For now, I guess I'll have to settle for some of this," I said as I handed half to her.

Food was becoming more of a concern. We now had only two protein bars left, and there was no foreseeable way to replenish our larder. I knew there was game around, somewhere out in this vast tundra, but hunting took time, skill, and a thorough knowledge of the land. While I had some skill, the other two traits were in short supply. Secretly, I hoped we could find a stream that had some fish in it, but even if we managed to do so, catching them might prove difficult, or even impossible, since we had no fishing tackle, no line, and no bait. Pushing these thoughts aside, we began our trek again.

Our bodies protested under the weight as we shouldered our packs. We were both still sore from the crash, and trudging through the rocky expanse of tundra grass with the extra weight of our packs on our backs only served to increase our discomfort.

Giving one last glance toward the little creek that had supplied us with water, we walked toward the ever-receding eastern horizon, which marked the way toward civilization.

As we walked, Bailey's final words by her father's grave continued to plague me. I wasn't sure whether it was appropriate to ask her about it, but the desire to know more about her life eventually won out over my fear of reopening any emotional wounds that she might have. Also, I somehow felt that hearing about Harold's life might give me a little more peace about his death.

"Tell me about your father," I ventured. "With all that we've gone through, I feel like I should know him a little better."

"There's not much to tell," she replied, after a long, awkward pause. "He and my mom were divorced when I was six."

Hesitating, she continued, "After he came back from the Persian Gulf War, my mom got pregnant with me. Soon, he started drinking. Just a little at first, but, before long, it began to take over his life. My mom said that he had trouble coping with what he had seen over there, and he never really felt like he had anyone he could talk to about it. So, slowly, he became more and more consumed by his internal struggle and drank to ease the pain. Things started getting worse between him and my mom. They were always arguing and fighting about one thing or another. Anyway, one day, when I was six, he hit my mom while he was in a drunken rage. That afternoon, my mom left him and took me to California, where she and I lived with my grandparents.

"My dad and I never really talked much growing up. He stayed up in Alaska, and we stayed down in California. He'd send a card every once in awhile, for my birthday or for Christmas... when he wasn't too drunk to remember," she stopped, embarrassed that she had shared so much.

"But you two seemed to have a decent relationship now," I said, confused by the tenderness that I had witnessed during his last moments on earth.

"Yeah. A few months ago he called me out of the blue. He said that he was sorry for the way he had been living and for how that must have affected me and my mom. He explained that he had been going to church and to Alcoholics Anonymous and that he'd been sober for almost a year now. He told me that he wanted to try to start over again with me and get to know me again, and he asked if I would be willing to come up to see him over my summer break."

A sudden, startling change came over her face. "I hated him for calling. I hated him for asking. I *hated* him." She paused as tears welled up in her eyes. "I hung up on him then and there and vowed that I'd never go to see him, and that I'd never talk to him ever again, as long as I lived. But, over the course of the next couple of months, my attitude toward him softened, and I hated that too. I had been so angry with him for so long that I wasn't even sure why I hated him. My conscience began to tell me that maybe I was wrong for hating him, and maybe I should give him a chance. I went through a pretty bitter internal struggle for a while. I felt like if I relented, even if I just called him, it would be like I was saying that everything he had done in the past was OK. Deep down, I knew that wasn't true.

"It took a few weeks, but, eventually, I worked up the courage to call him. It was pretty awkward at first, but after a few conversations with him, despite my vow, I decided I would go visit him, but for only a couple of days. Well, a couple of days turned into a couple of weeks, a couple of good weeks... until now." A stream of tears was falling as she finished.

I was overwhelmed. Her story was even more tragic than I had ever imagined. Unable to respond right away, all I could eventually manage was, "I'm sorry."

"Me too," she said through her tears.

We walked on in silence for quite some time after this exchange. For my part, I was at a loss about what I could say, fearing that anything I could offer would seem inconsequential.

By mid-afternoon, we had covered about six miles, as far as I could tell. My feet were aching, and my shoulders were protesting under the weight of my pack. We needed to stop soon, but I was hoping to make it to what appeared to be a wooded area a couple of miles ahead. We hadn't seen it earlier in the day, since it was beyond the horizon at the time, and, even now, we couldn't be sure that it wasn't just a broad patch of darker scrub grass.

Stopping for a moment, I took more time to consider whether or not we should push onward toward the forest or stop for the day, giving our bodies ample opportunity to rest for tomorrow's journey.

Although we were both tired, and would have liked nothing more than to stop, I thought of several reasons why we should keep moving. First, we were exposed to the elements out here on the open tundra. Plus, if we did stop for the night, we didn't have anything to use for pegs and posts to secure the tarp, so we wouldn't be able to have a roof over our heads. Furthermore, there was nothing to make a fire with out here on the plain, and we could use a good fire this evening, if for no other reason than to boost our morale.

After Bailey and I discussed the matter for a few minutes, we decided to push on until we made it to what we hoped was a band of woods, even if that meant making a hasty camp in the dark when we finally got there.

The sun was just beginning to disappear under the western horizon when we finally reached the edge of what, fortunately for us, ended up being a forest. Bailey and I were both exhausted, making the idea of setting up camp seem almost torturous. By this point, neither of us had slept for at least a day and a half, and we had just walked close to eight miles. This would have been difficult under normal circumstances, but our bodies were stiff and sore from the crash, making every movement an exercise in pain tolerance. Not to mention, we had only had a few bites of food since the crash, so our bodies were running on an empty tank. These factors combined to make even the simplest tasks seem daunting.

By the time we dropped our packs, it was almost completely dark under the cover of the pine trees. We hastily searched for a suitable place to make camp.

"This looks like as good a spot as any," I said, shining my flashlight onto a level piece of ground a few yards within the wooded area. "Let's get the tarp set up, then we can work on getting a fire started."

The light was slowly fading and night had almost completely settled over the plain as we finished setting up our shelter. The beam from my headlamp, while casting a bright swath of light for several yards, was quickly swallowed by the utter darkness within the woods.

"How are you feeling?" I asked as we spread out Bailey's bed roll and the garbage bag that served as my insulation bed.

"I'm pretty sore and tired..." she hesitated, "and hungry."

"How's your head?" I asked, trying my best not to think about food.

"The bump only hurts when I touch it, and I still have a little headache. But my whole body is so sore that I can't really tell what hurts and what doesn't."

"Well, let's get some wood together, then; once we get a fire started, we can split a protein bar. Maybe that will make us both feel a lot better," I said, hoping that the thought of a meal, however small, would motivate us to work more quickly.

First, we cleared the ground a few feet in front of the tarp, moving anything that might inadvertently spread the fire. Laying down some large chunks of bark for a base, to keep our tinder and kindling off of the ground, we proceeded to gather wood.

"Why don't you collect the small stuff? Try to gather dry twigs from the ends of dead branches, about the width of a piece of pencil lead. Grab a few handfuls, and put them on the bark base that we laid down. While you're doing that, I'll work on collecting the pencil-sized and thumb-thick wood. After that, maybe we can both try to find some bigger pieces. However, while we're working, let's make sure that neither of us goes too far from the shelter," I suggested.

What normally would have taken a few minutes, even in the dark, ended up taking almost a half an hour. But, despite the delay, we had a generous pile of wood by the end of that time. All I had to do now was make some shavings for tinder, and, with a little bit of luck, we would have a roaring fire in no time.

Unsheathing my Stilwell Knives Model Five, I began making some very fine shavings from a piece of fatwood I had found on a nearby pine. The fatwood, crystalized with rich, flammable pine resin, would burn much more vigorously than most other wood, giving us a much-needed advantage. I breathed in deeply as I made the pile of shavings, savoring the pungent smell that I had grown to love.

"Just start the fire," Bailey said in frustration as she watched me making the shavings.

"Despite what you may have seen on TV and in movies, just because you have wood and matches doesn't mean that you can start a fire," I replied. "You have to prepare the wood so that it will easily catch a spark. That's what I'm doing now by making shavings…. There, that ought to do the trick," I said, looking up at Bailey, forgetful of the headlamp's bright rays emanating from my forehead. After a quick apology for nearly blinding her, I pulled the ferro rod out of my pocket and prepared to start the fire.

"Why don't you just use a match?" she asked as my first shower of sparks was unsuccessful.

"Because we only have 25 matches," I retorted, "and when they're gone, they're gone. I want to try to save them for when we actually need them."

Another shower of sparks rained down onto my tinder pile as I slid the striker along the length of the ferro rod. The shavings still did not catch. It was late. It was dark. We were tired, hungry, and scared, and we needed this fire. No, *I* needed this fire. I had started fires with my firesteel hundreds, maybe even thousands of times, but the stakes weren't quite as high then.

Focus, I chided myself, *focus on what you are doing. Don't let your emotions get the better of you.*

Taking a deep, calming breath, I tried again. A cry of triumph escaped from my lips as a small tongue of yellow flame leapt to life among the shavings. Quickly, I placed a handful of the smallest kindling over the flame and watched with excitement as the smallest twigs began to burn. Next, I added the pencil-thick wood, and, waiting until it was fully aflame, I arranged the thumb-thick wood over the growing fire. Within a few minutes, all of the effort that we put into gathering and preparing the wood was rewarded by a small, but steadily crackling fire.

"Too bad we don't have any marshmallows," I said, smiling as I handed half of our second-to-last protein bar to Bailey. The warmth of the fire somehow seemed to make everything we had suffered feel more distant, more bearable. Even Bailey, who had been taciturn ever since she had opened up about her childhood, managed a half-hearted smile.

Despite the fact that we were both exhausted, neither of us seemed to have much of a desire to turn in for the night. It felt almost as if the disquieting thoughts from the night before were just waiting to assail us. However, since neither of us had slept for nearly 48 hours, sleep was probably what we needed most.

"We should probably get some rest," I opined.

Bailey seemed more than a little apprehensive about this idea, and just sat by the fire, lost in thought.

"I'm not tired," she replied, not bothering to look over at me.

"How can you not be tired?"

"I'm just not!" she shot back defensively.

"What's this all about?" I barked, letting my frustration get the better of me. I couldn't make her go to sleep, and normally, I wouldn't have cared, but our exhaustion was only going to slow us down, at best, or could get us killed, at worst. Tired people make stupid mistakes, and out here there was little room for error.

"It's just... It's just... It's..." she stammered. "How do I know that I can trust you?" she said, with a look mixed with shame for feeling the need to ask the question, and anger that there may be truth to her doubts. There was good deal more implied in that simple question than her words conveyed, but her demeanor made her meaning crystal clear.

"What? Where... where is this coming from?"

"You're a man, aren't you?" she shot back derisively. "I've been around enough of you to know what you're all like. And, now you have me here, alone, in the middle of who-knows-where... so, how do I know I can trust you?"

"You don't. But, I think that deep down you're convinced you can. Otherwise, why would you have come along with me?"

"It's not like I had much of a choice," she said, a slow fire kindling in her eyes, made even sharper by the yellowish light of the flames reflected in them. "You've got the food, you've got the map, you've got the guns, and you've got the gear. What was I supposed to do, stay behind and die?"

A feeling of pity, mixed with indignation at her suspicions, began to grow within me. What horrible experiences must she have had to make her distrust men so much? And, in this particular case, she was partially right, not about my character, but about her position. I did have the map, gear, food, and guns. Her situation wasn't very tenable. She needed me to survive... me, a guy she hardly knew, with whom she was stuck far from the outside world, far from home, far from anyone who could help her if I was the kind of man she feared that I might be.

"Have I done anything to show you that I can't be trusted? Haven't I taken care of you so far? Haven't I shown you respect?" I stopped, letting these points sink in. "Don't judge me by your past experiences, whatever they may be; judge me by my actions."

"Sure, that's easy for you to say..." she trailed off, leaving the rest of her statement unfinished.

I was trying to be understanding, but I was physically and emotionally drained.

Getting up, I walked over to the pile of gear, and hastily retrieved the AR-7. Bailey recoiled a bit as I marched back toward her, holding the gun.

"Here," I said, handing it to her, "Now *you* have a gun." She looked up at me, confusion on her face, as, opening my pack, I retrieved the Survive Knives GSO 5.1, and placed it by her side. "And, now you have a knife. So, even if you can't trust me, you can at least defend yourself."

She sat silently for a moment, looking back and forth between the gun sitting across her knees, and the knife resting by her feet. "I'm sorry," she said, avoiding my gaze. "This isn't who I normally am. I'm just having trouble coping with everything that's happened in the past couple of days. My emotions are just a jumbled mess right now."

"Don't be sorry," I responded. "You have been through a lot lately. And, you're right about the fact that we really don't know anything about each other. It must be hard being stuck out here with a strange man as your only companion. Just do me a favor," I said, moving on from this topic. "Don't mess with the gun too much until I show you how to use it in the morning."

"How do you know I don't know how to use it?" she asked, surprised by the accuracy of my intuition.

I laughed out loud. "The fact that you're holding it like a snake that might just jump up and bite you."

After this exchange, we made our way to the shelter and laid down for the night. As I closed my eyes, I couldn't help but wonder how my friends and family were taking the news that I was missing. That was, of course, assuming that anyone had realized we actually were missing. For all I knew, everyone might think I was safe and sound in Fort Yukon, enjoying the wild countryside while I fished, hiked, and canoed in relative safety.

The last image my waking mind saw was my mother, weeping as she heard the news about the crash, juxtaposed with the picture of my former boss smugly gloating that I had received my "just desserts." Then, sleep took me, and I knew no more.

Chapter 7

Hunter or Hunted?

Suddenly, I was startled out of the depths of sleep. "What was that?" I asked, struggling to regain consciousness. In vain, I reached for the lamp on my nightstand, hoping that turning on the light would help me make sense of everything. In confusion, I began to realize that the lamp wasn't there and neither were my clock and my nightstand. None of this made any sense.

Where am I? Why are there trees everywhere? What am I doing here? My mind struggled to process the situation. Then, the awful realization came as a blow. *I remember....*

A long, mournful howling broke the stillness of the night, and nearby, it was answered by another howl. A few hundred yards away, on the grassy tundra, a horrid sound reverberated on the calm night air. Some poor animal was screaming its death knell.

Bailey bolted upright as the muffled sound of growls mixed with the piercing squeals of some dying animal that was being massacred out on the plain.

"What is that?" Bailey whispered, the embers of the dying fire illuminating her face just enough for me to read the terror that was written there.

"Wolves," I whispered back in a voice full of concern. Slowly, I got up, and, as quietly as possible, I grabbed the Mossberg Persuader from where it lay, near at hand. Quietly, I sat back down on my sleeping bag, holding my index finger to my lips, letting Bailey know that she should be quiet. I didn't know enough about wolves to know whether or not we should remain silent, or if we should make noise to alert them to our presence. However, I felt that the wisest option was to be as quiet as possible and make some preparations for defense, just in case.

Thinking we might need to move away from this area if the wolves decided to visit our camp, I hastily put my socks and boots on and motioned to Bailey that she should do the same. Next, I put my headlamp on my forehead, but left it off. I was afraid that turning it on, while allowing me to see any approaching wolves, would attract their attention, which was the last thing we wanted right now.

Faint sounds of yipping and the occasional growl were the only noises that we heard for several minutes, as the wolves gorged themselves on the flesh of their prey. I tried not to picture that scene in my mind. I could tell by the death grip she had on the AR-7 Bailey was thinking the same thing. Back at work, less than a week ago, there was a picture of a wolf pack on my desk with the quote, "Throw me to the wolves, and I'll come back leading the pack." Now, here in the darkness of night, as the wolf pack mercilessly shredded the flesh of their prey, there was much less power in these words.

Staring into the trees around me, by the light of the moon and the dull, eerie glow of the dying fire, I sat, picturing the dreadful wolf pack stealthily closing in on us for the kill.

Straining my senses, I waited, desperately trying to see or hear any sign of approaching wolves. After what seemed like hours, a full chorus of fresh howls broke out. The ominous howling lasted for less than a minute, then died away as the faint echoes reverberated throughout the forest. An oppressive, brooding silence, full of dread, filled the void left by the retreating howls.

I sat like a statue, barely moving or breathing, clutching my shotgun, until the first rays of dawn slowly began to fill the woods.

The fire had died sometime in the night, but Bailey and I had been too afraid to rekindle it. As soon as it was light enough, we walked toward the plain, where last night's tragic scene had unfolded, more out of morbid curiosity than for any other reason.

About 500 yards west of our camp, the torn remains of a moose were scattered in a wide circle, and the blood-stained grass around the body was nearly trampled flat. I was mostly disturbed by the thought of how easily this could have been us. Bailey and I had little desire to linger around this disturbing scene, so we hastily made our way back to camp.

"Can you show me how to use my gun?" Bailey asked as we walked back toward the shelter. There was little doubt that this was prompted by the terror of last night, listening to the moose's slaughter on the open plain and knowing that she had no way to defend herself.

"Sure," I replied. "Once we get back to camp, I'll give you a safety lesson, then show you how to use your rifle."

Once we returned to our shelter, I explained the four universal rules of firearm safety to Bailey.

"Treat all guns as if they are loaded," I began, sounding a bit too much like a stodgy, old professor for my liking.

"Don't point your gun at anything you don't want to shoot. Keep your finger off the trigger until you are ready to shoot. This means that your finger shouldn't touch the trigger until your sights are on target."

"Ok," she replied, digesting the information.

"Lastly," I said, continuing the lesson, "know your target and what is beyond it. This means it is not good enough just to identify something that you intend to shoot. You need to make sure there is nothing beyond your target that could be injured by the shot if you miss, or if the bullet passes through your intended target. Do you have any questions about these rules?"

"No, I think I've got it," she said, repeating each of the rules out loud.

"Alright," I replied, encouraged by the speed with which she had memorized the rules, "let me show you how to use your gun."

I proceeded to show her how to load and unload the chamber, how to engage and disengage the safety, how to load and change magazines, and, lastly, how to properly align the sights on a target.

"Focus on the front sight," I coached, as she aimed at a poor, unsuspecting tree about 20 yards away.

"The target should be blurry, and the rear sight should be blurry, but the front sight should be absolutely crisp. Now slowly press the trigger straight back."

Crack! A shot rang out.

"Good shot!" I exclaimed. Her shot had hit an inch below the knot in the tree at which she had been aiming.

"Really?" she asked, filled with excitement.

"Really. Are you sure you've never shot a gun before?"

"I'm sure," she smiled.

"Well, that was the best first shot I've ever seen."

"I had a good teacher," she replied.

"So you think I've got a future as a firearms instructor?" I asked, returning her smile.

"Sure! Why not open a school right here?"

"And do what, teach moose and caribou how to shoot?"

"Why not?" she chuckled.

"I guess it's better than nothing. Want some breakfast?" I asked, opening our last protein bar.

"Is this the last of it?" she inquired. She seemed very hesitant to eat the last of our food.

"This is it," I replied somberly. "However, I think that it's best to eat it now, to give us some energy for today's walk."

We quickly ate the last protein bar and found that our stomachs felt even emptier than they had before our meager breakfast. Both Bailey and I had become much more somber as we prepared for the day's march, our depression redoubling as we looked down at our packs, thinking of the long march that lay ahead. We both had blisters on our feet from yesterday's trek and our backs ached from our exertions, so we knew that today's walk would be filled with discomfort.

Opening the first aid kit, we both put Band-Aids over the blistered parts of our feet, hoping to protect them from the abuse that they would surely take today. We also each wore a pair of the wool socks from my pack, since the cotton socks that we had been wearing were still wet with a combination of dew and perspiration.

"I could use a walking stick," I said. "You want one?"

"Umm... sure, I guess."

I quickly cut two birch saplings to size and removed the tiny branches from them. Before we had started on our day's journey, I went back out to open plain to get a better idea of which way we should go as we walked through the forest. Now, as we walked through the woods, I tried to find a tree, log, or other landmark that lay ahead to use as a guide, so that we didn't get turned around and end up heading in the wrong direction.

After we had been walking for about an hour, Bailey broke the silence, asking, "What would you be doing right now if you weren't stuck out here with me?"

A laugh escaped from my lips as I considered the irony.

"You know what? I never thought about it like this, but I'd actually be doing almost the exact same thing. I came out to Alaska so that I could go on a wilderness adventure. You know, hiking, camping, fishing, canoeing – that sort of thing."

I thought that the only real difference between what I was doing now and what I would have been doing if we hadn't crashed was that I'd have more food.

"Wait, you mean you were going to pay someone to make you live in crappy conditions like this?" she asked in disbelief.

"Pretty much." I said, thinking that somehow it didn't sounds as glamorous when presented in that light.

"Why?"

"Have you ever felt unhappy in life?" I asked after a minute's reflection.

"Yes," she replied, stopping.

"Have you ever felt like you just needed to get away from everything, from the life that you're living... or, really, the life that you feel trapped in?" I explained.

"So you were trying to escape from something?"

"Yes... well... no, not exactly." I struggled to find the words to explain my thoughts.

"It's like this. I was 'living the dream,' or at least that's what everyone told me. I had a great job, with lots of room for advancement. I earned a decent salary and lived in an upscale neighborhood. But, to me, it wasn't great... it wasn't even good. I hated it! Don't get me wrong, I was glad to have a job, especially when not everyone is as fortunate, but I felt like I was just a pawn in the system. Nothing I was doing in life, except for my leisure, was giving me any satisfaction, or providing me with any sense of purpose. Instead, I found it draining, like it was sucking my very soul from me. I was tired of going to a job I didn't like and working with people who didn't understand me, people who looked down on me because I was different from them."

"And?" she prodded.

"And, I thought that if I could get away from it all, if I could do something I had always wanted to do, if I could fulfill a childhood dream, then maybe I would be able to make sense of it all. I thought that maybe, just maybe, I could figure out where I fit in in this thing we call 'life.' Does that make sense?"

"It makes perfect sense," she quietly replied.

It felt awkward having shared so much of myself with someone I hardly even knew, but somehow, it had come so naturally.

I hadn't expected her to understand. In fact, I half-expected her to scoff at my search for meaning in life. But, instead of scoffing, she seemed to genuinely understand, and even to sympathize with what I was feeling. Sensing that the conversation had come to an end, I started walking again, as Bailey followed along silently.

It was nearly noon, judging by the sun, when we emerged from the woods. Before us was another undulating plain of rocky grassland, stretching for miles, broken only by the serpentine form of a river off in the distance.

"Well, there's more water out there," I said as I pointed, filled with fresh hope at the sight of another source of clean water. "Now let's hope we can find some food."

When we eventually made it to river, we had been walking for hours, but we had only come two or maybe three miles by my estimation. We were starving, and our feet had been battered by the landscape, making the hike to the river a painful, tiring endeavor.

There, on the western bank of the river, we met with our first major check. The river, although no more than 20 yards wide, was swift and deep in spots. I was confident that we could find a place to safely cross, but such a spot might be miles in either direction.

Sitting down on the edge of the bank, we give our tired bodies a well-deserved rest.

"You know," I mused, watching the water run swiftly by, "if I wasn't so hungry, I think I would really enjoy this."

Bailey gave me a perplexed look, so I attempted to explain further. "What we're doing contains a lot of the components everyone needs in life: danger, excitement, challenge, beauty, solitude, and simplicity. For instance, just look at this river! How many people do you think have been here, in this same spot, looking at this river?"

"I don't know," she replied, seeming entirely disinterested.

"I'd be willing to wager that it's not very many. We're here, in a spot that few people even know about, and probably only a handful have ever seen. Doesn't that excite you at all?" I asked, amazed at her apathetic demeanor.

"A little, I guess," she said, more to pacify me than because it was true, "but not as much as the thought of a good meal, or a warm bed."

Looking at the water, I cursed myself for not packing my Pen Rod Extreme - a small, but strong collapsible fishing rod and reel that would have taken up next to no space in my pack. A rod and reel would have been a major asset, allowing us a realistic chance at feeding ourselves. Right now, it was sitting at home, in a drawer, collecting dust. The thought galled me!

Well, I'd better at least try something, I thought. In response, I stood up and drew my knife from its sheath.

"What are you doing?" asked Bailey.

"Making a fishing spear. Can I borrow your walking stick?"

"Don't you have one of your own?" she objected, strangely possessive of something she had only had for a few hours.

"Yeah, but I need to borrow yours. You'll get it back in one piece," I reassured.

I was going to use her walking stick as a baton, to help me pound the edge of my knife's blade into the end of my walking stick. I planned to split the end of my staff into four equal segments, and then use my knife to carve a sharp point onto each of these segments. Having four sharp points would hopefully increase my chances of catching a fish, assuming there actually were any fish in this river. I knew that I could have lashed my knife onto my walking stick and used that as a spear, but I wasn't willing to risk losing my knife when the wooden points would serve my purposes just as well.

"Why don't you just use your axe to split the end of your walking stick?" asked Bailey.

"I could, but using my knife, both of my hands are out of the way, which is much safer in case the blade slips. If I use my axe, I have to hold my walking stick with one hand while swinging the axe with the other. Have you ever seen what an axe can do to a hand that gets in the way?"

"No, but I understand why you're doing it this way now," she replied.

After I split the end of my staff into four equal parts and sharpened them into formidable points, I tied the end of the nylon cordage just below the splits in the staff. I then wrapped the cordage between the two pieces closest to me several times, widening the gap between them to ensure that they would stay open. Turning the staff, I repeated the process again, then wound the rest of the nylon cordage around the length walking stick.

This would serve two purposes. First, it would give me a leash that would keep me from losing my newly made fishing spear. Second, it allowed me to improve the function of the spear by separating the points from one another, without cutting any of the cordage. There was the risk that if the leash, which I would tie to myself, came loose from my wrist, we would lose all of our nylon cordage, but the risk was so minimal I was willing to take it.

"Let's see if we can put this thing to good use," I said, grinning with pride at the spear I had fashioned.

I knew that spearfishing was a tenuous proposition at best, but it wasn't like we had very many options. We hadn't seen any game yet, except for the mauled moose, and we were completely out of food. So this seemed like the only reasonable choice we had for feeding ourselves.

As I considered how to go about using my fishing spear, I was well aware of the risk of drowning, and also had considered the chances of injuring myself by twisting a knee or an ankle while wading into the river. There was also the risk of hypothermia, especially if I didn't dry out by tonight. Still, if I didn't try, we most likely weren't going to eat, and fatigue (from hunger or any other factor) could be just as deadly as any of the other risks out here.

"Let's try to find a place to cross this river," I advised. "We'll keep an eye out along the way for any pools that might contain fish."

Once my spear was finished, we shouldered our packs again and walked southward, following the course of the river. Within 30 minutes, we found a place that looked shallow enough to cross. However, the current was moving swiftly there.

"I'll wade out into the river to see if it is shallow enough for us to safely cross," I said, unwinding some nylon cordage from my walking stick. "Hold onto this; in case I fall, that way I won't be swept away if the water is deeper or swifter than it looks." Pausing for a moment, I added, "If I do get swept downstream, and you can't hold onto the rope, or if it starts to pull you in, just let go. I don't want both of us getting carried away by the current."

"OK," she anxiously replied.

For this trial run, I had left my pack and shotgun on the shore, planning to come back to get them once I was sure we could safely cross the river. Slowly, I waded out into rushing water, which rose up to my calves after the first couple of steps. By the time I was several yards out, the swift current was pushing against the backs of my knees, trying to force me downstream.

"It's really cold!" I shouted back to Bailey, with a slight smile on my face. "Let's hope we don't…" The words died on my lips, as, to my horror, a massive brown figure lumbered around a bend in the river, less than 40 yards away.

The thought that flashed through my mind contained one single, disconcerting word, *Bear!*

Chapter 8

Split-Second Survival

Time seemed to slow to an unnatural pace as my mind struggled to process this situation. Retreat wasn't really an option. I couldn't leave Bailey all alone to fend off one of the world's largest predators. I also knew that I couldn't stay where I was. So, making my way back to the shore and finding a new place to cross this river, one where there wasn't a giant bear nearby, seemed like the only thing that we could do.

I knew that grizzly bears can sometimes be territorial, so I was afraid that this one might charge. That was something that I definitely wasn't prepared for. Sure, I had my 10mm pistol on my hip, but if it actually came down to using my handgun in this situation, the chances were slim that it would do any good. Hitting a moving target with a handgun was very difficult, even in the best of conditions, but now, standing in a frigid river, fighting to maintain my balance as I moved, it would be next to impossible. And, assuming my shot hit the bear, there was a good chance that a 10mm bullet wouldn't have the power to kill it, even if it was well-placed. And, the last thing I wanted to do was to wound the bear, only to face the full extent of its rage.

Mere seconds had passed as I processed these thoughts, while the bear lumbered along the shore, seeming completely oblivious to our presence.

Suddenly, the bear paused in its tracks. It had seen me. Slowly, I began to make my way back toward the shore. As I made my way closer to the bank, I glanced over at Bailey. The color had totally drained from her face, and a look of terror was fixed upon her features.

"Don't make any sudden movements," I called, trying not to raise my voice too loudly, fearing that it would provoke the bear.

The grizzly now began to walk straight toward us, very deliberately, at a moderate, lumbering pace. It was now only 30 yards away as I started to come ashore. It began grunting in short, intermittent, low growls as it approached.

Everything I had ever learned about how to deal with bears had been momentarily erased from my mind, otherwise, I would have waved my arms and shouted, "Hey bear," and tried to make myself look as big as possible. However, for now, all I could think about was getting to my shotgun, which was now only 20 feet away on the bank leaning against my pack. The closer this imposing grizzly bear got, the bigger it seemed, and the more I was impressed by the fact that *it* was at the top of the food chain out here, and I might just be what was for dinner.

Suddenly, everything seemed to happen at once. The massive grizzly broke into a furious charge. Its low growls were punctuated by its efforts to quickly gain momentum as it bore down upon us. Bailey let out a shrill scream, and, turning around, began to run away while I dashed toward my shotgun, as fast as my sodden boots would take me over the wet silt of the bank.

The bear had me beat... I was sure of it. There was no way I was going to be able to make it to the shotgun, get it to my shoulder, disengage the safety, and fire a well-placed shot before the enormous bear would be on top of me, mauling me to death.

In spite of my fear, I was amazed at how quickly the colossal, clumsy animal was closing the distance. In another couple of seconds, it would be on top of me.

Instinctively, I began to draw my Glock 20 as the charging grizzly filled my field of vision.

Every sense seemed to be distorted as I struggled to bring my handgun into action. As if my sense of sight was failing me, the bear was just a confused blur of brown, speeding toward me. And, despite the fact that my ears had been working just fine a moment ago, all sound had turned into a cacophony of indistinguishable noises.

To make matters worse, time was completely distorted. My actions seemed to be slowing down to an unnaturally sluggish pace, while the bear's movements were sped up to a mind-numbing blur. It was almost like I was stuck inside of a nightmare, only one from which there was no waking.

Nothing seemed to be working in my favor. I needed more speed, more distance, more time.

Any millisecond now, I expected to be trampled down, and ripped limb from limb in a violent, agonizing death.

Bang! Finally bringing my pistol into play, I fired a hasty, un-aimed shot.

Before I had time to pull the trigger again, the bear suddenly broke its charge and veered past me, off into the shallows of the river about five yards away. Had it continued its charge, instead of turning aside and running past me, I would have been bowled over before I even had a chance to think about firing a second shot.

The grizzly quickly began to circle back around, moving several yards downstream of me. Then, it stopped, seeming unsure whether to charge again, or to give up and lumber off to some other less populated section of the river.

Shaking with fear, and from the effects of the adrenaline dump I was experiencing, I placed my sights over the bear's chest, ready to fire if it moved toward me, when another thought occurred to me. Here was food – literally hundreds of pounds of meat. And, here we were, starving, with no prospect of another meal, possibly for the entire time we were stuck out here in this wilderness.

I knew that this was dangerous thinking. Sure, we could eat this bear, assuming I could kill it without it killing me first. But, a misplaced shot could mean a quick, but painful death by being mauled by a wounded and enraged grizzly. However, a well-placed shot could literally mean life for Bailey and me.

Slowly, I backpedaled toward my pack, keeping my eyes firmly fixed upon the brooding bear. It had now turned to face me, and was grunting and popping its jaws, making a loud snapping sound. Drool poured from its lips, as it tried its best to intimidate me.

As I continued backward, the bear became less aggressive, seeming content with the fact that it was scaring me off, since I was backing away from it. Little did it know what was in store for it. Reaching down, I carefully holstered my pistol, then, snatching up the shotgun, I hastily brought it up to my shoulder.

Part of me thought that it was a shame to shoot such a majestic and powerful creature, especially now that it no longer seemed to be an immediate threat to my safety, but I also realized that we desperately needed food.

I disengaged the safety, as the front sight came to rest over the stationary form of the bear.

I didn't have a good shot, since it was facing me head on. I stood irresolute for a moment, searching my mind for some way to get the bear to move, giving me a better shot. Then, having come up with a strategy, I deliberately took a step forward.

The bear, in another effort to intimidate me, took a couple of steps toward me, then stood up on its hind legs, presenting me with a perfect shot.

BOOM! The shotgun let out a deafening roar as I pulled the trigger. Instinctively, I chambered another round, in case I had to shoot the bear again, but there was no need to do so. The grizzly had fallen over and was now gasping out its last breaths.

I had hunted for years, but in all of my time in the woods, I had never felt more remorse than I did at this moment. Maybe it was because before, when I was hunting back at home, I was warm, well-fed, and adequately clothed. But here, now, fighting for my life in the wild, I somehow pitied the bear, realizing that it was engaged in the very same struggle to survive. Just like me, it had fought with every fiber of its being to withstand the rigors of nature. It had known both cold and hunger, just as I knew them now. It had finally lost that struggle, and I was the one who killed it.

My conscience pained me as I watched the bear in its death throes.

Bailey had walked up beside me while I was lost in contemplation, staring at the body of the grizzly whose life I had taken, lying with its hind legs in the river and its head on the shore.

"Is it dead?" she asked with a tremble in her voice.

"Yeah," I said, still struggling with the feeling of guilt, "I think it's dead. Let me make sure though. You stay here."

I approached the grizzly bear's body with my shotgun ready. I was confident that it was dead, having seen it breathe its last, but I also knew that hunters have been injured or killed by animals that they were certain were "dead."

When I got within a pace of the body, I leaned down with the barrel of my gun pointed at the grizzly's head, and poked its eye with the tip of the barrel. It was definitely dead.

Reengaging the safety on the shotgun, I slung it to my back and called to Bailey, "It's safe. You can come on over now!"

"I'm not coming anywhere near that thing, dead or not!" she said, recoiling in fear and disgust.

"Do you want to starve to death then?" I snapped.

"You want me to eat *that?*" she replied, even more disgusted.

"At this point, I don't care what *you* eat, but I'm hungry, and this is fresh meat."

After several minutes of work with my Model Five, I had managed to harvest about 30 pounds of meat, probably enough for the next two or three days, and placed it in the garbage bag I had been using for a bed roll. I had thought about putting some extra meat in the other garbage bag, and having Bailey carry it, but I knew that this extra meat would spoil over the course of the next couple of days, making it inedible, so we ultimately decided against it. It was a shame to leave all the rest of that meat there to rot, but I just didn't think we could spare the time to try to preserve any of it.

Finishing the task of harvesting the meat, I hastily rinsed both the knife and my hands off and prepared for the rest of the day's journey.

"We really need to get going," I said, noticing that the sun was riding its downward course toward the western horizon.

I held my hands up in front of my eyes, resting my left hand on the visible horizon line to the west. Next, I placed my right hand on top of my left. Then, moving my bottom hand so that it rested on top of my right hand, I gauged how many hours were left before sundown.

"Three hand widths between the sun and the horizon. That means we have about three hours before the sun sets. So, we need hustle if we're to find a way to cross this river safely and make it to those woods before it gets dark," I said, pointing eastward.

We shouldered our packs while we considered what the best course of action would be. After a couple of minutes, both Bailey and I came to the conclusion that we should walk a little further south, to see if we could find a safer place to cross this river. My first attempt, even if it hadn't been interrupted by the bear, would have been cut short anyway, since the water was too swift to safely cross. However, we decided that if we couldn't find a safer crossing within 15 minutes, we would turn around, come back to this spot, and take the risk of fording the river here.

Walking was much more laborious now that I was carrying the bag of bear meat, hoisted over my left shoulder like some kind of meat-bearing Santa Claus. I knew that many backpackers frequently carried as much weight as I was carrying, but the combined 60 pounds was taking a heavy toll on my tired body.

About a quarter mile downstream, we found a broad, shallow shoal where we thought we could cross with minimal risk. The water still moved swiftly here, but it seemed to only be about knee-deep in its deepest spot.

After some discussion about who should go first, we carefully made our way to the other side of the river, and struggled up the opposite bank.

We had been walking for a few minutes when Bailey asked, "Why didn't you run away from the bear?"

"I wouldn't have gotten very far if I did," I reasoned.

"I know, but you could have run away anyway. Weren't you scared?"

The thought occurred to me that she might be feeling guilty because she had run away and left me all alone to face the charging bear.

"Of course I was scared. I was terrified," I explained, "but I knew that if I ran I was going to die, but if I stayed and fought, there was a chance, however remote, that I would live. Besides," I added, "there was also a chance the bear was just trying to scare us off, and didn't actually want to hurt us."

"But you didn't know that."

"No, I didn't know that. In fact, I was pretty sure I was going to die," I explained, reliving some of the terror from earlier in the day. "Look, I'm not saying I didn't feel like running away. In all actuality, I did. But, I also didn't want to go out without a fight. If you feel bad about running away, you shouldn't. You followed your instincts. Your brain told your legs to get out of there, and you ran. There's no shame in that."

Bailey became silent for a moment, then said, "So, you're not mad at me then, for running away... for leaving you alone?"

"No," I replied honestly. "Quite frankly, I think it would have been harder for me to concentrate on dealing with the bear if you would have stayed. When you ran, I knew you were safe for the time being, so I was able to concentrate on stopping the bear from killing me."

"OK," she said, relieved by my answer.

It was nearly sunset by the time we reached the edge of this newest patch of forest. Being more exhausted than either of us had been up to this point, it took us nearly an hour to make camp. After our shelter was set up, we worked, with as much energy as we could muster, on collecting wood to make a fire so that we could cook our supper of grizzly bear meat. The prudent thing to do out here in bear country would have been to make a separate cooking fire, at least 100 feet (but preferably 100 yards) away from where we were going to sleep, but we were far too tired to be prudent.

It had been dark for a couple of hours by the time the fire was big enough to cook the bear meat. I cut a steak into manageable chunks and skewered several of these with a pine branch. Before long, the meat began to sizzle, filling the air around us with the tantalizing smell of broiling meat. This smell, after having eaten so little for the past couple of days, made our stomachs ache with hunger.

"Let's just eat it now!" said Bailey, frustrated at how long it was taking the meat to cook.

In all reality, the meat had only been over the fire for a few minutes, but watching the steamy juices drip off into the fire, while we were racked with hunger, made even seconds seem like an eternity.

"Suit yourself," I replied, handing the stick over to Bailey. She looked at the meat for a moment, seeming to have second thoughts about eating it before it was fully cooked. Then, her hunger getting the better of her, she took a ravenous bite. A smile of pure delight spread across her lips as she chewed the piping-hot meat.

"This is really good!" she exclaimed, then quickly took another greedy bite. How much we ate that night would be the source of legend, if someone else had been there to witness it. The more we ate, the better we felt, both physically and emotionally. Our moods shifted from morose and contemplative to lighthearted and contented. We ate and chatted and joked and laughed into the early hours of the morning, and then, when we couldn't eat another bite, we went to bed, falling into a deep, dreamless sleep.

****

Despite the terrifying encounter with the grizzly bear earlier in the day, with full stomachs, a decent shelter, and a glowing fire, the night seemed almost inviting. For the first time since the plane crash, we slept without fear. It seemed odd when I reflected on it the next morning. It would have made more sense if we had both lain awake all night, remembering the howling of the wolves and the bear's desperate charge, waiting for some fresh terror to befall us. However, either from sheer exhaustion or maybe from a sense of empowerment, having scored a temporary victory in our fight with nature, both Bailey and I slept well into the morning.

The sun was already up in the sky and the woods were fully alight when I awoke. Bailey was just beginning to stir as I put my boots on.

Last night, as we ate and talked, I remembered that I had a Field Notes booklet in my pack. (Bailey also remembered her copy of "Rogue States;" however, I didn't think *that* was worth much, except maybe as fire starting material.) We both thought that it might not be a bad idea to keep a crude journal of our trip.

As I sat, collecting my thoughts for the day, I began to make my first entries in the little booklet:

Bailey Reynolds & Ryan McQuaid

Aug. 2 – plane crash – Harold died of suspected heart attack. We stayed at crash site.

Aug. 3 – walked 8 miles east – wolves at night – keep predators in mind during rest of trip.

Aug 4 - walked 5 miles – Bear charged by river. Killed bear. Fresh meat!

It wasn't a very detailed journal, but it would help us keep track of the days, our progress along the way, and, in case we didn't make it, it might clear up some of the mystery that would surely surround the discovery of our bodies, assuming anyone ever did discover them.

I had just finished the journal entries when Bailey walked up beside me. "What are you doing?" she asked, filled with curiosity.

"Working on the journal of our trip," I replied, showing her the entries.

"Not much to it," she said after reading the entries.

"It's a journal, not a diary," I retorted.

"Whatever you say. What time is it?" she asked, changing the subject.

"I have no idea. Mid-morning, judging from the sun. You could always check your phone."

"I hadn't thought of that," she replied, shocked by that fact.

A quick glance showed that the battery was dead. It was a little too late now, but it would have been a good idea to have turned off her phone, saving the battery, and, obviously, not to have destroyed my phone in a fit of rage. We may have been able to find a place out here with cell phone service and used one of the phones to call for help. However the odds of getting service anywhere out here on the North Slope were extremely remote.

After taking a few minutes to gather some wood and get the fire going again, we began cooking some of the remaining bear meat to eat throughout the day. We huddled around the fire as we cooked the rest of the meat, eating as we went.

Both of us were glad to have a fire this morning, since it was much colder than it had been on any of the previous mornings. In fact, it was so chilly that I was surprised we hadn't seen any frost on the ground.

Once we had eaten our fill, we began placing the cooked meat in the other remaining garbage bag, which I had used for a bedroll last night. We thought it would be imprudent to put it back in the bag that had been filled with the raw bear meat.

"Your head is looking better," I observed, noticing that the bruising from her injury was starting to heal. "How have you been feeling?"

"Sore and tired, but I feel a lot better now that I have a full stomach," she replied, as she nibbled on a piece of bear meat.

"Just think of the soreness as part of the process of getting home," I encouraged, trying to sound wise, but feeling like I had failed in the attempt.

"Yeah," she responded, not convinced by my logic.

"Wonder what our friends and family are going through right now," I said, giving voice to this thought which continually troubled me. They had to know by now that the plane carrying us to Point Barrow had never reached its destination. They also had to know that we had yet to be found. Since no one had heard from us yet, everyone probably assumed that we were dead.

"My mom's probably too busy with work to care," Bailey began, obviously jaded toward the idea of parental affection. "If I know my friends, most of them have posted something on Twitter or Facebook about how sad they are and have moved on with their lives... assuming their posts got enough likes. And my stepdad... well, he's probably on the couch playing video games and eating junk food, since he's too lazy to actually get a job."

"Do you really think that everyone has moved on? I mean, it's only been a few days, you know," I retorted.

"I know," she said, coldly. "Do *you* think *your* friends and family are pining away for you?" she added derisively.

"Yes, actually, I do. My mom is probably a wreck right now," I replied, unfazed by her cynicism. "My dad is, I'm sure, doing his best to be strong. I don't have very many friends, but I know that the ones that I do have are praying for me and for my family." I paused, seeing her eyes tear up. "Now, my former coworkers, they're probably oblivious; and my former boss... I honestly wouldn't be surprised if he is throwing a party right now in celebration of my demise," I chuckled at the mental image of Paul cutting the "Happy Landings" cake in my memory.

"Well, nobody is praying for me," she snapped, with a mixture of jealousy and despondency.

"I am," I replied.

She began to cry.

I've sure got a way with women, I said to myself as I helplessly watched Bailey bury her head in her knees, sobbing.

"We're going to make it," I encouraged, hoping to calm her down. "We're already at least 10 miles closer to civilization, maybe even 15. Besides, it's not that bad; just think of it like a vacation... a vacation, exercise program, and diet plan, all rolled into one. I bet celebrities would even pay millions to do this, as long as it had a cool name."

She looked up, laughing a little through her tears. "You're a horrible liar, but I appreciate it. This whole situation is just so overwhelming."

"Well, it might be a little less overwhelming if we gave it a cool name. Let's call it the... hmmm... the... no... the..."

"The North Slope Diet?"

I laughed out loud, and she soon joined in, forgetful of her sorrow a few moments ago. From this point on, we referred to our journey as the North Slope Diet.

We had finished cooking the meat, packed all of our gear up, and began our eastward journey by early afternoon. After a couple of hours of walking, we came to the end of woods and were once again walking on a wide open plain.

As I surveyed our surroundings, I was beginning to think that we were actually walking southeast, because the rugged wall of mountains to the south appeared slightly more pronounced than it previously had. However, this could have just been some kind of optical illusion.

We took a brief break at the edge of the woods. "It looks like it's going to be a while before we see another band of forest," I observed gravely.

The tundra swept on before us and seemed to extend to the horizon many miles to the east. This was a discouraging prospect. No forest meant no shelter from the elements, and, more importantly, it also meant that we had no way to make a fire.

I stopped to consider the best course of action.

"I'm not really sure what to do now," I said, voicing my concerns to Bailey. "We could keep walking, but we'll probably only make it three or four more miles before sunset. Also, unless we bring some poles with us, we won't be able to make a shelter, and, even if we do make a shelter, we won't be able to start a fire to keep ourselves warm tonight. This fact alone concerns me, especially with how cold it's been today. However, if we stop here for the night, we'll most likely still have to camp out there on the open plain at least one night, maybe more."

"I'm not sure I like either option," Bailey replied.

"That sums up my thoughts on the matter as well," I responded. "However, there is one thing that makes me think we should keep pushing forward." I paused for effect.

"Which is?" she asked, implying that I should just get to the point.

"Right now we have food, but it is going to gone by morning. We're not sure we're going to get any more for the rest of the trip. So, the longer we delay now could directly correlate to the amount of time we have to press on without any food in our stomachs."

"Then let's get to walking," she exclaimed, standing up and shouldering her pack.

"Let me cut a few sticks and tie them to the top of my pack," I said, digging the saw out of my pack. I intended to use these branches for poles and pegs so that we could set our tarp up out on the plain.

Within a few minutes, we were on our way again. While we both looked out upon the landscape, neither of us really were in the mood to appreciate the amazing beauty of the sea of tundra grass, dotted by various small lakes and ponds, and interspersed with small, but vibrant patches of wild flowers of all colors.

We had trudged on in silence for over an hour when I felt the need to lift our sagging spirits. A song came to mind that was very relevant to our situation - "500 Miles." Without a word of warning, I began singing at the top of my lungs, in my best British accent. I didn't bother to look over my shoulder at Bailey, who was walking a couple of steps behind me, but I'm sure she was more than a little surprised, and possibly also afraid that I was losing it.

After I had finished the entire song, Bailey asked, with a mix of laughter and surprise in her voice, "What the heck was that?"

"What?" I asked, shocked by her question. "Don't tell me you don't know that song? It's a classic!"

"Nope," she replied, even more amused now. "I can honestly say I've never heard it."

"You need some culture," I teased. "Alright then, what do you have to bring to the table?" I challenged, curious to see what she thought a good walking song would be.

"I don't know. You seem to be the song expert."

"Know any Billy Joel?"

"I don't think so," she replied, mildly ashamed at striking out twice in a row.

"Well, you're about to," I said, giving my best rendition of "You May Be Right," as we trudged along.

By evening, we were starting to get low on water again, but there were enough lakes and ponds dotting the landscape that we weren't worried about our ability to resupply.

The lower edge of the sun was just starting to touch the western horizon when we decided to stop for the night. Before we went to work setting up our shelter for the night, I gazed eastward, surveying the land that we would have to walk through in the morning. Out in the distance, the fading light glimmered with a reddish hue along the serpentine thread of a river, wider than the one we had crossed the day before. While it was difficult to tell anything for sure from this distance, I was worried that it would be an imposing barrier to our progress.

We'll cross that bridge when we get to it, I said to myself, not looking forward to the prospect of fording another stream.

Since we were out in the open, I thought it would be best to set our shelter up a little differently than we had while we were in the woods. Instead of setting it up in a rectangular shape, with two level front posts and two level rear pegs, I set it up in a diamond configuration, with three of the posts close to ground level and the fourth between waist and chest high at the opening of the shelter. I put the rear of the shelter facing in the direction of the prevailing wind, which allowed us to be protected from the elements out here on the open plain.

It was almost too dark to see without the aid of our flashlights by the time we had finished arranging our sleeping bags and bed rolls. Since there were no pine needles on the plain, I stuffed the bag that had housed the raw bear meat with an ample amount of the various plants that grew all around on this plain. While I knew that using the bear meat bag for a bed roll wasn't the best idea, since it might attract predators, there weren't very many other options.

After crawling inside the newly built structure, we ate a cheerless dinner, consisting solely of the last of the bear meat that we had cooked that morning. Neither of us had much to say, both being distracted by our own thoughts.

I found a new annoyance that was plaguing me that evening. I hadn't had an opportunity to shave since the accident, and now my facial hair was at that awkward length where it was constantly itching. As I lay in my sleeping bag, contemplating the next stage of our trip, my thoughts were constantly interrupted by the incessant urge to scratch. This was, by all accounts, a minor inconvenience, but it galled me nonetheless.

As night wore on, my mind was beginning to give way to the feeling of exhaustion which had been creeping over me. I was in that strange limbo between waking and sleeping, when my eyes seemed to catch a movement somewhere outside the shelter. I sat up, feeling a sense of urgency to protect myself from a possible threat. As the fog slowly lifted from my mind, I began to make sense of what was happening; there were vast bands of light performing an elegant dance across the starry night sky.

My fear gave way to wonder as I watched the scene unfold. Varying shades of green and red blended into a tantalizing kaleidoscope of color. After staring in wonder for several moments, I woke Bailey. She started, fearing some new danger had fallen upon us.

"Look!" I said, pointing toward the breathtaking display.

We sat for several minutes, watching the lights change in color and intensity. I had never seen the Northern Lights before, and the sight was nothing short of awe-inspiring.

Gradually, they melted away, until all that could be seen was the starry night sky. For the few moments that we had watched in silent wonder, all of our problems had seemed so remote, so inconsequential. There was a poignant sense of amazement that we felt about being the only people to witness such an extravagant show, which nature seemed to be putting on just for us.

Reluctantly, we crawled back inside our sleeping bags and laid back down for the night.

Morning came, cold and cheerless. A veil of fog had settled over the plain, and the sun vainly struggled to penetrate the gloom. After waking, we took the shelter down as quickly as possible, hoping that getting on the trail would help us warm our chilled bodies.

The moisture in the air made it feel much colder that it actually was, and, dripping with condensation, we shivered as we put our packs on and made our way eastward.

I had an extremely difficult time judging the direction that we should go, since the sun was hidden from view, but hoped that my guess would be good enough to guide us until we could be more certain of our bearing.

"We need to be careful walking," I said, breaking the heavy silence of the gloomy morning. "With as little light as we have, we could easily trip, step into a hole, or something else equally as bad."

"Ok," she replied, crestfallen.

"Go easy on the water too," I cautioned. "We probably won't be able to refill our bottles until we get to the river, which hopefully we'll do in a couple of hours."

We had to walk very slowly because of the fog, but the slower we walked, the colder we felt. About an hour into the day's walk, I began to wonder if it would be more prudent to hunker down until the fog burnt off. We were in a tight spot though. The longer we waited, the later in the day we would come to the river, and, if we didn't have enough time, we might not be able to find a safe place to cross until the next day. And there was always the problem of our lack of food, forcing us to walk onward whether or not we wanted to.

By mid-morning, the fog was beginning to lift, and the sun was peeking through intermittent gaps in the mist. We decided to take a short break to rest our feet, hoping that in a few minutes we would be able to see how far we had come.

While we waited, I warmed my hands, which were stinging from the cold, by placing them in the front pockets of my pants. Despite the fact that I was wearing my work gloves, my hands were still suffering from the harshness of the climate. I had put my wool cap on last night, but this morning I gave it to Bailey, reasoning that it would be cruel to protect my head and hands, while allowing her to suffer. So, my ears were red and aching, and her hands were all but numb, despite the fact that she had kept them in her jacket pockets for most of the day's trek.

"Let's hope the sun warms this place up soon," I shivered.

"Yeah, I can't take much more of this cold," Bailey replied, her teeth chattering.

As we stood, shivering, Bailey and I naturally gravitated toward one another, hoping to preserve our body heat by being in close proximity. The dew-laden grass had soaked our shoes and pant-legs and had added to our distress, so the combined warmth of our bodies as we huddled together was a welcome change.

There was something almost electric about being so close to her. However, I wasn't really sure about her yet, so I fought to keep my feelings in check.

Initially, I thought that I wouldn't like her, since she and I obviously came from different worlds. She was a liberal college girl, and I was a conservative outdoorsman. Yet, in all of our interactions, both the good and the bad, I always ended up feeling drawn to her, whether through sympathy, compassion, or infatuation. But, as I struggled to make sense of what I was feeling, I knew that it was dangerous to go down this road right now. Our main priority out here was survival, and anything that might complicate our lives right now had to be avoided.

Passing the time while we waited for the fog to finally lift, I tightened my belt a notch. Yesterday, I had noticed that despite the legendary feast of bear meat, my pants were beginning to fit more loosely than they had a few days ago.

"Chalk up a win for the North Slope Diet," I said sarcastically.

Bailey cracked a joyless smile. She knew that our weight loss wasn't a good thing.

"You OK today?" I asked, seeing her gloomy expression.

"I don't know.... Why did this happen to us? I mean, why *us*? What did we do to deserve this?" she asked, struggling to make sense of our plight.

"I'm not sure that we'll ever know the answer to those questions. I've given up trying to figure out why things happen. I've found that all I end up doing is driving myself crazy by trying to figure it out. In the end, I'm not even sure that 'why' matters, or at least it doesn't matter nearly as much as 'what?' By that, I mean, 'what are we going to do about it?'"

"I just want to go home," she said, glancing up at me momentarily.

How could I not pity her? I wanted to go home just as badly, and I was doing something that, under normal circumstances, I loved to do. Not to mention, she was still dealing with the loss of her father, had gone through a terrifying encounter with a bear and was constantly faced with the dangers of starvation and hypothermia. I wished there was something I could do for her, but I knew that there wasn't. The only thing that I could do right now was to try to keep both of our minds occupied, to keep them from wandering into dark and depressing contemplation.

"We're getting there," I replied. "Just think of a hot shower and a steaming-hot bacon cheeseburger waiting for you when we do."

"Cheese..." she said, with longing in her voice. "I think I'd honestly pay a million dollars for some cheese right now... especially if it was on some french fries!"

"Ooh," I replied, picturing a huge plate of chili cheese fries, showered in bacon. "You're on. As soon as we get back, let's get some chili cheese fries, bacon cheeseburgers, jalapeno poppers, and coffee.... Oh, coffee. I think that's what I miss the most right now."

I awoke from my daydream of a giant mug of coffee, with wisps of steam rising from the mouth of the mug, to see that the morning sun was now fully breaking through the large gaps in the fog. The images of the cold, hard landscape before me were a sharp contrast to my recent thoughts. Mountains of food were replaced by drifting banks of fog and sodden, grass-covered, rock-strewn hills. We had rested long enough, too long, and it was time to begin the second leg of our morning's journey.

We had walked in silence again for another hour when we finally came to the river that I had espied yesterday. Much to our surprise, it was actually narrower than it had appeared from afar, and we found a crossing after only 15 minutes of searching. This good fortune was much appreciated and took a great weight off of my already troubled mind.

Once we were on the eastern shore, I wanted to look for a place where I could try out my fishing spear and hopefully catch some fresh meat. After another 10 or 15 minutes of searching, we came upon a pool where some large salmon were swimming lazily.

Now I was faced with a dilemma. I knew that I should keep my clothes as dry as possible, but doing so would require me to remove them and leave them on the shore while I fished. However, I wasn't alone out here in the wilderness, and removing my clothes would mean that I would be naked in front of the only girl for miles around. The very thought of this made me feel awkward. Maybe I am just old-fashioned, but I decided to split the difference and remain partially clothed. I left my pants and shirt on the shore by my pack and proceeded to enter the water wearing my boxer shorts. Bailey seemed too caught up in her own thoughts to care one way or the other, but I, at least, felt better about this arrangement.

I crept stealthily into the river. The freezing cold water in the pool quickly came up to my waist, and I struggled to keep up my resolve to score fresh meat as my legs rapidly became numb.

Slowly, I came within striking distance of one of the salmon. Dipping the tip of my spear very gingerly below the surface of the water, I poised to strike. Splash! In one fluid motion, I had thrust the spear vigorously into where I thought the fish was, but when I looked down, the tip of my spear was empty. I swore under my breath, frustrated by this fruitless attempt to spear the fish.

I waited a couple of minutes for some of the fish to return, which, in this icy current, felt like an eternity. Seeing a promising target, I poised to strike again... Splash! This time I completely lost my balance and fell headfirst into the water. When I broke the surface of the pool, sputtering and splashing, all I could think about was getting warm. Bailey was seated on the bank a few yards away, shaking with laughter, and taunting me good-naturedly.

"Have a nice trip?" she called through her laughter.

"You keep that up, and I'll show you what it feels like," I threatened, only half-joking. Her taunts had hardened my resolve to catch a fish or freeze to death in the attempt, which, under the circumstances, was a real possibility.

I waited a couple more minutes, hoping I hadn't totally blown it, but eventually a couple of the fish returned to the pool. As I waited for an opportunity to strike, I thought back to my high school science class and remembered something about the fact that light bent in water. This meant that what I thought I was seeing was not what was actually occurring under the surface. However, I wasn't sure whether that meant the fish were above or below where they appeared to be. Despite the fact that I didn't know whether to aim higher or lower than I had been, I had a 50/50 chance of getting it right. So, after a moment's deliberation, I decided that I would try to aim lower.

As an unsuspecting salmon swam closer, I poised to strike... Splash! I immediately felt resistance as I raised my spear out of the water. It worked! Amazed, I realized that I had actually caught a fish. I couldn't believe it!

"It's about time!" Bailed quipped.

"Hey, it's a lot harder than it looks!" I retorted. "In fact, I'm kind of surprised it actually...NO!" I screamed as the fish fell off the spear onto the shore. It wriggled toward the water as I chased after it, desperately trying to keep it from escaping. Every time I grabbed it, its slimy body wriggled free, propelling it closer to the water. Finally, diving on top of it, I pinned it under my chest. Then, getting a firm grasp on it, I stood in triumph.

"Hah!" I yelled. "Thought you could get away, huh?"

I looked up, and Bailey was literally in tears from laughing so hard. I must have been quite a sight. I was covered in silt from my knees to my neck, standing in nothing but my boxer shorts, holding onto a wriggling fish, and sporting an ear-splitting grin. I'm sure I would have laughed at her if the roles had been reversed, and, quite frankly, I was so pleased with myself, I didn't care a bit about the humor at my expense.

Grabbing my walking stick and pinning the fish down against the shore with my knee, I gave it a couple of sharp smacks on the head, to put it out of its misery. After that, I brought the fish over to Bailey, placing it in her care so I could rinse all of the muddy silt from my body.

I dashed into the river, rinsed as quickly as I could, then ran over to my clothes, and dressed faster than I had ever done before in my life.

Despite the fact that I was nearly frozen solid, I was elated! We had fresh meat again. We weren't going to starve… at least, not today.

"I wish you could have seen yourself," laughed Bailey, "chasing after that fish, and diving onto the bank. It was priceless."

"I'm glad I was so entertaining," I returned with a smile. "Now let's get back on the road again, before I freeze to death."

Chapter 9

Enjoying the Ride

The fog had completely vanished, and the sun warmed my chilled body as we walked along the rugged plain. A couple of small mountains stood out against the horizon, a few miles east, slightly south of our intended path. They looked majestic and savagely beautiful, not nearly as forbidding as the wall of the Brooks Range mountains many miles to the south.

"Don't those mountains look beautiful?" I asked as we walked. "It's almost like I feel drawn to them."

"Yeah," she said, "they're nice, but I'd still rather be home."

"If we can stay at our current pace, we might be able to make 10 miles by the end of the day," I encouraged. "That means, by tonight, we might be 1/5th of the way there. If we keep this up, we'll be home in a couple of weeks at the most." I continued with enthusiasm.

In fact, the idea that we had a couple more weeks of this ahead of us was somewhat depressing, but, for Bailey's sake, I thought if I put up a good front, maybe she would feel excited too.

"Two weeks? I can't do this for another two weeks!" she cried in despair.

"What choice do you have... stay here and die?"

She said nothing in response, but began walking faster, hoping to shorten our time out in here the wilderness. I thought maybe that walking in silence was not such a good thing, since it gave us too much time to dwell on all of the negative things that we had been experiencing. So, I tried to start a conversation to distract the both of us.

"If you could be stuck out here with any celebrity, who would you pick?" I inquired.

"What kind of question is that?" she asked, taken aback.

"A simple one," I quipped. "Who would it be?"

"I don't know..." she replied evasively.

"Oh, come on. Be a good sport."

I don't know... maybe Chris Hemsworth. What about you?"

"I don't really go for the Hollywood types," I replied honestly.

"You can't get out of your own question that easily."

"OK," I sighed, "I guess Kate Beckinsale."

"Oh?"

"Yeah, I've got a thing for brunettes," I joked.

We kept the banter going until mid-afternoon, when we came upon another patch of trees. It wasn't a forest, like we had walked through before. It was an oblong circle of stunted deciduous and pine trees, about 100 yards long by about 60 yards wide.

I knew we should probably make camp here, where we could at least make a fire to take away the chill from this morning. Despite our exertions, the cold of both the fog and the river had yet to go away. However, staying would mean that we would lose at least three, maybe four, miles of potential progress. There was a chance that we could find another group of trees, or even a forest somewhere along the route today, but this patch of trees that we were in right now was a sure thing.

"I think we should make camp here for the night," I said, matter-of-factly. "But, if you can think of a really good reason why we shouldn't, I'm open to discussion."

"No, let's camp," she replied in agreement.

We dropped our packs as I began to survey the landscape around us. There was a large, pristine lake about a quarter of a mile away, and an imposing river a little more than mile beyond that.

We had filled our water bottles earlier in the day, when we crossed the last river, but since we had two sources of water so near, I thought it would be best to drink as much as we could, to avoid getting dehydrated.

Early into our journey, we had found a use for the handkerchief from my pack as we filled our bottles. Silt and sediment from the water could have easily clogged our water filter. However, by placing the handkerchief over the mouth of the filter's squeezable bag, we were able to keep the larger particles from getting into the filter, which prolonged its life and kept us from having to flush it out after every use.

After setting up our shelter, we made a separate cooking fire about 100 feet from where we planned to sleep.

"What do you think about the idea of fresh fish cooked over an open fire?" I asked as my stomach growled audibly.

"I hope it tastes good," she said, not convinced that the fish was going to be worth eating.

"Are you saying you don't like my cooking?" I feigned being hurt.

"Well, it could use some variety, and maybe some spices... and side dishes."

"You'll be singing a different tune after you've tasted this," I replied with confidence.

I thought it would be best to gut the fish and rinse it off as far from camp as possible, so we wouldn't attract any predators. Bailey didn't want to be left alone, so we both walked over to the lake. I was uncomfortable with the idea of leaving my pack unattended, so I lugged it along, just in case, despite the fact that my body was worn out.

When we got to the lake, we were immediately struck by how crystal clear the water was. We could see minute details on the lake floor, even in the deeper parts of the water. It was almost like we were looking through a pane of glass instead of through the placid depths of an undefiled lake.

Recovering from my wonder at the sheer beauty of this scene, I proceeded to gut the fish, while Bailey surveyed the landscape around us.

"It's beautiful!" she exclaimed.

"It sure is," I said, momentarily looking up from my work.

"I think I'll wade out a little bit," she said, after staring in wonder at our surroundings.

"Sure! Go for it. It's going to be really cold though."

She soon put her words into action after taking off her shoes and socks. She had rolled her jeans up to her knees and was walking around in the shallows. Bailey's spirits seemed to lift as she walked around in the cool, clear water of the lake. Within moments, despite the cold, she was smiling, and she even began to hum softly to herself.

This sudden change in her demeanor, while shocking, was certainly a welcome sight. I had been concerned about her today, since she had, at times, been very withdrawn and contemplative.

"I might join you in a minute," I called out. "I just had an idea that I'd like to try out. I think I might be able to catch another fish or two."

After I gutted the fish and rinsed it off, I placed it next to my pack and shotgun, then took off my boots and socks and walked toward the water. My plan was a bit of a long shot, but I thought if I took some of the fish guts and put them in the water around me, I might be able to attract some fish, and maybe, with a little bit of luck, spear another one.

Bailey continued to wade in the water, seeming deeply affected by this magical scene. Thinking it best to give her some space, I walked about 100 yards away from her, along the bank, and waded in, hoping my plan would work. Wading out between waist and chest deep, I dropped the guts in a semi-circle around me, praying that some fish would swim along.

Within a few seconds, what appeared to be two large trout raced over toward the bait. They came so quickly that I didn't have time to get the tip my fishing spear into the water before they were right beside to me. Afraid that doing so now would scare them away, I took a wild stab at one of the fish. Immediately, I flipped the spear up, feeling the weight of the fish fighting wildly on the end. I had only gotten him with one point, so I raced as quickly as possible to the shore, hoping to get onto dry ground before he flopped off.

"What's wrong?" Bailey asked, scared by my mad dash to the shore.

"Fish!" was all I could manage to get out.

After cleaning the second fish, we lingered by the lake, drinking in the majestic scenery around us. The shore was lined with stunted birch trees, their white bark reflecting off of the placid surface of the water. The vegetation on the plane waved gently in the breeze, making the sunlight seem to ripple along the rolling hills beyond.

As we sat side-by-side, a moose entered the water a few hundred yards away, and we watched as it walked through the shallows, stopping periodically to nibble on some vegetation. Eventually, it wandered out of sight, and, thinking it best to get back to camp, we made our way to the shelter.

We made a fire in our cooking camp and roasted the fish on a stone that Bailey carried back from the lake. We made sure that the rock was totally dry before we placed it over the coals, since I had learned from experience that moisture-laden rocks can explode if placed over an open fire.

Rather than trying to filet the salmon, I cut it into steaks. The trout I skewered on a stick and placed over the fire, cooking it whole.

We sat impatiently as the fish steamed and sizzled on our improvised grill. While Bailey had expressed some misgivings about the fish earlier in the day, they ended up being entirely baseless. The salmon steaks were juicy and tender, and tasted better than anything either of us had ever gotten from the grocery store. And the trout was sweet, succulent, and flaky.

With full stomachs, a warm fire, and the leisure time earlier beside the lake, the prospect of spending two more weeks out here seemed almost pleasant.

After we had eaten, I placed a large piece of punk wood on the fire, allowing it to catch a spark so that it burned with a strong ember. Holding the punk wood carefully, I carried it over to our shelter. I placed the glowing punk wood into a bird's nest of tundra vegetation and gently blew on it, meticulously coaxing the tinder bundle into a flame. Within minutes, we had a small, crackling fire a few feet from the entrance of our shelter.

After our campfire was steadily burning, I made sure the cooking fire was out. Then, Bailey and I sat beside the fire and talked as we stared at the dancing flames.

"What did you like so much about the lake today? I haven't seen you respond like that about anything we've seen so far," I asked, full of curiosity.

"I don't know," she said, searching for the right words. "It just seemed like the perfect place. The water was so clear, and the sky's reflection was so crisp on its surface. The landscape was so beautiful, and there were mountains off in the distance. It just made me feel happy... happy like I haven't felt in a long time."

"Why do you think so many of the beautiful things in life are hidden away where very few people will ever find them?" I reflected, thinking that the lake was somehow a representation of so many of the truly good things in life; so hard to find, but so worth the effort when you do finally discover them.

"I guess maybe they are just the things that haven't been spoiled by mankind yet."

"That's so true. Maybe, at some point in the past, there were places like this everywhere, and slowly, they were polluted, or turned into gaudy resort towns, or cheapened by the fact that so many people could come and see them with so little effort.... Maybe this lake is so beautiful simply because it is unknown and untouched, unsullied by the masses of mankind." I trailed off, not knowing how to put into words what I was thinking.

"I didn't know you were so philosophical," she said with surprise.

"I wouldn't say that I'm philosophical. I'm just trying to make sense of all of this." I explained, waving my hand. "To make sense of life."

"Good luck with that."

"Yeah... I know. But, I feel like I've at least got to try," I said.

The moon was rising high into the starlit sky when we finally went to bed. As I settled in for the night, I couldn't help but be uncomfortable about our current sleeping situation. I was laying on the bag that had held the raw bear meat, and we had some leftover fish inside our shelter, to keep it from being eaten by scavengers. Under any other circumstances, I would never have kept food inside our shelter, since it could attract bears, wolves, and other carnivores. However, without knowing where our next meal would come from, we couldn't afford to let some wild animal eat the rest of our meat. Sure, we could have rigged up a bear bag, but in this section of woods, there weren't any trees tall enough or strong enough to support a bear bag and still manage to keep the food out of a bear's reach, since all of the trees in this patch of woods were nothing more than glorified bushes. I just hoped and prayed that no curious creatures came to visit us in the middle of the night.

Chapter 10

A Howl in the Darkness

I woke as the sun was just beginning to peek over the edge of the eastern horizon. Bailey was already wide awake and was seated at the edge of the shelter watching the sunrise. Fortunately, we hadn't had any unwelcomed visitors at night, at least as far as either of us knew.

As I roused myself from sleep, I was amazed at how quickly we were able to adapt to sleeping so soundly out here in the wilderness, despite the constant threat of predators. Our first night in the wild, our thoughts had magnified the slightest noise into the steps of some horrible creature intent on devouring us in the darkness of night. But now we paid little heed to any sound in the darkness.

Once I was fully awake, I started the task of reviving the fire. We didn't really need it, other than to ward off the chill of the morning, but I have always found fire to be one of the best things to lift my spirits.

Making some wood shavings for kindling, I stirred the dying embers to life, and small flames quickly leapt up to meet the fresh curls of wood. Bailey and I sat by the fire eating a hearty breakfast of fish steaks as we watched the sun's slow climb into the morning sky.

"What's the plan for today?" she asked, nibbling on her fish steak.

"The first order of business is to rinse out these two garbage bags," I explained as I wrinkled my nose. "The past couple of nights the idea, not to mention the smell, of sleeping on top of a bag full of rancid blood has been somewhat disconcerting."

"Ew! I thought I smelled something last night, but I figured it might be us, since neither of us has bathed for a few days," Bailey replied in disgust.

"You have a good point," I reasoned. "It might not be a bad idea to wash ourselves off in the lake before we go. It is going to be a cold walk down, and an even colder walk back up, but if we get the fire nice and hot, we should be able to dry off quickly and be ready to get on the trail by mid-morning. One of the biggest threats out here, aside from hypothermia and starvation, is infection... so the more attention we can pay to hygiene, the better our chances of staying healthy."

My old fashioned ideals made this proposition a little difficult for me. Bailey teased me as I explained my position, but I think, in reality, she appreciated the fact that I wanted to respect her privacy. We decided that I would try to hunt for some fresh game while she bathed and dried off by the fire, then she would hunt while I took my turn bathing in the frigid lake. However, we would make sure to stay within shouting distance of one another at all times, in case of emergency.

My hunt didn't go very well. In fact, I didn't see a thing. Bailey seemed to feel better after her plunge in the lake, but warned me that the walk back up to the shelter was brutal.

Despite my reservations about plunging into the frigid waters of the lake, I actually enjoyed bathing, except for the miserable 400 meter dash back to camp. It somehow made me feel a little more like a normal human being, and less like someone who was fighting to survive in the wilderness. One thing did concern me, though, during my bath. I knew that I was losing weight, but I was surprised to see just how much weight I had actually lost in less than a week. Before the plane crash, I was lean but not scrawny by any stretch of the imagination. Now, despite having eaten, albeit not regularly, over the past several days, I was able to see most of my ribs. I knew that if this trend kept up for too long, I was going to run out of fat for my body to burn, which was potentially fatal. I was also sure that Bailey was experiencing similar weight loss. In light of these facts, my prognosis for our chances of survival was not good.

While I sat by the fire waiting to dry off, I busied myself by making some journal entries:

Aug 5 – walked 6 miles, slept on open plain, saw Northern Lights.

Aug 6 – walked 7 miles, caught fish, camped by small lake, beautiful.

With the journaling completed, I placed the Field Notes booklet back inside of my pack and proceeded to put my clothes back on. I was just getting ready to call for Bailey to let her know that she could come back to camp, when the report of her rifle rent the still morning air.

Crack!

Silence.

My heart began to race.

Crack! Crack! Crack!

I grabbed my shotgun and sped toward the direction of the shots.

"Bailey? Bailey!" I called. I thought the shots had come from the direction of the lake, but I wasn't certain.

"Bailey! Are you OK?" I yelled as I sprinted, gun in hand, toward the lake. As I burst through our little patch of woods, I could see the small, distant figure of Bailey kneeling on the ground a few hundred yards away.

"Bailey!" I called, scanning the area for danger.

She looked up at me from over her shoulder, and shock began to spread across her features as I sprinted toward her, as fast as my legs would carry me.

"What happened? Are you OK?" I cried, as I huffed and puffed, closing the distance.

"What's wrong?" she shouted to me, with a voice full of fright.

I slackened my pace a little, *"What's wrong? That's what I'm trying to figure out!"*

"What are you talking about?"

I walked steadily forward. "The shots!" I panted, catching my breath.

Slowly, I started to piece the puzzle together. There, at her feet, near the edge of the lake, was a large, white bird, lying dead. It looked like a goose in shape and size, but its feathers were totally white, and it had a solid black beak with a little patch of yellow toward the rear, where the beak meets the head.

"You scared me half to death!" I said, full of relief at what I saw. "I thought you were in trouble... I thought..." I trailed off.

She looked up and smiled, full of pride. "Nope. No trouble here. I was just sitting here, looking at the lake, when this bird landed by the shore, about 10 yards away from me. A week ago, I would have thought 'look how beautiful that bird is,' but now, I just thought about how good it would taste.

"Anyway," she continued, "I slowly put my gun to my shoulder, and lined the sights up like you taught me. He was busy plucking at his feathers with his beak and didn't even seem to notice that I was there. So, I steadily squeezed the trigger and shot him. At first, I thought I missed, since he looked like he wanted to take off and flapped his wings furiously, but no matter how hard he tried, he just couldn't get off the ground. I was afraid he would get away, so I fired a few more shots to make sure he didn't. I was just getting ready to pick him up and bring him back, when I saw you running toward me like a madman. I thought you were being chased by a bear or something."

"No," I laughed, "if I was being chased by a bear, I think you would have heard a little more shooting, and a lot more screaming." Looking down at the bird, I added, "Well, let's get this thing back to camp, and get your gun reloaded. You did good!"

We took the bird back to camp and field dressed it. After some deliberation, we decided that it would be best to take it with us, and hopefully find a way to cook it when we made camp in the evening. It probably would have been more prudent to cook it immediately, but it would have cost us a lot of time, and time was something we didn't have much of to spare. So far, we were making good progress toward civilization, but the more we delayed, the longer it would take to reach the outside world, and, more importantly, we were in a race against the onset of the brutal winter of this region, so any unnecessary delay could be fatal.

Despite our best efforts, it was getting close to noon by the time we got on our way. I had rinsed out both of the garbage bags before we left and turned them inside out to let them dry. We placed the field-dressed bird inside one of these bags, and I carried it over my shoulder as we walked, just as I had done with the bear meat.

Within about a half an hour, we had covered the distance between our camp and the river that we had seen yesterday. Fortunately, it appeared to be both shallow and slow enough to cross safely.

Thus far we had been very fortunate. No stream or river we had encountered had been the daunting obstacle that I feared it would be. However, I knew that our luck couldn't hold out forever.

Before crossing the river, we took about 20 minutes to rearrange our gear, including my pistol and shotgun. While the river looked both shallow and slow enough to safely cross, it was still deep enough that we would need to protect our gear from being soaked. I was particularly concerned about the firearms getting wet, so I placed my pistol inside my pack and tied the shotgun across the top. Bailey also strapped her rifle to the top of her pack, using her makeshift sling to help with this process.

Both Bailey and I held our packs above our heads as we slowly and carefully picked our path across the river. The water was deeper than it looked, rising up to my chest, and covering Bailey all the way to her neck.

Not wanting to carry too much at once and risk accidentally dumping it all into the river, I left the bag containing the goose on the other side of the river, intending to return for it.

Once everything was safely across, we rearranged our gear and tried our best not to be bothered by our packs pressing our sopping-wet clothes against our backs. Had we known how deep the water was before we began to cross, we would have placed our clothes inside our backpacks, so that they would be warm and dry once we crossed the river, but it was a little too late for that now.

The mountains we had seen in the distance yesterday were now coming into sharper focus as we made our way to within a couple of miles of them. We decided that, as tempting as it was to camp beside these mountains tonight, we should probably keep going, passing them on the northern side. However, the beauty of the mountains was hard to resist as we continued on our journey. Their rugged majesty seemed to draw me toward them, as if they were inviting me to explore their untrodden slopes.

The landscape was captivating as we walked under the afternoon sun. The sky, an azure blue dotted with puffy white clouds, met with the variegated brown plain in the distance. Flowers in full bloom dotted the grassy plain with vibrant red, purple, and white blooms. Streams, lakes, and ponds dotted the plain in all directions, while here and there small copses of alder and willow trees could be seen. Whereas previously our only concern had been survival, for the present both Bailey and I gave ourselves over to the full enjoyment of this majestic scene.

Passing a small lake to our north during the mid-afternoon, we stopped to refill our water bottles and continued onward as swiftly as we could. I was tempted to try my hand at fishing again, but I thought the delay wouldn't be worth it, since we already had meat for the night.

Shortly after passing the lake, we came to a small creek with a thin patch of scraggly willows running along either side. This we crossed without hardly even wetting our feet and continued our eastward journey until early evening.

When we stopped for the night, I guessed that, despite our late start, we had made about 10 miles of progress during the course of the day. After crossing another small creek, we decided that the patch of woods on the eastern shore would suffice for a campsite.

I was beginning to grow tired of setting up the tarp shelter every night, only to take it down again in the morning. The whole process took about an hour, and, thus far, we hadn't needed a roof over our heads. However, the weather was inevitably going to bring rain, or even snow (something it could easily do this far north, despite the fact that it was early August), and if we were left out in the open, we could die from hypothermia.

Despite my lack of motivation, we set up the tarp shelter before sundown and then worked on gathering wood for a fire, so we could cook the goose that Bailey had shot earlier in the day.

We sacrificed a couple of pages from Bailey's copy of "Rogue States" to get the campfire going. I know it may be wrong, but I got a warm, fuzzy feeling as I saw the pages from Noam Chomsky's work go up in smoke; it somehow seemed appropriate. Much to my surprise, Bailey didn't object to using her book for tinder, especially since it meant we would have a fire several minutes faster than if we used natural tinder.

Soon, our bird was roasting on a rotisserie of my own making. I had pounded two forked sticks into the ground, one on either side of the fire, then skewered the bird, which weighed about 10 pounds, with another stick. I then duct taped another stick to the skewer to make a handle for rotating the meat. I was rather pleased with this invention, but Bailey seemed more concerned with eating than with any ingenuity I had exhibited.

We didn't make a separate cooking fire this night, since both of us were exhausted from the day's long hike. We hadn't encountered a predator for several days, which further influenced this decision. Bailey and I knew we were taking a risk, but neither of us seemed to think there was any real danger in cooking right next to camp this evening.

The bird was still cooking when Bailey and I, racked with hunger, decided we could wait no longer. To say that the goose tasted heavenly would be an understatement. Anything would have tasted wonderful after our day's long march, but this goose was succulent, far better than the bear meat we had eaten and even more flavorful than the salmon, if such a thing were possible. We both ate without saying a word until we thought we were going to be sick, and by the time we were finished, there was hardly any meat left on the bones.

After our dinner, we piled the wood high on the fire, hoping it would last well into the night, and then we laid down in our sleeping bags, ready for sleep.

The crescent moon was rising as we laid down for bed, adding to the beauty of the clear night sky, dotted with innumerable stars.

"You know," I reflected, "if we were able to be picked up this minute, I don't think I would want to go, but the very fact that I *can't* leave, makes me wish that I could. Isn't that odd?"

"Yeah. I think that's how I feel too. At least, it's how I feel right at this moment." Bailey replied. "I just don't like being trapped."

"Yeah. Same here," I agreed. "Several years ago, I read the journals of Lewis and Clark. Talk about being trapped. At one point, they were well over a thousand miles away from the nearest European settlement. They walked, rode, and paddled thousands of miles through previously unexplored territory. They faced starvation, exposure to the elements, predators, and even had a couple of close scrapes with some unfriendly Native Americans. What we are doing is child's play compared to what they did."

"And they made it back, right?" she asked.

"Yeah," I laughed, "but not before Lewis was shot in the butt by one of his own men."

"Really?" she giggled.

"Yeah," I chuckled. "I'm sure he wasn't very happy about it. Let's hope that doesn't happen to either one of us." I said, adding, "I don't want either of us being the butt of everyone's jokes."

"Ugh," she groaned, "Are your puns always this bad?"

"Pretty much," I smiled.

After this exchange we quieted down for the night.

I was in a deep, sound sleep, when the intense feeling of danger suddenly brought me back to consciousness. I knew that something was terribly wrong, but everything around us was absolutely still. I heard no movement, no rustling in the woods, no sounds at all, except for the gentle rise and fall of Bailey's breathing.

I slowly sat up and scanned the area around our camp, but I was unable to see anything by the dim light of the dying fire. Satisfied that my misgivings were mistaken, I was just about to lay back down when an almost imperceptible movement caught my eye. I wasn't certain that I had seen anything, but I thought that a momentary band of light had appeared, and just as suddenly disappeared, about 20 yards away from our shelter. It wasn't bright, like a light from some lamp or flashlight, but rather, it was grey and ghostly, almost how I would expect some kind of other-worldly specter to appear, if I believed in such things.

I sat, staring into the eerie darkness, made all the more disquieting by the ever-changing patterns of reddish-orange light emitted by the glowing embers of the fire. I began to believe that maybe I was just imagining things, when a sudden, startling sound shattered the still night air. My heart began to race as I heard a long, mournful howl reverberate throughout the woods around us. My blood ran cold at the sound, made all the more daunting by the darkness from which it emanated. It wasn't so much the sound that caused my terror, but rather what that sound meant: fur, muscle, and teeth... hungry, hunting... possibly for us... for me... for Bailey.

The last echo of the lonely howl had just begun to fade from the cold night air when another cry broke out, much closer than the last. Bailey startled awake, bolting upright, her eyes wide with terror. She looked over at me for an explanation.

"Wolves," I mouthed, as I tried to see the animal that had just emitted this uncomfortably close howl. After a couple of seconds, I pinpointed the area from which the sound was coming. It was right on the edge of where the faintest hints of light from the glowing coals of the fire melded into darkness, no more than 20 yards away from the opening of our shelter.

Slowly, I worked my way out of my sleeping bag and stealthily reached for my shotgun, which was propped up at the entrance of our shelter. I had continued the practice of sleeping with my Glock 20 holstered on my right hip and my Stilwell Model Five sheathed on my left hip, so I wasn't completely unprepared for this impending danger, but I wanted to be as thoroughly armed as possible in case we had to fend off these ghostly predators. Bailey, seeing what I was doing, also slowly and cautiously worked her way out of her sleeping bag, grabbing her AR-7 and GSO 5.1, both of which she had been keeping beside her while she slept.

As this closer howl died away, I caught another furtive movement out in the darkness of the trees. A greyish specter glided between the trunks of two trees, about 15 yards from the entrance of our shelter, off to the left. A brief succession of yips was exchanged between the two closest wolves, both just outside of the ring of light cast by the fire, then another howl rent the night off to our right. We were being surrounded.

I cursed myself for not putting the food in a bag and suspending it between two trees, because I was almost certain that the smell of our evening meal was the cause our current situation.

Hindsight is 20/20... but it won't help you if you're dead, I thought as I tried to formulate a plan of action.

Another stealthy movement caught my attention. A blackish-grey figure flitted into the ring of dying firelight, then quickly disappeared again. The yips and barks coming from the darkness increased in frequency, and the number of our foes had grown to at least a half-dozen, judging by the noise.

Suddenly, a massive black wolf, braver than the rest, trotted out of the ring of darkness and steadily approached the entrance of our shelter. Its yellow eyes were steadily fixed upon me as it sized me up with an unflinching, malicious stare.

In response, I stood up, taking a step out from under the shelter of the tarp.

The wolf halted, shuffling his front paws, as if undecided about whether he should proceed forward or retreat, all the while keeping its eyes focused upon me.

"Get out of here!" I yelled, taking a step forward.

The wolf retreated a few paces, then stood staring at me, malevolently. The light shone strangely in his eyes, reflecting the deep red hue of the smoldering embers as he bared his teeth at his prey... at me. This monstrous wolf was almost other-worldly, standing there with that crimson light reflected in his maleficent eyes.

This image unnerved me for a moment, adding a primal sense of fear to the growing dread that I already felt. I could fight flesh and blood, but this wolf seemed, in this very moment, to be filled with an evil, powerful malice beyond that of a mere mortal creature.

Sensing my fear, the beast growled, a low, menacing, guttural growl that made my heart pound inside of my chest. He wanted to kill me, to eat me, to sink his teeth into my living flesh and drink my blood as the life ebbed from my body. Now, he was only trying to decide when and how to attack.

As I beheld my foe, I heard the footfalls of the other wolves, veiled by the darkness, shuffling off to the right and the left. There could be little doubt now we were completely surrounded.

Bailey stayed within the shelter, poised on one knee, her rifle raised at the ready.

We were now in a standoff, neither side willing to open hostilities for the time being. Taking advantage of this delay, I turned on my headlamp and moved my head from side to side, quickly surveying the scene. As the light fell upon the wolves, they recoiled slightly, averting their eyes from the bright beam that was cutting through the darkness. But, as soon as the beam moved away, they began to bark to one another, moving around impatiently among the cover of the surrounding trees.

The massive black wolf was standing still, like a statue, now only 10 yards away from me. With his teeth bared, he stared fixedly at me, still emitting that low, menacing growl.

When I focused the beam of my headlamp on him, unlike the other wolves, he held his ground, unfazed. If anything, the light seemed to embolden him. After the beam had rested upon him for a moment, he wriggled his body, as if readying himself to attack.

Seeing that his attack was imminent, my courage, which had all but abandoned me a few moments ago, returned.

Raising the shotgun to my shoulder, I clicked the safety off and brought my finger quickly to the trigger. Deliberately, I squeezed the trigger, waiting for the night-rending boom that would send a 1 oz. lead slug into the heart of this dark and menacing wolf. As I braced my body for the inevitable recoil, I heard a frantic rustle coming from just over my right shoulder. I knew what was coming, but there was nothing I could do about it...

BOOM! My world began to spin just as the shotgun let out a deafening roar. The split second before my shot had broken, another wolf had hit me from behind, knocking me from my feet and sending me sprawling to the ground. The Mossberg had fallen from my hands in the tussle and lay somewhere on the ground, out of my reach.

My mind struggled to catch up to the situation that was unfolding. I was on my back, desperately clutching the fur on the sides of the face of the wolf that had just ambushed me. It stood with one paw on my chest and the other planted firmly on the ground between my ribs and my right arm. It shook its head in a violent struggle to free its face from my grasp, growling as it bared its teeth, desperately trying to sink them into my exposed neck.

Only a second or two had passed since I was knocked from my feet, and already I was literally inches away from having my throat ripped out. I had to do something quickly, before any of his companions arrived on the scene to help their struggling cohort. I shuddered at the thought of being torn limb-from-limb, like some poor defenseless creature of the forest.

Realizing that its efforts to free its head from my grasp weren't working, the wolf brought all of his weight to bear down on his head, trying to get his teeth even closer to my throat.

Its nose was almost touching my chin, when I pushed my left forearm into its face with all of my might, dealing it a stunning blow. At the same time, my right hand grasped at the grip of my Glock. As quick as lightning, the wolf recovered from the blow, and hungrily sank its teeth into the flesh of my raised forearm.

Bang! Bang! Bang! Bang! Four shots rang out in rapid succession as I pressed the muzzle of my pistol into the wolf's chest.

A piercing yelp broke from its mouth as it released my arm and fell onto my legs, kicking in desperation to get away from whatever had dealt it so painful a blow. However, all of its kicking was in vain as its lifeblood poured from its fatal wounds. The wolf's kicking slowed to a halt, and was replaced by a series of low whimpers as I struggled to my feet.

Standing, I looked down upon the wolf that, just a few seconds ago, had desperately tried to take my life.

The whimpers slowed, becoming weaker and quieter, and then, after becoming almost inaudible, they ceased.

The wolf had died.

Silence reigned once more.

Looking up from the body of the wolf, I scanned the woods around me, fearing a fresh attack. Nothing now could be seen but trees and shadows. As quickly as they had come, the wolves were gone.

Believing that the attack was over, I looked toward the shelter, and saw Bailey standing wide-eyed, staring in my direction.

"Are you OK?" she asked, snapped back to reality by the beam of my headlamp shining in her eyes.

"I think so," I said, holstering my pistol.

Immediately, I searched for my shotgun, and picking it up from the ground, I chambered a fresh round, just in case the wolves decided to come back.

With my Mossberg at the ready, I looked out toward where the imposing black wolf had stood only a moment ago. He too had gone. Apparently, my shot had missed him. I figured that the wolf that attacked me had jarred me just enough to make my shot go wide, missing its intended target. The malevolent wolf would live on then, striking fear into the hearts of its victims, until mortality eventually took its toll on the dreadful beast, if indeed it was mortal.

"It was terrible!" Bailey exclaimed, as I sat down on my sleeping bag, trying to calm myself from the building surge of adrenaline. "The wolf jumped on you, and then you disappeared. One second you were standing up, holding your gun, and the next second, you were gone. I rushed out to help you, but I wasn't ready for what I saw. The wolf was on top of you, with drool dripping from its fangs as it tried to maul you to death. I started to scream, then I heard the shots, and saw the wolf fall off of you. I knew you had to be alive, but was certain that you were injured. Are you hurt badly?" Bailey asked, obviously shaken by what had just happened.

"I don't think so," I replied, looking down at my arm. "I think I shot the wolf before he had a chance to do too much damage, but we should probably take a closer look, just to be sure."

Upon a closer inspection, we found that the wolf's teeth had managed to tear several holes in the sleeve of my shirt, and had left scrapes and bruises on my arm. Also, I had one minor puncture wound on the top of my left forearm, from which a steady trickle of blood was flowing.

"It could have been a lot worse," I explained, relieved to see that my arm wasn't badly damaged. "If that wolf would have had a chance to shake its head after it clamped down on my arm, I think I would be in pretty bad shape right now."

"Let's get this cleaned up," Bailey said as she retrieved the first aid kit.

We poured a little bit of fresh water from our water bottles over my arm, then I used the inside of my other sleeve to pat it dry. We had a couple of gauze pads, but I didn't want to waste one on drying my arm, especially when we may need them later. Bailey used one of the precious few alcohol swabs to sterilize the wound, which felt like fire in my fresh cut. After that, we placed one of the two packets of antibiotic ointment on my cut and dressed it with a 4"X4" gauze pad. To keep the gauze on, we had to use the one and only roll of gauze wrapping. I was pretty sure that, under normal circumstances, I would have gotten a couple of stiches at the local emergency room, but this would have to suffice for now.

"I'm not sure if the wolves will come back or not, but I would feel a lot better if we rekindled the fire, if for no other reason, than to allow us to see better," I advised.

So, I cut some more branches to throw on the fire, while Bailey kept an eye out for any fresh signs of trouble. Both of us knew that there was little chance of getting back to sleep after this incident, so we sat awake by the fire until the first inklings of dawn began to show in the forest around us. Whatever this day would bring, we both hoped that it would be better than the terror that the night had brought us.

Chapter 11

The North Slope Diet

During the course of the seemingly endless night, Bailey and I kept ourselves busy, trying to distract our minds from the horror that the wolves had instilled in us. We still kept a sharp eye out for any signs that they were returning, but nothing was seen or heard from them again that night.

After my arm was dressed, I made sure to replace the rounds that I had shot from my pistol and the shotgun. We only had 20 rounds left for the pistol, and 13 left for the shotgun. This was something that greatly concerned me, considering that we still had many days left to walk in this wild and savage land. Bailey still had 45 rounds left for her AR-7, but that would be of little use for defense... still, it was better than nothing.

"Can you imagine where we would be if we didn't have any of this equipment?" I asked Bailey, as I checked the action of my shotgun, to make sure it hadn't gotten any dirt in it when it was dropped.

"Yeah..." she responded solemnly, "probably in the belly of some animal by now, whether from not being able to defend ourselves or because we had starved to death."

I had expected some resistance or argument against my comment, but to my surprise, Bailey seemed to recognize the necessity of being armed out here. Just a few days ago, she was terrified by the very sight of a firearm, but now, she was carrying one of her own, and had even used it to kill an animal so that we could eat.

Changing the subject, I nervously chuckled, "It sure was a close one tonight, wasn't it? I think we really need to be more careful about food preparation and storage, since I'm pretty sure that's what did us in."

"What should we do?"

"Put any food in one of the garbage bags and hang it between two trees, about a hundred yards from camp," I replied, wishing we would have done this last night.

"I bet those wolves would have been pretty disappointed if they had gotten ahold of the goose inside of our shelter. There's hardly any meat left on it," Bailey said, pointing out the irony.

"Yeah, but if they had gotten the bird, it would probably be because they had gotten us too," I replied without humor. "Then the joke would have been on us, only it wouldn't have been very funny."

Talking about the bird carcass gave me an idea for how to hopefully catch some more fish. I thought that maybe I could make an improvised fishing hook out of the bones. With this in mind, I grabbed a couple of the wing bones, and went to work.

I used the poll of my axe to shatter a bone and picked out several of the sharper, more promising-looking splinters, each between 1.5" and 2.5" long. Next, with great sorrow, I cut a 25' section of paracord from the 100' hank that I carried in my pack. After sealing the end that was still attached to the main length of cord by placing it briefly in the fire, I began the process of "gutting" the 25' section of cordage by removing each of the 7 smaller interior strands from the protection of the outer nylon sheathing.

Next, using the file on my multi-tool, I made two generous notches toward the middle of the bone fragments, one on each side. It probably would have been better to bore a hole through the center and attach the line there, but that would have required sacrificing the tip of one of my knives, and that was something I wasn't prepared to do.

After an hour's work, I had three finished "hooks." It was a long shot that they would actually catch anything, but so was everything else we were doing out here.

We packed up before it was fully light, eager to leave the place where we had almost become wolf chow. Before we left, I quickly added another entry in our makeshift journal:

Aug. 7 – walked 10 miles, ate goose, wolf attack.

It was a clear and cool morning as we started our day's journey. Despite the fact that the sun was shining full and bright, our exertions were the only thing that warmed us as we trudged along.

"How can it be so cold in the middle of the summer?" Bailey asked, frustrated by this frigid weather.

"Well, we are above the Arctic Circle," I reasoned, "but you are right, it is really too cold to be called summer. Maybe up here they should just call it 'not winter'."

After nearly an hour of walking, we came to a little creek which was only a few yards wide. I was anxious to test out my new fishing tackle, but the creek seemed too small to contain any sizeable fish, so we quickly moved on.

We walked for another half an hour and came to an odd little river, or rather series of rivers. Instead of being one main body of water, it was a confused and jumbled mess of many rivulets separated by marshy islands. It was almost like a river delta, only we were far from the mouth of this winding river.

Because there were so many separate streams, crossing this river, which would have been difficult, if not impossible, had it been one solid current, was a simple task.

Once we reached the eastern bank, I thought I would try my hand at fishing with my line and "hooks." It took nearly 10 minutes to find a pool that contained any fish. I had saved a few pieces of our cooked goose, in hopes of sacrificing it to catch a bigger meal. Taking some of this meat, I pressed it onto the point of one of the hooks and tossed the line into the water. Within seconds, a small salmon darted toward the bait and swallowed it, hook and all.

Surprised, I jerked on the line, which, rather than setting the hook, yanked it from the fish's mouth. Frustrated, I pulled the line in. The bait had fallen off when I jerked the line, so now I had to use another piece of goose meat to try again.

I cast the line out into the pool again and prayed that one of the fish would take the bait. I held my breath as I saw a salmon about a foot and a half long dart at the bait, then greedily suck it into its mouth. This time, I let it hold it in its mouth a little longer, hoping it would completely swallow the hook. Instead of tugging on the line this time to try to set the hook, I began to pull it in steadily. The fish resisted mightily, jumping, flopping, and wriggling as I pulled the line toward where I was standing. Excited by my success, I pulled the fish out of the water, and, using the line, flopped it on shore.

The salmon continued to struggle, and, in its excitement, it snapped the line, shredding it with his teeth as it flopped its body from side to side. I struggled to keep the fish from getting back to the water, and after a few tense moments, I had the salmon effectively pinned beneath my foot, and dealt him a few firm whacks on the head. I picked up the broken piece of string, doubled it up, and weaved it through his gill, then secured the salmon to the outside of my pack.

I was elated about having something to eat for the day, but one fish was surely not going to replace the calories that we were going to burn over the course of the 10 miles we hoped to make.

Not enough, I thought to myself as we started on our journey again. *This North Slope Diet is going to be the death of us.*

We had made about five miles of progress by the time we stopped for a break at midday. It was finally beginning to warm up, and the sky looked blue and inviting. Bailey and I lounged, basking in the sun.

"Let's hope this weather holds," I said, thinking of how miserable it would be to walk all of these miles in the rain.

"Yeah," Bailey replied, with a slight smile, "I could get used to this."

Over the next few minutes, we surveyed the scenery around us. To the south, about four miles away, two lone peaks rose up to meet the afternoon sky. Many miles beyond them, the ever-present wall of the Brooks Range loomed. To the east, several miles distant, was a patch of lesser mountains that we would either have to pass by going slightly north or by going several miles out of our way to the south. They looked almost as if they jutted out from the Brooks Range, but neither my eyes nor the map made that point very clear. We had yet another river to cross, about a quarter mile away, but it didn't look or sound very swift from where we were sitting. Away to the north, the land looked much the same as it did to the west, only the landscape was interrupted by protruding ridges of small mountains.

The stream proved to be more of a big creek than a small river, and we easily crossed it. We walked north for about 15 minutes in search of a pool containing fish. However, try as we could, we found none and abandoned the search, thinking it best to move on while we were still able to walk at such a good pace.

The mountains that we had surveyed earlier in the day were quickly approaching by mid-afternoon, and Bailey and I stopped to decide whether we should alter our route, walking slightly to the north, or go several miles south and hope that they weren't part of the massive Brooks Range.

"I think the best decision is to head north. We're pretty sure that we can get through that way, whereas, if we go south, we may walk for a couple of days, only to find that our way is blocked by a solid wall of mountains," I said, thinking aloud.

"That makes sense to me," Bailey replied. "When are we stopping for the night? My feet are killing me!"

I pointed a half mile eastward. "I'd like to get a couple of miles into that band of trees. We've done very well so far, and I'd like to push it as far as we can today. Just think, the sooner we get back to civilization, the sooner we can have our epic feast."

"Yeah," she retorted, "but the sooner we stop for the night, the sooner we can eat something *today*."

The thought of food had been foremost in our minds today. We had only had a couple of scavenged bites of goose meat the entire day, and our stomachs were protesting the lack of nourishment. People are prone to think about food even when they are full, so imagine our distress after having been unfed for most of the day. Not to mention, in addition to being underfed, we had walked many miles, which made our hunger all the more severe.

"I hear you," I agreed. "Just let that thought of a fish dinner motivate you to walk a little faster."

We entered the band of trees about 15 minutes later, and were soon engulfed in a dense forest of many different kinds of trees. There were patches of birch, willow, and alder, but the majority of the trees were evergreen. I don't know why, but somehow I had the impression that this wood was a large, broad forest, at least compared to what we had encountered so far. It was well-fed with streams and springs occurring at least every mile, and often much more frequently. As the afternoon wore on, we found ourselves stopping more and more often at these stream crossings, either to refill our water bottles or to rest our weary feet.

We walked until evening, and then, utterly exhausted, we stopped to make camp for the night. Once we got the tarp set up, I worked on getting a fire started while Bailey got the bedrolls and sleeping bags arranged. We typically had been working together on most projects, but tonight we were famished, and this allowed us to eat sooner.

As I cut some hefty branches to size for the fire, I reflected on how difficult this process would be without my Silky saw. Sure, I could scavenge for wood, and break it into manageable pieces for fire-making, but the saw made quick work of harvesting wood. Its extra-large teeth quickly ate through wood, and its 10.5-inch blade allowed me to cut through logs as thick as 7 inches with no problem. I had used this saw many times and knew I could count on it to perform, and now I was thankful that I had such a tool in my pack when we went down in the plane crash.

Another tool that was proving to be very handy was my Gransfors Bruks Small Forest Axe. While we may have been able to get along without it, it certainly made splitting firewood into kindling much easier. Also, it made light work of any pounding task that we had to do, such as pounding in tent pegs, support poles, and even the braces for the rotisserie that I had made.

As I made the pile of shavings that would serve as the fine kindling for the fire, I also considered where we would be if not for my most useful tool, my Stilwell Knives Model Five. It had excellent blade geometry and kept a sharp edge for a very long time, much longer than some of the other knives I owned. I had used this knife a lot already out here and had not even had to touch the edge up with the small sharpening stone I had in my pack, although I made sure to wipe the blade down and strop it after every use.

There is a saying that goes, "Take good care of your tools, and they'll take good care of you." Well, I always took good care of my tools, and now they were taking good care of us when we needed it most. As I contemplated these things, I decided that when we got back to civilization, I would personally thank the makers of these tools that were helping to keep us alive out here.

Even more useful than the tools were the skills that I had learned over the years. Tasks like making wood shavings for a fire, shelter set-up, and batoning were entirely foreign to me until a couple of years ago. Skills like using a firesteel to catch natural tinder, proper wood selection, and knot-tying, which we were using every day out here to keep us alive, were skills that I had been taught by other outdoorsmen. In fact, most of the skills and knowledge I had been using had come from Terry Barney, the creator of the BushClass USA courses, and from other notable members of the BushCraft USA community. These free online classes had allowed me to build a skillset that, before, had been very valuable, but now was literally saving our lives. If we made it back to civilization alive, I would have a lot of people to thank for the skills that they had helped me learn.

While I worked to get the fire started, I noticed that my arm still ached from my encounter with the wolf. It had been less than 24 hours since that frightful encounter, but it already seemed like a distant memory. As I continued with the fire prep, I made a mental note to check my wounds and change my bandage before it got dark.

The sun was beginning to set, and the woods were growing dim as Bailey and I sat beside the fire devouring the fish that I had caught earlier in the day. We had discussed saving some of it for the morning, but we ultimately decided to trust in providence for tomorrow's meal. We ate the entire fish, minus the bones, and then carried a coal from our cooking fire over to our camp.

We hadn't really thought about or mentioned the wolf attack during the day's march, but now that darkness was creeping over the forest, we became increasingly nervous.

"Do you think they'll come back?" Bailey asked, trying to mask the tremor of fear in her voice.

"I don't know," I replied, plagued by the same thought. "I don't think they were really after us in the first place last night. I think the smell of our food brought them to our camp; then, seeing us as a target of opportunity, they thought that they could fill their empty stomachs with us."

Disturbed by this thought, I continued, "I don't think wolves are supposed to be very aggressive towards humans, especially this time of year, when they are usually well-fed. However, I'm not sure that the 'rules' apply out here."

"I don't think that I'm going to be able to sleep at all tonight," Bailey confessed.

"It's going to be hard to fight off the scary thoughts," I replied, "but I'm so tired, I don't think I could stay awake tonight even if all of the wolves in Alaska were out to get us."

With those words, I threw plenty of fuel on the fire and laid down, hoping that sleep would soon overtake me. However, with no activities to distract me now, my mind became a tangled mess of troubling thoughts.

How are my parents and friends doing? Is anybody still looking for us? Where is our next meal going to come from? What if the wolves come back? What if a bear wanders into camp? How is Bailey coping with everything? Does she blame me for everything that has happened? If so, will she ever forgive me? Why did I go on this trip in the first place? Thoughts of this kind ebbed and flowed throughout my semi-conscious mind, until, finally, utterly exhausted, I gave way to sleep.

Chapter 12

Wasting Away

A hissing whisper cut through the darkness as I struggled to rouse myself from sleep. "Ryan. Ryan!"

"What?"

"I thought I heard something," Bailey said plaintively.

"What was it?" I asked, not sure whether to be annoyed or concerned.

"I don't know. It sounded like something moving in the woods," she explained, still whispering.

We listened in silence for a moment, but neither of us heard anything, other than the normal nightly noises one expects to hear in the woods.

"Wake me if you hear it again."

"You're going back to sleep?" she asked incredulously.

"I don't see any reason not to," I replied, unsuccessfully trying to hide my frustration.

Bailey said no more, but I could tell that she was lying awake, worried about what might lay hidden in the darkness, beyond our vision.

After a couple of moments, I knew there was no hope of falling back to sleep, so I got up and, throwing some more wood on the fire, I sat down beside the warmth of the glowing flames.

Throughout our journey, I had been plotting what I thought our approximate course was on the map. I had checked the map periodically during the early stages of the trip, but now that we had been making decent progress, I checked much more frequently, to make sure we weren't going either too far to the north or the south, and needlessly wasting time and energy.

After comparing the landmarks on my map with those that we had encountered during the previous day's journey, I drew a line to represent the distance we had covered. I figured that we had traveled about 12 miles the previous day, which was the best we had done so far.

After I marked the map, I turned my attention to our journal, making an entry for yesterday's march. The entry read:

Aug 8 – walked 12 miles, 1 fish, need more food.

I don't know what made me write that last part of the entry, since I had purposely avoided writing any similar comments before; however, that was the truth of the matter. Right now we were in a race against starvation, and I couldn't truthfully tell who was going to win. This point was made even clearer to me as I had tightened my belt another notch before we had gone to bed. Throughout our journey, Bailey and I had been joking about the North Slope Diet, but it didn't seem very funny right now.

After turning my attention back to the map and comparing it with the entries I had made in the journal, I guessed that we had made 50 miles of eastward progress so far. This was great news; however, it also meant that we still had 100 miles to go, and I had already lost a dangerous amount of weight just during the first third of our journey. My lean frame was beginning to look more and more scrawny with each passing day.

Bailey, who didn't have any excess weight to begin with, was also starting to notice that her clothes were fitting more loosely as her body rapidly shed weight.

Night seemed to linger as a blanket of clouds obscured the rising of the sun. We did our best to get packed up and on the move as quickly as possible this morning.

Hunger was a great motivator. The hungrier we got, the more we wanted to rush to get back to civilization. However, we both were aware that our bodies wouldn't be able to keep this heightened pace up for long, at least not without a significant amount of calories to keep them fueled.

We crossed a couple of small creeks in the first hours of this morning's journey, but only stopped once to refill our water bottles. Before mid-morning, we had come to a small river and searched for nearly an hour, hoping to find a pool that contained fish, but finding none, we moved on.

Despondent, we continued on without a break until nearly noon. The landscape had changed once again, and, shortly after leaving the Fishless River, which was what we named it, we came again into a vast expanse of open and treeless grassland.

Even the sun, who had been an almost constant companion on our journey thus far, seemed to turn against us, being hidden behind a wall of gloomy clouds that appeared ready at any minute to release a heavy deluge of frigid rain.

"Looks like we might get rained on today," I said as we trudged along.

"I hope not," Bailey replied, looking suspiciously at the sky. "This is bad enough already; I can't imagine that adding rain to the mix would make it any better."

"No, my guess is it's going make it a lot worse," I added.

We trudged on until noon, when we stopped on a grass-covered knoll to take a much-needed break. However, we didn't rest for long, because at least while we were moving, we were able to distract ourselves from the all-consuming thought of food. Furthermore, a cold wind was blowing over the plain, almost freezing us to the core, and making us utterly miserable. While we sat on the grassy plain, all of our thoughts and conversations revolved around food: foods we liked, foods we missed, foods we have never tried, etc.

"Your girlfriend must be an emotional mess right now," Bailey said, steering the conversation to more personal matters.

"Well," I replied tentatively, "she would be, if I had one."

I wasn't sure whether I should feel slightly ashamed that I was 28 and single, or whether I should explain that I'd never really found the kind of girl that I was looking for, and that at this point in my life, I wasn't even sure that she existed.

"Oh," she replied simply, then paused as if unsure whether or not to pursue the matter further. "Are you divorced then?"

"No," I answered, thankful that I hadn't had to go through so painful a process. "I've dated off and on, but I've never been able to find what I was looking for in a girl. I don't know, maybe I'm just too picky. I know what I want, or at least I think I do, but I just can't seem to find anyone who measures up."

"Well, what *do* you want in a girl?" she asked, genuinely curious.

I felt awkward opening up like this, but I didn't really have anything better to do, and it wasn't like I could make some lame excuse about not having the time to talk about it right now. So, hesitantly, I began, "I want a girl who is compassionate and kind, but won't coddle me. I want a girl who is more concerned about raising a family than climbing the corporate ladder. I want a girl who will love me for who I really am, and not what she thinks she can change me into. I want a girl who is as proud of her mind as she is of her body, not that a nice body is a bad thing," I added with a sidelong glance and an embarrassed smile. "In short, I want a girl who knows who she is and what she wants out of life, and wants the same from me… someone who isn't afraid to ask the hard questions about life… someone who…" I stopped, embarrassed from sharing too much.

Quickly, before she could probe any further, I put the question to her. "How do you think your boyfriend is taking things?

"I don't have a boyfriend," she replied, with a hint of anger in her voice.

"Oh," I said, apologetically, "I meant no offense."

"Oh, no. I'm not offended. It's just complicated, like everything else in my life. I dated a guy from college for about a year, but I broke up with him after I found out he had been cheating on me with my best friends," she explained with bitterness in her voice.

"Friends? Plural?" I asked, raising an eyebrow to emphasize my amazement.

"Yeah… plural. As in three." Her eyes narrowed in disgust.

"Nice guy," I said, my voice dripping with disdain.

"My thoughts exactly," she agreed, then changed the topic yet again. "You know, you'll probably be flooded with marriage proposals when we get back to society."

"What?" I laughed.

She laughed in her turn, then explained, "You're a living story-book hero. Boy meets girl. Boy and girl get into trouble. Boy saves girl. Boy takes care of girl. Boy... Well, you get the point," she trailed off.

"I'm pretty sure the excitement would taper off pretty quickly if they could catch a whiff of me right now," I replied with a laugh. "Not to mention, I don't think too many women would be interested in an unemployed accountant who moonlights as a mountain man."

"Oh... when did you lose your job?" she asked sympathetically.

"Just before I went on this trip. In fact, it was this trip that cost me my job. We have a strict, but unwritten, no vacation policy, which I broke. At the time I was glad I did it, but now I'm trying to decide what would be worse, starving out here in the wilderness or still being stuck in a job that I hate, working for a boss that I despise."

"I'm sorry," she replied, unsure of how to respond.

"I'm not," I answered coolly. "I've known for quite some time that accounting wasn't for me. At least, not with some company that is more concerned about having the proper social connections than with having integrity. Quite frankly, I'm kind of glad to be free. Now I can figure out what I really want to do in life, and then pour myself into it."

The conversation turned to less serious matters as we continued our walk until mid-afternoon, when we took another brief break. We had made about seven miles of progress so far and had potential to make between two and three more, but, as we looked to the east, we both saw a serious impediment to progressing much further today. There was a river, wider than any we had encountered thus far, cutting across our route about a mile and a half away. I didn't mention it to Bailey at the time, but I was fairly certain that any attempt to cross it would be fraught with danger.

Our hunger pangs, which had decreased somewhat as the day progressed, were redoubled now as we sat, or rather sprawled out, on the grassy plain. About 500 yards to the north, a few caribou were wandering toward the river. Seeing such a large source of meat out on the open plain, beyond our reach, was almost torturous.

"If we only had a rifle," I muttered aloud as Bailey and I watched them move further and further eastward.

"We do have a rifle," she said, thinking I had somehow forgotten about her little AR-7.

"No, I meant a big rifle, one that I could use to shoot us one of those caribou," I replied.

"Oh."

"If I had my Remington 7600, we'd be eating venison in no time, but as it stands now, we'll just have to be content to watch them wander toward the river. Maybe," I said doubtfully, "maybe we'll get a chance to surprise them up close later, and I can shoot one with my shotgun."

With great effort, we shouldered our packs again and continued our trek toward the river, hoping that we would be able to find both food and a way to cross the water safely before nightfall, but holding out little hope of finding either.

The ominous clouds had thus far only threatened rain, but they still looked as if they would let loose a raging torrent at any moment.

Slowly, we trudged on, pausing more and more often as afternoon wore on into evening. We stopped for the night at around 7:00 p.m., as best as I could judge, using my hand against the horizon to gauge the amount of daylight remaining.

We found a decent spot on the downward slope of a grass-covered hill, a couple hundred yards west of the river, and began to set up our tarp shelter, using the same poles and pegs we had used a couple of nights ago, the last time we had camped on an open plain.

All-in-all, I estimated our day's progress to be about 8 miles, which, considering our hunger and lack of sleep, was pretty decent. However, assuming we could cross the river tomorrow, I knew that without some food to give us a boost of energy, our eastward progress would soon taper to a crawl.

Dozens of small lakes and ponds dotted the plain around us. The landscape didn't offer any fuel for a fire, so after we set up camp, we had a little over an hour before sunset to refill our water bottles and check some of these bodies of water for fish or other sources of food.

While the surrounding scenery was nothing short of breath-taking, our appreciation for this stunning land was dampened by our utter failure to find anything to eat in the ponds and lakes. Apparently not all of the bodies of water out here were teeming with life.

Now I began to wish that I had some knowledge about wild edibles. I was sure some of the vegetation around us was edible, but which plants would nourish us and which would poison us I didn't know. So, much to our disappointment, we made our way back to the shelter, exhausted, hungry, and downtrodden. It was going to be a long night, probably filled with thoughts of unattainable food as we lay, tortured by empty stomachs. Neither of us was looking forward to it.

When we got back to the shelter just after sunset, I thought that I should tend to my arm again, which I hadn't done since we applied the initial dressing. Delicately, I unwrapped the gauze and lifted the bandage, concerned about what I would find. The bruising was healing nicely, but the wound was red and irritated. It didn't necessarily look infected, but it didn't look like it was healing like it should either. I rinsed my arm with a little bit of fresh water, then wiped it off with an alcohol wipe. After the burning sensation died away, Bailey helped me apply the only remaining 4X4 gauze pad, and then we wrapped my arm up again.

"You need to take better care of that, or it's going to get infected!" Bailey chided.

"I know," I admitted. "I just hate to open the bandages up too often because that could also lead to infection, which is the last thing either of us needs right now."

Having tended to my arm, Bailey and I settled into our sleeping bags and lay down for the night – a cold, cheerless, restless night.

Chapter 13

Sink or Swim?

"What is that?" Bailey asked, waking me from a vivid dream for the second night in a row.

"What is what?" I snapped, thoroughly annoyed.

"That sound?" she said, not adding any clarity to the issue. I listened for a moment and heard the sound of rain steadily falling on the tarp above us.

"Rain," I replied, then rolled over in an attempt to go back to sleep.

"Should we do anything about it?" she asked, obviously never having been in this scenario before.

"There's not much we can do, other than make sure our packs are off of the ground. We're near the top of a hill, so we don't need to worry too much about runoff, and we're a few hundred yards away from the river, so we don't need to worry about flooding, at least not yet." I stopped to consider if I was forgetting anything. "If the tarp starts to leak, I've got a poncho we can shelter under, but, until that happens, I suggest you try to get some sleep."

"Aren't you worried?"

"What's there to worry about?" I asked with a chuckle, amused by her concern about so common an occurrence as rain.

"I don't know..." she said, sounding sheepish.

"Look," I started, trying to explain the situation as best as I could, hoping to allay some of her fear, "it rains all the time. I bet you've been in the rain dozens, if not hundreds, of times. Has anything bad ever come of it?"

"No," she answered hesitantly.

"So why is this any different?"

"Because we're out in the middle of nowhere, under a tarp!" she snapped, her voice rising in emphasis as she finished.

"Are you getting wet?"

"No," she replied reluctantly.

"OK. So the only difference between this rainstorm and the other ones that you've been in is the thickness of shelter separating you from the rain," I said, hoping my point would comfort her, or at least give her something to ponder so I could get back to sleep.

"I guess. It just somehow seems more threatening out here."

"Well, in some ways it is. However, we're dry, and that's our main concern. Now, if we were getting soaked, with as cold as it is, that would be a major problem," I said, trying to avoid using the word deadly, since she was already unsettled. "So, be happy we're dry, and get some rest so we can get back to real buildings to shelter us from any future storms."

The conversation ended, but try as I might, I couldn't fall back to sleep. Visions of my recent dream began to haunt me as I tried to quiet my mind.

Before Bailey had awakened me, I had been in the midst of a vivid and troubling dream. Bailey was standing over my prostrate body, crying, her tears falling in a steady stream over my motionless form. Instantly, the scene changed to my parents' house, where both my mother and father were looking at a picture of me and sobbing uncontrollably. I tried to comfort them, but they couldn't hear me. This vision faded and was replaced by my former boss chuckling to himself as he read the newspaper headline, which said, "Local Man Lost in Tragic Plane Crash, Presumed Dead." This image faded, and in its place I saw, slowly materializing, a vision of Kyle, my coworker whose death had precipitated my trip. He looked at me, with sadness in his eyes, and silently shook his head slowly as if to say, "Poor fool." He was just opening his mouth to speak when I was suddenly awakened by Bailey.

I lay awake, puzzling over the meaning of the dream.

Was it prophetic? Was there some message of warning for me? Was it just my fears coming to me in my sleep, where I couldn't fend them off? I couldn't be sure. Maybe it was just the lack of food. I had heard that when someone has gone without eating for a day or two, their dreams can be shockingly vivid. I hoped that this was the case, rather than a portent of something to come.

I tossed and turned, consumed with my thoughts, until the blackness of night faded into the colorless grey of dawn. Sometime in the night, Bailey had fallen back to sleep and was still lost in the land of dreams as I watched the dawn slowly illuminate the plain. I hoped that whatever she was seeing in her dreams was of more comfort than what I had seen in mine.

It was still raining, or rather misting, and the sun was hidden behind a solid wall of clouds. The pangs of hunger had dissipated sometime during the night, and were replaced by an empty, hollow feeling in my stomach. This scared me more than the hunger, and I resolved to find something to eat once we got on the other side of the river.

I awakened Bailey about an hour after dawn, anxious to tackle the challenge of crossing the river. I figured we were probably going to have to swim across it, so I wasn't very concerned about walking in the rain, since we were likely going to get soaked soon anyway. The threat of hypothermia was very real, but I figured that if we stripped to our underwear and kept our packs dry, we would be able to warm up after some brisk walking. The only real dangers I saw in the plan of swimming the river, assuming it came to that, were being swept away by the current or getting our clothes wet, either of which could mean the end for us, especially with no possibility of starting a fire. I did hold out hope that, even if our clothes and gear got soaked, we could fend off hypothermia by sheltering inside the Mylar emergency blanket I had stowed in my pack.

"We'd better get an early start," I said, as Bailey struggled to reenter the land of wakefulness.

"What about the river?" she asked.

"We're probably going to have to swim it," I replied somberly. "That is..." I said, startled by a new thought, "that is, assuming that you can swim."

"I can swim a little bit," she replied, smiling slightly at the obvious look of relief on my face.

Reassured, I explained my plan to Bailey. "We'll hike to the shore of the river, strip off our outer clothes, put them in the packs, and then put each of our packs inside of a garbage bag. We'll try to cross in a spot that has an island separating the river, so we don't have as far to swim, and so we can rest for a minute before we swim the second part of the river. Then, once we get across, we'll dress and get on the road, or on the path... well, you know what I mean," I said, with a half-hearted chuckle. Somehow, despite our current circumstances, I was able to manage a bit of humor.

"What about the guns?" Bailey asked, posing an astute question. "I thought that guns weren't supposed to get wet."

"Good point," I replied, pleased that she was thinking about things like that. "It's OK if they get rained on, but we probably shouldn't submerge them in the river. I had planned to put my pistol in my pack, and to strap each of our guns to the top of the garbage bags, so that, unless the whole bag goes under, they'll stay relatively dry."

"But what if we need to use them like we did at the other river?" Her face took on a look of intense fear as she recalled the encounter with the grizzly bear.

I was really impressed with how she was thinking through the possibilities instead of relying on me to make all of the decisions for us.

"We should each keep a knife on us. I plan to hold my multi-tool in my hand as I swim. It's not much, but it's better than nothing. I don't know how you feel about trying to swim with my folding knife in your hand. Worst-case scenario, we could always duct tape it to you." I replied, only half-joking.

"What if one of us gets swept away?" Bailey asked very seriously.

"Here's the part I'm not very comfortable with, and it's another reason I want you to have your knife on you. I plan to use the paracord to tie us together, that way if you have any difficulty, I can help you out. However, if I get into trouble, it is going to be much more difficult for you to help me. So, if I start dragging you down, I want you to cut the rope."

"What?" she shouted in surprise.

"If I'm getting swept away, and I start dragging you down, I want you to cut the rope," I said slowly and deliberately, looking her in the eye for emphasis.

"No way!" she yelled indignantly. "I'm not going to do that."

"I'd do it myself, but my guess is, if I'm getting swept away I'll probably have already lost my multi-tool in an attempt to swim for my life," I reasoned. "There's no sense in both of us getting swept downstream. Not to mention, you increase both of our chances for survival if you cut the rope. There's a chance the current will carry me to the shore downstream, but if I drag you downstream too, we'll both become anchors, carrying each other down to the bottom."

She didn't respond, so assuming we were done with this conversation, I started getting my bag packed. Bailey followed suit, and, within 20 minutes, we were ready to start our walk to the river. The terrain was very rough along the short hike to the river, full of many short, but steep, hills.

As we got closer to the river, I noticed that the ground on the opposite side of the river was anything but encouraging. There were many steep hills, cut with rifts, where small streams issued into the larger river. I hoped that this wasn't a permanent change in the landscape, which would surely make the rest of our journey next to impossible. I put the thought aside and tended to more immediate matters.

When we got to the shore, we noticed that the current was moving very swiftly, the river being swollen from last night's rain. The mist had slowed to a very light, almost imperceptible spray.

The only positive factor that I saw in this whole endeavor of crossing the river was that there was a barren island, more like a gravel bar, several hundred yards long, straight across from where we were now positioned.

"We should probably walk another hundred yards upstream," I said, hoping that this would give us enough of a buffer so that we wouldn't be swept past the island by the current and end up having to fight across the whole width of the river at once.

"OK," Bailey replied, too distracted by the flowing current to give much heed to what I had said.

We would only have to swim about 40 yards between this shore and the closest edge of the island. It didn't seem that far, but with each of us trying to keep our packs afloat and struggling against the strength of the racing current at the same time, it would be no easy task.

"Alright, let's get our clothes off and into the packs, then get our packs into the bags," I instructed, trying to get Bailey to focus on the task at hand, and not on her growing fear of the river.

"Alight," she replied, and reluctantly complied.

I used some duct tape to seal the ends of the bags shut, and almost forgot to throw the small roll inside the second bag before I sealed it. Having done that, I used the rope to lash my shotgun and fishing spear to my bag, and used the empty sheathing from the gutted paracord to secure Bailey's gun and our shelter poles to her bag. Lastly, I uncoiled the 75-foot length of paracord and tied one end around my waist.

"Here," I said, handing the other end to Bailey. "Make sure you tie it tightly enough that it stays on, but not so tight that it restricts any of your movement."

"OK," she answered, her eyes wide with fear. "Are you sure about this?"

"No," I responded frankly. "However, I don't think we really have any other option. Just remember, use smooth, steady kicks. Don't panic... and, if you get into trouble, yell for me as loud as you can."

I checked and rechecked the rope that bound us together, then I double-checked the lashings that held our guns to our bags.

"Hey," I said with a smile, "at least you're not sitting in some boring classroom right now."

She managed a nervous laugh and a half-hearted smile. "Yeah, and I bet this beats being stuck in the office, right?"

It was my turn for a nervous laugh. "Haven't you ever heard the saying, 'A bad day in the field beats a good day in the office.'?"

"No, but let's hope it's true," she said doubtfully as we walked to the edge of the water.

The first thing I noticed as my feet touched the water was how icily cold it was. Immediately, alarm bells began to sound in my mind, trying to convince me to go back to the safety of the shore. I fought against the instinct to retreat from the frigid danger of the surging flow, and quickly waded a couple of yards out into the river, until the water was up past my waist. Then, with a quick spring, I lunged forward into the rushing current.

The water was so cold that it nearly took my breath away as the rest of my body, with the exception of my head and hands, plunged beneath the surface. I was shocked by how quickly the current was carrying me downstream, and instantly realized that I had grossly underestimated the danger of crossing the river. In that moment I also realized that holding the pack while still keeping my head above water was much more difficult than I had anticipated. Every time I kicked to propel myself forward, my face and hands would dip slightly below the surface of the muddy effluence.

I had made it about a third of the way across, when I hazarded a glance over my left shoulder to make sure Bailey was still above water. She was struggling to make forward progress, just as I was, but she still managed to somehow keep her face and pack above the surface.

"You're doing good!" I shouted in encouragement.

We had started out about 100 yards beyond the near edge of the island, so that we had an additional buffer against being swept past the land. I thought this would give us plenty of room for error. However, I was now beginning to worry as we struggled to the halfway point of this portion of the river, and were already past to nearest edge of the island, being quickly carried downstream.

"Kick harder!" I shouted aloud to myself.

We hadn't been in the water for more than a moment, but I could already feel that my muscles were nearing the point of exhaustion. I kicked again, as powerfully as I could manage, and then stole another look over my shoulder. Bailey was starting to panic and was in the process of doing the worst possible thing she could do, trying to stand up and touch bottom.

"Keep kicking," I yelled to her as I put my own words into action.

My face was sinking lower and lower in the water with every kick, and my pack was dipping deeper and deeper into the stream. We were two-thirds of the way across, and already at least half of the island had passed us by. My entire body ached from the cold, and my strongest efforts now had hardly any effect.

"Got to make it!" I shouted to myself again, hoping to rally my strength, "Kick! Kick!"

In desperation, I kicked much faster and much harder than I had thought myself capable of. My chest began to burn in protest, as I heaved, struggling to fill my greedy lungs with air. My heart was pounding so hard and with such rapidity that I thought it was going to burst.

Suddenly, the world disappeared into a swirling eddy of brown as my head unexpectedly dipped entirely below the surface. My limbs felt like jelly, now entirely numbed by a combination of cold and exertion, as I struggled to inch forward against the irresistible force of the river. Realizing that I was now fighting for my life, my head broke the surface, and spitting out a mouthful of silty water, I gasped for breath. A violent fit of coughing choked me as a scene of solid brown quickly met my eyes again, my head plunging below the surface yet again.

Another kick, weaker than the last, brought my eyes above water for a fraction of a second, then everything was swallowed by the roiling torrent of muddy water once more.

In this moment, a terrifying realization hit me: I was drowning! If something didn't change in the next couple of seconds, I was going to die. Last night's vision of Kyle came to my mind again, as I vividly saw him shaking his head. "Poor Ryan," I heard him say as the sound of the rushing water grew softer and my senses dulled. My body began to go limp and the scene of muddy, turbid water faded to black. I was losing consciousness.

"No!" I screamed under the water, fighting to survive with the last of my waning strength.

I kicked with all of my might, breaking the surface and taking a brief, desperate gasp of air. Franticly, I struggled to make it the last few yards to the island, but my best efforts were of no avail. Almost immediately, I began to sink again. In my heart, I knew that I was going down for the last time, and there was nothing anyone could do to save me now. The only person around for miles was probably gasping out her last breaths as well, engaged in a futile struggle against the unassailable might of nature.

Instinctively, I stood up in the river, subconsciously hoping to find the bottom of this raging flow.

"Hah!" I shouted in triumph as I discovered that I was able to stand, now being in only chest deep water. However, my elation was short-lived as the swift current ripped my legs from the bottom, sending me quickly downstream yet again.

Empowered by the realization that I was so close to the island, so close to solid ground, so close to surviving, I readied myself for one final, herculean kick, hoping to propel myself to shore. With all of the strength I had in my battered body, I plunged forward. Planting my feet on the bottom, I struggled to stand.

I might just make it yet, I thought, as my feet stayed planted firmly on the bottom of the river, and I stood now in waist deep water. I fought against the current as I walked toward the shore of the island, heaving, and bent with weakness. I was almost there, almost to the shore, just another couple of steps, and I'd be safe.

Suddenly, I felt myself jerked off of my feet as my body was propelled into the air.

Thud! My body made a hollow sound as it struck the ground.

My mind raced to understand this new dilemma.

Somehow I had landed on my back, with my waist in the water, and my head on the shore of the farthest edge of the island.

The rope! I thought, as I began to understand what was happening.

I knew that this could only mean one thing - Bailey had overshot the island and was being swiftly carried downstream. I planted my feet firmly in the mud at the edge of the island as I struggled to sit up, fighting against the force that was trying to drag me from the safety of the island and pull me back into the deadly current of the river.

"Help!" I faintly heard Bailey scream over the sound of the rushing water.

I looked up to see her still clutching her pack, as a drowning man would cling to a life preserver. She had indeed been swept past the island, and was now caught in the crosscurrent as the two halves of the river met together again after flowing past the island.

"Keep kicking!" I yelled as I struggled to reel the paracord in. I hoped that it would hold against the strain, knowing that the cordage was being taxed well beyond its limits.

Little by little, foot by foot, with the combined efforts of her kicking and my pulling, I was able to pull her out of the current and into the natural eddy that was formed by the island. Faster now, I pulled, and she kicked, until, utterly spent, she struggled to the tip of the island, and collapsed.

We lay there for several minutes, our chests heaving, too exhausted to move. Somehow, neither of us had drowned, and we had both managed to get our packs across the first half of the river.

"Are you OK?" I asked, after managing to catch my breath enough to speak.

"I think so," she replied, still breathless.

"Well, that was easy," I chuckled as I struggled to sit up.

"It's not funny," Bailey snapped. "I almost died!"

"*We* almost died," I shot back. "And, it's not like this is the first time we've had a close call. Remember how we got into this mess?"

She didn't respond, but just lay there catching her breath for another moment.

I looked across the island, to the eastern shore of the river. The remaining portion that we had to cross was narrower, only about 25 yards wide, and didn't look any more perilous than the half of the river we had already crossed. However, we were much weaker now, and I had serious doubts about our chances of crossing this remaining half of the river.

"We're in a bit of a jam," I said, hoping that talking through the problem would provide new insight.

"Yeah, and it's *your* fault," she growled, with eyes full of anger. "You almost got me killed."

"Did you have a better idea?" I retorted.

She looked down. If she had a reply, she kept it to herself.

"As I was saying," I continued, "we're in a tight spot here. I don't know about you, but I'm pretty wiped out after that swim. However..." I chattered, noticing for the first time that I had been shivering.

"However, we need to warm up, now!" Changing my thought midsentence, I realized that we were probably already in the early stages of hypothermia. I quickly peeled the duct tape off of the garbage bag covering my pack, and hastily located the Mylar emergency blanket inside. I also had to open the garbage bag covering Bailey's pack to retrieve the bedroll, hoping to insulate us from the ground, protecting us from losing more body heat.

Coming back beside her, I opened the two-person emergency blanket, and looked over at Bailey, who was shaking from head to foot from the cold.

"Get in," I said, the urgency in my voice leaving no room for argument.

She silently complied.

After she was situated, I squeezed in and pulled the blanket close around my body, including the top of my head, leaving only my face exposed. We sat silently, side-by-side, facing the western shore of the river, hoping that our body heat, reflected and trapped by the Mylar blanket, would warm us up enough to stave off the potentially deadly effects of hypothermia. After several minutes, our teeth began to chatter less, and our bodies shook less violently as we were slowly being warmed.

"That was a close call," I reflected, not bothering to look over at Bailey.

"Yeah," she quietly replied. "I'm sorry I yelled at you. I was just overwhelmed. I really thought I was going to die out there in that river."

"It's OK. I wasn't talking about the swim, though, I meant hypothermia. We should have warmed up right away, but I think that both of us were just too tired to move, let alone think about the dangerous situation we were in by allowing ourselves to get too cold. The thing about hypothermia is, just about the time you realize that something is wrong, your mind is confused from the shock, and even if you know what you need to do to get warm, you can't figure out how to do it. Another couple of minutes, and I think we would have been in really serious trouble," I finished, as a spasm of cold shook my body again.

"So what do we do now?" she asked.

"Well, what do we know?" I mused aloud, reasoning through the problem.

"That we can't stay here," she replied, the Mylar loudly crinkling as she shifted positions.

"And, that we can't go back," I emphasized, motioning with my head toward the western shore. She nodded silently in assent.

"What do we have?" I asked next, hoping that maybe we had overlooked some item or strategy that would help us get across.

"Our packs, our guns, and the rest of our gear," Bailey responded.

"And ourselves," I replied, thinking that we were the best resource to tackle this problem rather than any of the gear we had. "So, what can we do?"

"Swim," Bailey said, with dread in her voice.

"That's about it. I don't think there is a whole lot else we can do," I agreed.

"But we barely made it across the first time!"

"And we might not make it across the second, but it beats either freezing to death or slowly starving on some barren island in the middle of a river, doesn't it?"

After some thought, she reluctantly admitted, "Yeah, I guess it does, but I just wish there was some other way."

"So do I, but there isn't. Let's deal with reality now, and save the wishing for later. We've got to swim, so the sooner we do it, the better chance we have of making it across alive."

We sat in silence for several minutes, allowing our bodies to warm up enough so that it would be safe to attempt to cross this second half of the river.

Trying to formulate a better plan of attack this time, I said, "Let's try to jump out as far into the current as we can. I think we waded out too far the last time and lost the advantage that a strong lunge across the water would have given us. Let's plan to let the water get just above our knees, then jump into the river with every bit of strength that we can muster. Also, let's try to swim more diagonally, with the current, this time. I feel like we wasted a lot of energy trying to swim straight across, fighting against the current, instead of letting it work for us. Does that make sense?"

"Yeah, I guess so. I don't really know if there is a right way to do this, but whatever we can do to increase our chances of making it across is worth a shot," she reasoned.

We sat in silence for a few more moments, watching the water rush by as we allowed our bodies to absorb the ambient heat under the cover of the blanket. However, I was growing restless, fearful that the longer we put this off, the harder it would be to actually finish crossing the river. So, with a great effort of willpower, I got up and stepped out of the comfort of the emergency blanket. As quickly as I could, I stuffed the blanket and bedroll back inside my garbage bag, and sealed it back up again. Next, I sealed Bailey's bag and lashed our guns back to our packs.

During this time, I found my multi-tool on the shore, much to my surprise. I figured that I must have dropped it when I was swept off my feet by the force of the rope. How I managed to keep ahold of it that long, I'll never know, but I was very happy to discover that it wasn't lost forever. In the struggle for her life, Bailey had managed to hold onto her pack, saving us from a disastrous loss of gear. However, my beloved Spyderco Endura was somewhere at the bottom of the raging river, and neither of us had any interest in trying to recover it (if such a thing was even possible). It was a tough blow to lose a piece of gear that was both useful and had such sentimental value, but it was a small loss when compared to our lives.

With our gear packed up and ready to go, we walked to the other end of the island and tied the paracord around ourselves again. I looked across at Bailey, whose face was filled with terror. It was a difficult thing to face the river again so soon after it had nearly taken both of our lives.

"Remember, this side isn't as wide. It's really not that far across; maybe 80 feet at the most. We can do this. Just don't panic. If I get across before you do, I'll do my best to pull you in.... One more swim, then we're home free." I coached as we waded into the raging current again. I just prayed that what little strength remained in our bodies would be enough to carry us to the eastern shore.

Chapter 14

Running on Empty

Already cold from our previous swim, the chill of the water cut to the bone as we waded into the surging effluence. My heart was beating so fast already, I was afraid it was going to beat through my chest. I began to feel lightheaded as my chest tightened from the anxiety of facing death so soon again. I had underestimated this river the first time, so now I was struggling to keep my courage up as the water quickly came up to my knees. Taking another reluctant step, I felt the current trying its best to sweep my legs out from under me, as if the very water itself was affronted by my attempt to resist its power.

"On three!" I yelled to Bailey, who was standing a few feet to my left, staring at the water as if it was a writhing mass of venomous snakes, poised to strike at any second.

"Bailey!" I shouted. "On three! And remember, swim diagonally, and yell if you need me. Oh, and don't let go of your bag, or you'll be wearing just your underwear for the rest of the trip," I quipped, hoping to add a touch of levity to a very serious situation.

Taking a deep breath, I slowly let it out. "One… Two…" I hesitated. It was now or never, but the terror of the river was still too fresh in my mind.

I took another deep breath, and slowly letting it out, I tried my best to push my fears aside.

Looking at Bailey, I gave a firm nod, "Three!"

Splash! Immediately, the current took us, speeding us downstream with violent rapidity. I kicked and pushed and kicked and pushed, keeping my eyes fixed on the water just ahead of me, and trying my best to convince myself that I would be to the shore with each renewed effort.

This new method of letting the current work for us, instead of trying to fight against it, seemed to be working. After what seemed like just a few seconds, I looked up to see that we were already in the middle of the stream. Stealing a glance toward Bailey, I noticed that she was trailing a couple of yards behind me.

"You're doing great!" I yelled, hoping that my encouragement would ease her fear, which was still written very plainly on her face.

The frigid water, combined with my exhaustion from the previous swim, made catching my breath a futile endeavor. It seemed like the faster my lungs worked, the more oxygen my body craved.

After another 15 seconds of kicking and pushing, my limbs began to get than familiar jelly-like feeling, and my head began to sink lower and lower in the water. This is how my problems began the last time, so I knew that unless I reached the shore soon, I was going to be swallowed by the river, never to rise above the surface again.

Desperate, I looked up, hoping the shore was just ahead.

Five yards, I thought. *I can do five yards.*

With that encouragement, I found fresh strength and redoubled my efforts.

With a few more firm kicks, I found myself staggering toward the shore, my lungs heaving like a bellows. I dropped my bag on the muddy shoreline and stumbled to a half-seated, half-leaning position. I had nothing left to give, but I knew that Bailey would need my help; so in a supreme act of willpower, I grabbed ahold of the rope, intent on pulling Bailey toward shore. However, before I could begin to pull, and, really, before I even had a chance to look out into the river for her, I heard the splashing of footsteps coming ashore a few yards to my right. Bailey had made it on her own. Sometime during our brief swim, I had swam across her path, and she was now on the opposite side of me, where I least expected to see her.

"Piece of cake!" she said with a slight laugh as she lay gasping on the shore.

"Speak for yourself," I returned with a smile as I collapsed onto my side, my chest still heaving.

After a moment, I struggled to my feet and quickly retrieved the bedroll and emergency blanket back from my garbage bag.

Silently, we sat, side-by-side, on the eastern shore, looking out across the mighty river that had nearly taken our lives. Yet, somehow we had conquered it, at least that's how I viewed our successful swim, as an act of triumph over a worthy foe.

My muscles, utterly spent, could barely lift the limbs they supported, so I had my doubts about the amount of progress that we would make today. However, we had won a major victory; we were across the river and could resume our eastward trek, until we came across some other equally imposing barrier.

We remained on the shore for about a half an hour, resting our bodies and allowing them to warm up again (something I thought would never happen); then we prepared to move on again.

Despite the seeming eternity of our struggle against the river, it wasn't even mid-morning yet. Satisfied that the immediate risk of hypothermia was past, we quickly dressed, reloaded our guns, and packed up our remaining gear. Then, we slowly made our way up the steep incline of the eastern shore.

As we walked up the hill from the shoreline, the landscape leveled out for about 200 feet, then it curved sharply upward, leading to the peak of a great hill.

"It's going to be a long climb up that hill," I said, pointing to the grass-covered mound, more like a small mountain, several hundred feet high. "Nothing to it but to do it, I guess."

The mist had stopped all together now, and the clouds, though still covering the sky, were thinning, promising to reveal a glimpse of the sun.

"At least the weather might be better today," Bailey said, trying to be optimistic.

"Now if we could just get something to eat," I replied, realizing how thoroughly famished I was at that moment.

The walk up the hill took nearly an hour. Had anyone been there to see us, I would have been embarrassed by our sloth-like pace. We even had to stop and rest twice on the way up, which showed me just how weak we were becoming. However, despite the delay, we eventually made it to the top and were able to survey the fresh landscape around us. Beholding the land, I had mixed feelings about what I saw. Not much had changed to the north, south, and west, but eastward, the ground was rough and full of steep and rigid hills for at least the next mile. I thought I could see what looked like smoother ground several miles away, toward the horizon, but I couldn't be sure.

Two small bits of good fortune provided some comfort, despite the depressions I felt about the rugged terrain that lay ahead in our path. First, there were still several small lakes and ponds dotting the landscape, so we would have plenty of water along our immediate route. Second, there was a small patch of woods less than a mile to the northeast. At the very least, we could build a quick fire and drive some of the chill from our bones.

"How would you feel about warming up beside a nice fire?" I asked, pointing toward the newly discovered wood.

"I'd feel better about it if we had something to cook over it," she sulked.

I was concerned about how dark our moods were, simply because we hadn't eaten for a while. Everything seemed more difficult, more depressing, more dismal. In our minds, the possibility of ever making it home alive became less of a reality with each hour that passed with empty stomachs.

"I'm going to check every pond and lake along the way for fish, and either catch one, or die trying," I resolved aloud.

"Let me know how I can help," Bailey replied.

The thought of possibly finding some food was good motivation, and we came to the first pond within minutes. However, excitement soon turned to disappointment as we found the first pond devoid of any signs of life. We filled our water bottles, and moved on toward the next pond, but we were disappointed yet again. There was one more small lake almost directly in our path to the woods, and we held out some small shred of hope that there would be a big, juicy fish just waiting to be caught.

The short walk to this lake was filled with a mix of anticipation that we would finally get some food and dread that if we found none, we would be spending yet another day on the move with nothing to fuel our weary bodies.

I said a silent prayer as we neared the edge of the water. My eyes scanned the crystal-clear lake for any signs of motion. As I slowly walked the bank, my last inkling of hope began to die when, finally, I saw something flitting around out there in the water.

I focused my attention on the spot where I had seen a momentary flash of movement, and waited. There, plainly seen, was the shadowy figure of a large fish patrolling the waters near the shore. Little did it know that while it was looking for something to eat, so was I – I was looking to eat *it*.

I quickly dropped my pack, and took off my boots, socks, and pants. Fishing spear in hand, I waded into the water.

"Carefully, see if you can work around the shore line and get behind it, that way if it tries to swim off, you can corral it back toward me," I said to Bailey as she was taking her boots off, anxious to help.

Moving cautiously and deliberately in the freezing-cold water was torture. I was starving, and colder than I had ever been before in my life. Almost every fiber of my being was telling me to rush out there after the fish before it got away. However, a small, logical voice in my mind was wisely telling me to go slowly, otherwise I might ruin our only chance at a meal in days.

Doubt crept into my mind the closer I got to where the fish was lazily swimming. I knew my chances of catching him in this open lake were pretty slim, but I also knew if I didn't catch him, our chances of surviving were equally as slim.

As I felt the pressure of this moment, where our very lives were on the line, my mind harkened back to a high school basketball game I had played in, many years ago. It was the 4th quarter, and the game was tied at 62. There were 15 seconds left on the clock, and I had just been fouled while trying to take a jump shot. There I was at the foul line, knowing that the fate of the game rested on my shoulders. I took a deep breath, dribbled the ball a couple of times, scooted my toes up to the foul line, and mentally pictured ball going in. Struggling under the weight of this pressure, I took the first shot. Clang! It bounced off of the rim. After the referee handed me the ball for my second shot, I repeated my ritual again of dribbling the ball twice, scooting my toes to the line, and thinking positive thoughts. I shot the ball, and time seemed to slow down. The gym went quiet as everyone waited to see what would happen. The ball sailed in a beautiful, rainbow arc toward the net. I stood, willing the ball to go in. It was going to go in. It had to go in! Clang! The ball bounced off the front of the rim, and was immediately rebounded by the opposing team, who drove down for a last-second lay-up. We lost. I had choked.

As I recalled that memory, the stakes were much higher now, and the pressure much more intense, but I tried to push these thoughts aside and focus completely on the task at hand as I inched closer and closer to the fish.

Finally within striking distance, I ever so slowly dipped the tip of my makeshift fishing spear below the surface of the water. Then, I watched in horror as the fish readied himself to dart away.

I definitely wasn't prepared to strike, but I had no choice. In another nanosecond, he would be gone. I plunged my spear toward his body and instinctively closed my eyes as I tumbled off-balance and splashed into the water, still clutching the end of the spear with every ounce of strength I had. I felt the spear wriggle violently in my hand as I struggled to regain my footing, desperate to get the fish out of the water before he managed to shake himself free of the spear point.

Without giving much thought to what I was doing, I up-ended the spear and furiously swam toward the shore, splashing massive fountains of water as I went. I didn't focus my attention on the fish, the spear, Bailey, or anything else, I just ran toward the shore with everything I had.

When I finally got to the shoreline, in one fluid motion I stabbed the tip of the spear into the ground and knelt, pressing my knee against the body of the flopping fish. Fairly certain the fish could go nowhere, I pulled the spear from its body and gave its head two prodigious blows to ensure that it was dealt a swift and relatively painless death. Not even daring to breathe, I knelt, poised, ready to spring, in case the dying fish somehow managed to escape. Within a couple of moments, after it had given its last, limp flop, I jumped into the air and gave a whoop of elation.

"I didn't choke this time, did I?" I shouted to no one in particular.

Bailey was still standing in the lake, afraid to move. "Did you get it?"

"Did I get it?" I asked with a huge smile on my face. "Come and see for yourself!"

Immediately, all traces of fatigue seemed to fall away from us as I capered about while she dashed over to see the giant trout that I had caught. A sense of deep depression, which had clouded our hearts, was now replaced by a feeling of elation. I was amazed at the profound psychological effect the prospect of food had, but there would be time to reflect on this after our stomachs were filled.

It is a common occurrence that in a crisis situation, a person tends to get tunnel vision. Either this was the case, or I was extremely lucky, or both, because, as I examined the fish, I noticed that there was only one hole in him from the spear, and it was in the meaty portion of its tail, which was where I was focused right before I plunged the spear at it. A couple of inches up, down, or to the right, and we would have gone hungry yet again.

With our fish in hand, we quickly made a beeline for the woods, eager to make a fire and cook it. I was fairly certain that if there was one trout in this lake, there would be others and planned to go back to try to catch some more, either with my spear or with the makeshift fishing hooks. But, for now, the primary thought in our minds was filling our empty stomachs.

Once we got to the edge of the woods, I gave Bailey the folding saw and let her get started on harvesting some firewood while I gathered kindling to get the fire going. I decided that, even though it wasn't the wisest option, I would use a match and a couple of pages from *Rogue States* to get the fire started more quickly.

Within 15 minutes, we had a small fire going, and I left Bailey to feed it while I harvested as much wood as we would need for the next couple of hours. When this task was completed, I used my Model Five to clean the fish, saving the innards for bait. Then, I skewered the whole trout on a long, sturdy stick.

We couldn't find a suitable rock to use as a cooking surface, so I had to build another makeshift spit from two forked branches. All of this took about an hour to accomplish, but the time seemed to go very quickly. However, now, as the fish roasted over the open fire and we had little to do but to watch it sizzle, it seemed as if time stood still. Our stomachs began to ache as the scent of cooking trout filled the air.

Finally, we couldn't take it any longer and decided that, cooked or not, we were going to eat that fish. I could feel my mouth beginning to water as I pulled the trout off of the spit. Using my knife, I cut a piece of steaming, flaky meat from its side, and, oblivious to the slight burning sensation in my fingers as I grabbed the steaming meat, I brought it greedily to my lips.

There aren't words that can accurately describe the taste of that first bite of fish. It was sweet and succulent, and, in that moment, it rivaled the best cuisine from the best chefs that had ever graced a kitchen since the dawn of time.

"Oooh!" was all I could manage to say, as I chuckled with pleasure. Bailey quickly followed suit, and used her knife to cut a juicy chunk of flesh from the side of the fish.

"Mmmmm! This is amazing!" she said through a mouthful of piping-hot meat.

That was the last that we spoke for close to an hour, until, bite by bite, we had managed to reduce most of the 10 pound fish to a pile of discarded bones. Looking at the pile, I leaned back against my pack and breathed a heavy sigh of contentment.

"Now *that* was a meal!" I exclaimed with a smile of satisfaction as I looked across at Bailey.

"You're telling me!" she replied, returning the smile.

"What would you say to resting up for the remainder of the day, and hitting the trail early tomorrow morning?" I proposed.

"Yeah, I guess. But I thought you were wanting to push on as far as we could each day."

"I want to get as far as we can, but we've had a rough day, and now that we've had a good meal, I'd like to give our bodies a chance to recuperate. Plus, I'd like to take another crack at catching some more fish in the lake. The way I see it, the more food we can gather, the less likely it is that we'll starve."

Bailey relented, "OK. I'd do just about anything for another meal like the one we just had."

The clouds were slowly melting away, and the early afternoon sun tentatively peeked through the gaps, sending intermittent rays down upon the landscape as Bailey and I sauntered back toward the lake. I had baited the three bone hooks with some of the fish guts and was planning to try my hand at catching some dinner. I thought that a new strategy might work better than what I had previously done. This time, I had covered the whole hook with the bait, so there were no sharp edges protruding. This would hopefully keep the fish from spitting it out and prompt it to swallow the bait, hook and all, just like it would any other food. Then, when the bait and hook were in its stomach, I would reel the fish in, hoping that the bone would snag in its stomach, making it next to impossible for the fish to get free. It seemed like a good idea in my mind, but whether or not it would actually work was something that neither Bailey nor I knew. The only other fish that we had caught with a hook had partially swallowed it, so I took this as a good sign.

When we got to the water, both Bailey and I repeated the ritual of taking off our pants, boots, and socks, and then we waded out into the chilly water. It was something of a shock stepping into the lake, especially after having sat beside the warm fire for so long.

I gave Bailey one of the baited lines and explained what I thought the best tactic would be for catching a fish. I then waded about 25 yards down the shore, hoping to maximize our coverage of the lake. As I went, I trailed a baited hook in the water behind me, wanting the scent to attract some fish. I also carried my makeshift fishing spear, in case I was able to sneak up on some unsuspecting trout.

After being in the frigid lake for nearly 15 minutes, Bailey and I were beginning to shiver from the cold, and neither of us had anything to show for our efforts. I thought that maybe the other fish in the lake, assuming there actually were any, were further out toward the middle, in the deeper water. Based on this suspicion, I decided that I would wade out as far as I could, and give my line a cast or two before we gave up.

Walking ashore, I threw my shirt on the bank, then made my way several yards out into the water. Throwing both of the lines I was carrying as far as they would go, I waited in silence, shivering. I stayed out in this position for about two minutes, when I decided to get out and warm my body up. I was about halfway to shore, when I heard vigorous splashing off to my right.

"I've got one!" Bailey shouted as she struggled to reel her line in.

Excited, I raced to the shore and then rushed over to where Bailey was fighting to reel the fish in. This trout must have been big, judging from the difficulty she was having.

By the time I had waded out to her, Bailey only had a few more feet of line to pull in until the fish would be safely in hand.

Pop!

My heart sank as a stream of empty line flew back at us. Either the fish was too strong for the line, or its sharp teeth had sliced the nylon string into ribbons. Regardless of what had actually happened, the fish was gone, and we were going to go hungry tonight unless we could catch another one.

Dejected, we waded back to shore. I retrieved the bedroll and emergency blanket from my pack, figuring that we should warm up and then give it one more try before we headed back to camp empty-handed.

"Don't feel too bad," I said. "It wasn't your fault."

"I know. I'm just really disappointed. As soon as that fish was on the line, I had mentally caught, cooked, and eaten it, but now we're going to have to go hungry tonight. It would have been better if I hadn't caught it in the first place. At least then I wouldn't feel so let down," Bailey confessed.

"Yeah. Trust me, I understand. But, at least now we know there are more fish in this lake, and even if we don't catch any today, there's always tomorrow," I said, offering words of encouragement that I didn't necessarily believe in that moment.

After sitting for roughly 15 minutes within the warmth of the Mylar blanket, we decided to try our luck again. I handed Bailey both of the remaining lines, deciding to try to spear-fish while she used the two improvised hooks.

Somehow, I had the feeling that the only thing we would be catching today was cold, but I figured it couldn't hurt to keep trying. After nearly five minutes, I had walked half of the shoreline looking for signs of life in the lake and hadn't seen a single fish, when suddenly I heard the familiar sound of splashing coming from the opposite side of the lake.

"Got one again!" I heard Bailey yell.

I raced around the shore toward where she was stationed, hoping to help her land this trout. As I approached, she was pulling furiously, trying to get the fish in hand before the line snapped. I was almost at her side, and the fish was only a foot or two away from her grasp when... Pop! The line snapped. I made a desperate lunge with my fishing spear, but all I accomplished was soaking myself and splashing water all over Bailey.

I was livid! I didn't know at whom or at what, but I was afraid to open my mouth, lest I unleash a string of words that would make a sailor blush.

"I'm sorry," Bailey said, seeing my face turn red with anger.

"It's ok. It's not your fault. It's just so frustrating! We were so close!" I vented.

I felt bad for Bailey, and didn't want to make her feel any worse than she obviously did, so I changed the subject. "Well, we've still got the one line and hook, and there are few extra strands of string to make another line with. Maybe we can braid several of the strings together so that they won't snap as easily. Do you want to give it another shot, or do you want to go back by the fire and start setting up camp?"

"Let's go set up camp," she said, and then let out a little gasp. "Oh no! Where is the other line? I must have dropped it when I was trying to reel in the fish. It's got to be around here somewhere!"

We desperately searched for the line for the next couple of minutes. Losing it wouldn't have been a problem, except for the fact that it was tied to our last improvised hook. Search as we might, we couldn't see it floating anywhere on the surface, and the water was so cloudy from where we had disturbed the lakebed, that there was little hope of finding it in the water below.

"We can come back later to find it," I proposed, hoping to console her. "I was planning to come back anyway, hoping to find one of those fish that got away belly-up in the lake, so now this gives me another reason to come back."

The walk back to camp was cold and miserable, and much of the enthusiasm we had felt earlier had disappeared with the two fish that had gotten away. The one bit of good news was that the fire, which we had piled high with wood before we left, was warm, and we were able to comfortably dry off while sitting beside it.

Bailey and I sat silently beside the fire for quite some time, too contemplative to speak.

Toward evening, we set up camp, going a couple of hundred feet further into the woods to give us some distance from the cooking fire that we had used earlier. We transported a coal from this fire to get our campfire started. Then, after laying out sleeping bags, I decided to make one last trip back to the lake. I needed to refill our water bottles, and I wanted to look for the lost fishing line as well, even though I knew there was little chance of finding it now.

As I walked toward the lake, I also hoped that maybe, just maybe, I would find a dead fish floating on the surface of the placid waters. The chances were pretty slim, but this hope was all that was keeping me going at this point.

As I slowly walked westward, my mind was absorbed with the aggravating thought of how close we had come to catching those two trout this afternoon. Try as I might, I couldn't keep from feeling downtrodden by our ill fortune.

I was almost to the lake when the sharp crack of three rapid shots fired from a .22 rifle made me stop in my tracks. I had been around firearms enough to know that there weren't very many reasons to fire that many shots so quickly. This could only mean one thing, someone was in trouble.

Chapter 15

Feast or Famine?

Almost immediately, I knew that those shots had to have come from Bailey's rifle. There wasn't anyone else around for miles. However, I had no way of knowing for sure if she was in trouble. Part of me hoped that, just like the last time I heard her fire her rifle, she had just shot us something for dinner. However, the cadence of the shots seemed all wrong for that to have been the case. Hundreds of scenarios played out in my head as I raced back toward camp – most of them weren't good.

I began to ask myself questions as I sprinted the several hundred yards toward the camp. *Had the wolves come back? Was it a bear? What kind of game could she even take with a .22? Had she hurt herself and fired the shots to call me back? Were there other animals that were a danger to us out here?*

My mind, reluctant to dwell on these terrifying scenarios, kept flashing back to a few days ago, where, under very similar circumstances, I found myself sprinting toward the sound of shots from Bailey's rifle. Then, I had feared the worst, only to find out that, not only was Bailey unharmed, she had shot dinner for us. Maybe this time it would be the same... but I was almost certain that it wouldn't be. As I dashed toward the woods, I tried to think positive thoughts, but I couldn't help but have a bad feeling about things this time.

When I got about a hundred yards away from what had been our cooking fire, I began to shout. "Bailey! Bailey, are you OK?" I thought I heard a faint reply of "here," but I couldn't be sure.

I slowed my pace a little, and yelled again. "Bailey?"

The reply came louder this time.

"I'm here!" she shouted. "I'm OK, but come quick!"

I crashed through the stands of willow branches as I raced toward the sound of her voice, shotgun in hand. I slowed to take in the situation as I came within sight of our camp. Everything was undisturbed, the fire was still burning, and Bailey's pack was still sitting where I had seen it last. However, she was nowhere to be seen.

"Bailey? Where are you?" I called.

"Over here!" came the reply. She sounded like she was off to my left, about 40 yards away.

I looked over in the direction her voice came from and saw Bailey standing beside an alder tree, looking toward the sky.

"Come help me!" she said, not daring to take her eyes from the tree.

"What's going on?" I asked, as I worked my way toward her, fighting through the tangled mess of saplings and low-hanging branches.

Bailey glanced over at me, then directing her attention back toward the tree, explained, "I was walking over here to use the bathroom, when something moving in the woods startled me. I was already on edge from being all by myself, so when I saw it moving, I got scared, leveled my rifle, and tried to shoot it. I'm pretty sure I missed, because it ran away and climbed up this tree." She pointed skyward as I approached where she was standing. "Once I saw it climbing the tree, I realized that it was a lot smaller than I thought. It took a second for my heart to stop pounding and my mind to start working, but, eventually, I realized that this might be something we could eat.

"It's still right there in the tree," she pointed to a brown animal with a bristling coat of quills, "but every time I try to work around and get a shot at it, it scurries around to the opposite side of the tree. Can you try to scare it around to me so I can get a clean shot?"

"Sure!" I exclaimed, completely relieved that my premonitions proved to be false. We were safe for the time being, and with any luck, we might have dinner after all.

I worked my way around the trunk of the tree, hoping to scare the animal toward Bailey, but it had enough wit to sense the trap that we were setting and refused to budge. I thought about shouting and waving my arms to get its attention, but I was afraid of scaring it higher into the boughs of the tree, where getting a clean shot through all of the foliage would be next to impossible.

I began to walk slowly back over toward Bailey, hoping to come up with a new plan of attack. When I was a couple of yards away, I noticed that I had a clean shot on the creature.

"Give me your gun; I think I've got a shot," I whispered.

"Why don't you use *your* guns?" she hissed sharply.

"Because, if I use my shotgun, there won't be anything left to eat, and I want to save my handgun's rounds for a real emergency. Besides, we have more rounds for your rifle than for the other two guns. Come over here and take the shot yourself if you want, but whatever you're going to do, do it now, before he climbs any further up the tree."

Almost as if he had heard my words, our furry friend began to slowly, but deliberately climb further up the tree. Afraid that we were going to lose our meal, I started to draw my Glock, when my motion was interrupted by the crack of Bailey's rifle.

All was silent for a moment, then, as if pulled by an invisible magnet, the animal loosened its grip on the tree, and fell to the ground with a loud thump.

"Is that a porcupine?" Bailey asked, as we stood over it.

"Sure is!" I replied with a smile. "You know what else it is?"

"What?"

"Dinner!"

I didn't know how porcupine would taste, but I was fairly certain that it would be a lot better than going hungry.

The evening sun shone clear and bright as I field dressed the porcupine by our rekindled cooking fire. I thought that it would be a good idea if Bailey learned how to clean and skin an animal. So, instead of gathering more wood for the fire, she stood beside me while I showed her the steps involved in processing a game animal.

"First, you pinch the skin near the belly button, so it is raised up a little above the internal organs. Then, you use the point of your knife to make an opening in the stomach, like this," I said, demonstrating as I went. "Next, you cut the rest of the stomach open, up to the bottom of the ribcage, and down almost to the pelvis."

"Ew!" she exclaimed, putting hand to her mouth. "What's that smell?"

"That would be what the inside of a porcupine smells like," I chuckled, amused at her reaction.

"Now we turn this guy on his side, being careful not to get stuck by his quills..." I stopped, as Bailey interrupted me.

"Have you ever, what do you call it, 'field dressed' a porcupine?" She took her hand from her mouth long enough to use air quotes as she said the words "field dressed."

"No, but I've field dressed lots of other animals, and the process is basically the same, except deer, rabbits, and squirrels don't have pointy quills that can stab you. Ouch!" I said, just as one of the quills poked me in the hand.

I continued the lesson. "OK, now comes the gross part. You scoop out the innards, being careful not to tear the large intestine, at least not yet, otherwise the meat becomes tainted by the...." Thinking this might be a little too graphic of a description, I skipped the details, saying, "Well... just don't do it."

It took a moment to complete this stage of the process, and I had to focus completely on the task at hand. Once it was accomplished I looked up at Bailey, ready to explain the next step. I immediately noticed that she was becoming very pale.

"Alright, let's finish the lesson some other time. Why don't you go get some wood while I finish up here?" I instructed, trying to give her a graceful exit.

She was all too eager to comply and dashed off with the folding saw to cut down some of the standing trees that had died, many of which were so stunted from the cold climate that they were more like bushes. By the time she had returned with her first load of wood, I was almost done skinning the porcupine.

"Let's both run up to the lake and rinse this guy off before we cook him," I said.

After we returned from the lake, the sky was turning a deep and vibrant orange as the sun began to dip below the horizon, to the west. What had started as one of the worst days I had ever lived through was now ending on a high note. I thought it was strange how I could go from feeling utter despair, almost dreading every second that passed and fearing what disappointment each new moment might bring, to feeling pure joy at seeing the beauty of the sunset, all within so short a span of time.

"Well, let's hope it's going to taste better than it smells," I opined as I placed the body of the porcupine upon our makeshift spit.

"Yuck! I don't think I'll ever be able to get that nasty smell out of my nostrils," Bailey said as she wrinkled her nose.

I laughed a good, hearty laugh as Bailey looked over at me, full of chagrin.

"What?" she asked, slightly offended.

"Nothing," I chuckled. "You're just such a little princess sometimes. But, I guess I was a little grossed out the first time I had to field dress an animal." I said, trying to smooth any feathers that I may have ruffled with my comment.

"I am not a princess!" she gasped with a forced look of shock on her face.

"Suit yourself... princess," I grinned, unable to resist taking so easy a shot.

"Humph!" she pouted as she crossed her arms.

In all reality, I was actually very impressed with Bailey. She seemed to have changed a good deal since the first day we had met. Then, she had talked in vague platitudes about the problems of mankind, and how this or that government program would fix them. While winsome, she had seemed somewhat smug and condescending about the moral superiority of her positions. Now she focused on the issues related to keeping us alive and seemed to recognize that all the talking points in the world couldn't help with that. Then, she had cringed at the sight of a gun, and had a complete distrust of me because I was a man. Now, she was carrying her own gun, which she had even used to harvest food, and seemed to be comfortable with the thought of being completely alone with me. In fact, she seemed to have entirely changed the way she interacted with me. She was much more open and vulnerable now and seemed to genuinely care about me as an individual, and not just the means of getting her back to civilization. There was definitely more to Bailey than I had initially given her credit for.

And I was changing too, in my own way. I was no longer worried about where I fit in in life. I was simply concerned with staying alive, and was content to be living, even if it meant I had none of the answers to the existential questions that had plagued me for most of my life. Also, I was becoming more confident in myself, flaws and all. I had come to realize that all of the suffering I had gone through, all of my shortcomings, all that I both liked and disliked about myself had made me into who I was. During all of this time that Bailey and I had been struggling to survive, something had happened that all of my years of "normal life" had not been able to accomplish, I had become a man. Sure, I was already a fully grown adult male, but I had lacked the emotional and intellectual maturity and confidence of a man, being perpetually stuck in a state of mental adolescence. But now, through this experience, I had discovered within myself depths of courage and resolve that I had never known before. I didn't know what life would be like if we made it back to civilization, but I knew that I would never be the same again.

After a few minutes, the conversation resumed while we waited for the porcupine to finish cooking.

"You know, I've been meaning to ask you," Bailey began, "about that leather patch on your pack. I've noticed it as we've walked along, but I'm not sure that I know what it means."

"That's a patch that I got from an acquaintance of mine. It says, 'Not all those who wander are lost.' There is, of course the literal meaning, but my own personal interpretation is that a lot of people 'wander' in life because they lack direction, or, more accurately, they're lost. They have an idea of where they want to go, but they lack the understanding or the will to find the way to get them there. So, they wander aimlessly, hoping that someone will come along and put them on the right path. However, some people just weren't made for following the 'trail.' They may not take the conventional route to get to where they are going, but, not only do they know where they want to go, they know the way to get there, even if it lay through a trackless wilderness. Although, at first glance, it may be hard to tell them apart from those who are lost, they *choose* to not follow the trail, because they don't *need* to follow it. I'm doing a bad job of explaining, but I think you understand what I mean."

"No, I think you did a good job of explaining," she encouraged. "So, you don't think you're lost?"

"It depends," I replied. "If you mean literally, then, no, I don't think I'm lost. I have a good idea where we're headed, even though I may not know exactly how to get us there. But if, as I guess, you mean in life, then I most definitely was. But, the irony is that I thought that I wasn't. Before, I had the arrogance to think that while most of the people around me were lost, I was just a wanderer. But now I feel like, through the course of all that we've gone through so far, I'm beginning to find out who I really am... so, no, I don't think I'm lost. Or, at the very least, I'm finally beginning to find myself." I paused. "How about you? Are you lost?"

She looked away. She didn't mind asking me the question, but she seemed uncomfortable with having to answer it herself.

"I don't know…. I… It's hard to explain… I…"

"You think you're lost, but don't like what that means?" I asked, feeling like I understood.

"Something like that," she replied evasively.

Bailey and I sat for a moment, both of us staring contemplatively into the fire.

"It's just…" she began, having either gathered her thoughts, or worked up the courage to speak her mind. "It's just that everything I thought I knew, everything I was so sure of, everything I had based my understanding of the world upon… out here, having experienced everything that I have gone through over the past few days… everything I believed before just seems so trite and superficial. I feel like the ideological foundation of my life has been removed, and everything that I had built on top of it is crumbling around me. I just don't know what to think anymore. I don't even know if I'm lost, because I'm not even sure that I know where I want to go, let alone how to get there…. Why does life have to be so complicated?"

I had no reply, for that was a question that even the wise cannot answer.

We both reverted to gazing into the fire, wrestling with our own internal struggles. After quite a while of brooding silence, I felt the need to lighten the mood. Glancing over at Bailey, I said, "This guy should be just about ready to eat. Are you brave enough to take the first bite, or are you going to throw me under the bus and make me do it?"

"I'll do it," she replied stoically, as she cut a piece of the steaming meat from the porcupine's carcass. I watched as she reluctantly put it into her mouth, as if it were some piece of filth she was being forced to choke down. The look of disgust on her face changed to one of confusion, then to an expression of surprise.

"It's actually kind of good!" she exclaimed with a smile.

I wasn't sure whether or not to believe her, but there was only one way to find out. So, cutting a hunk of smoking meat from the porcupine, I hesitantly popped it into my mouth. She was right. It was good. Not nearly as succulent as the salmon we had earlier in the day, but it was definitely better than going hungry for the night.

The night wore on as we sat eating and talking, until the moon began to rise. Then, with full stomachs and tired bodies, we put out the cooking fire and headed back to camp. We still had a little bit of meat left over, which I hung in a bear bag by the cooking fire, hoping to eat it for breakfast in the morning. Before turning in for the night, I cut some more wood and threw it on our campfire and then headed to bed, where I fell into a deep and peaceful sleep.

The sun had already risen by the time I had woken up, and the woods were filled with the light of a new day. Bailey had awakened before me and had already packed up her sleeping bag and bedroll.

It was still very early in the morning, but judging from the preparations she had already made for departure, I could tell that she was anxious to get on the trail.

"What are you doing up so early?" I asked as Bailey came into camp carrying the bear bag.

"I woke up about a half hour ago, and thought I might as well get things ready to go. I figured that there was no sense in sitting around when I could be doing something productive."

"OK, well let's eat some of that porcupine meat for breakfast. Then we have to fill our water bottles and tear down camp before we can get going."

Within about ten minutes, we had finished the last of the porcupine and packed up everything except for the tarp and tent pegs. Before we went to fill our water bottles, I made two quick entries in our journal:

Aug. 9 – walked 8 miles, camped west of river, no food.

Aug 10 – only walked 1 mile, hard swim... close call, crossed river, caught fish and porcupine.

This meant that today was August 11. We had been stranded in the wilderness for nine days – nine long, terrible, depressing, and yet also glorious and exhilarating days. Despite what the journal said, it seemed like we had been out here for weeks or even months. Actually, in some ways, it felt like we had always been out here, living in the wild. I was roused from my musings by Bailey's voice.

"Are you ready to go fill our water bottles?" she asked impatiently.

"Yeah, let me just put my pen and notebook back inside my pack."

At the lake, we filled our water bottles in silence while I scanned the surface of the water, hoping to see a dead fish floating somewhere out in the lake, having been mortally wounded by one of our lost fishing hooks. However, we had no such luck. The surface of the water was as still as a sheet of glass, clear and inviting, but totally unobstructed by any object on its surface.

After filling our bottles, we walked back to camp and double-checked to make sure we hadn't left anything behind. Satisfied that everything was in order, we started our day's journey, hoping to make it one step closer to our families, friends, and homes.

Chapter 16

Between a Rock and a Hard Place

After walking only a hundred yard eastward, we came out of the little wood that we had camped in and were once again on a vast, open expanse of rugged grassland. The sky was clear, and the morning was the warmest one we had experienced so far, but it was still far too cool to be considered summer, at least by anyone who lived in the Lower 48.

The first mile of hiking was extremely difficult. The ground was a series of steep, rocky hills. Finding solid footing while climbing up and down these ridges was a tenuous proposition, and we had to go very slowly. Several times both Bailey and I lost our footing on the way down one of these hills, and were only saved from tumbling to the bottom by an instinctive use of our walking sticks.

After we finally made it through this nearly impassible series of peaks and valleys, the terrain became much less aggressive. In fact, if it wasn't for the snowcapped mountains jutting toward the sky to the south, and sporadically dotting the landscape to the east, I might have easily been convinced that I was looking out upon some vast rolling plain of sagebrush in the Midwest.

We walked steadily, talking seldom, until mid-morning, when we stopped for a brief rest. I hadn't checked my arm since the last bandage change, so I took advantage of the break to see if it was beginning to heal. The bruising had yellowed, and was even beginning to fade in some areas. However, I looked at the puncture wound with some concern. It was scabbed over now, but the area surrounding the scab was red and irritated. It still didn't look like a full-blown infection, but I realized that it could easily turn into one. Since the wound was closed, and we were out of gauze pads, I opted to put a large Band-Aid over it, hoping that this would keep the area clean and protected. However, we were also beginning to run low on Band-Aids too, since we had been using them throughout the course of the journey to cover blistered areas on our feet.

The longer we stayed out in the wilderness, the more I became convinced that we were dreadfully undersupplied. We were still a long way from home, and we were running low on almost everything. I tried not to dwell on this fact, but it was a concern that was steadily growing in my mind.

Once we got beyond the initial patch of brutally rough terrain, we made very good progress. When we stopped for a break around noon, I estimated that we had walked at least six miles already. However, the terrain, which had been very gentle for most of the day, was again becoming more difficult to navigate. About a half of a mile to the east, there was a steep, impassible ridge directly in our path. There appeared to be small gaps in it, where we might be able to get through, but we would have to walk at least one mile out of our way, to the south, before we came to such a spot. And, even when we got to the supposed gap in the ridge, we had no way of knowing whether or not it would provide us a way through to the other side.

After about 45 minutes of steady walking, we finally came to the gap in the ridge. Despite our earlier misgivings, we found the passage through the imposing wall of land to be relatively easy.

22

Once we came through the confining walls of the ridge, we encountered another welcome sight, water. After leaving the lake in the morning, we hadn't come across a single stream, pond, or lake during the day's march, and we were becoming concerned that we weren't going to be able to refill our water bottles for quite a while. However, the sight of the stream that now met our eyes allayed our fears.

We stopped to fill our bottles on the western shore, and waded across with relative ease, the stream only being a few yards wide.

"I doubt there are any fish in this little brook. At least, not here at any rate," I observed as we walked through the cool water.

"Yeah, the whole land, for as far as I can see, looks barren," she replied, dubiously scanning the horizon.

Having passed through the gap in the ridge, we were now in a gully, or small canyon, with a solid ridge behind us, and an impassible ridge before us. The new ridge, blocking our forward passage, extended, unbroken by any gaps or fissures, to the south for as far as we could see, but gently fell away the further north it went. There was no way we could continue eastward, unless we dared to climb the rocky walls directly in our path.

"Well, it looks like we've got to walk northward for a while," I said, disappointed at this delay in our eastward progress.

"Let's do what we've got to do to get out of there, then. I don't like being hemmed in like this," Bailey said, eyeing the ridges with obvious concern.

We had walked about a mile and a half before the eastern ridge had come back down to a level where we could finally proceed past it. However, any celebration we had about this apparent good fortune was soon cut short. After rounding a bend, with the western ridge still behind us, we discovered that what we had originally thought was a simple cliff to the east was actually a plateau, and we had just gotten past the initial edge. So, what we thought was a thin wall blocking our path was actually a completely solid wall, many miles thick. And, now we were stuck, like rats in a maze, in a valley that may or may not lead us to the plain beyond.

I stopped to survey the terrain ahead for several minutes before deciding what we should do. It looked like we could walk straight eastward for about a half of a mile, then we would have to bear north again, compelled to follow the contour of this canyon.

At this point, we seriously discussed attempting to climb over the ridge, but aside from the serious risk of falling, there was also the chance that we would just end up being dumped into a deeper valley or ravine once we got to the other side. So, in the end, we continued to walk with the contour of the terrain instead of fighting against it.

After walking for about a mile and a half, we finally came out from between the two enclosing ridges we had been trapped inside for the majority of the day, and the land before us opened up once again. I breathed a sigh of relief and hoped that we were out of the maze of canyons for good.

It had been very disconcerting being trapped in a valley between two massive walls of stone, especially since we had no way of knowing where they would ultimately lead. But, now that we were in the open air once again, the looming sense of claustrophobia began to leave us. However, despite our relief, new challenges lay in our path. All of the terrain around us, north, south, east, and west, looked anything but level.

With great effort, we walked along the rugged terrain until mid-afternoon when, taking the briefest of breaks, we continued our journey yet again.

We came upon another small stream, which was easily crossed, then proceeded on our journey eastward, making a detour around a mighty hill that must have been more than a mile in diameter and several hundred feet tall. The landscape, while it was as beautiful as it was rugged, became much more imposing. Both Bailey and I found it difficult to revel in its beauty, being discouraged by the slow progress we were making over the painfully uneven ground.

Once we rounded the massive hill, we espied another impassible ridge, rising high above the plain about two miles away. It was hard to tell for sure from this distance, but it looked like there was a small gap in the ridge, almost directly in our path.

I raised my hand and pointed, "Do you want to plan to head to that gap in the far ridge over there, then think about making camp for the night?"

"Yeah, I guess. Maybe there will be something to eat over there. I'm starving!" Bailey replied.

Her comment was disturbingly accurate. She was starving, literally, and so was I. Even though we had eaten a little bit of meat this morning, and had two solid meals the day before, the overall lack of food was taking its toll on us, physically, mentally, and emotionally. Throughout the day's walk, all I had been able to think about was food. It wasn't even so much about eating, but more about the calorie game that we were in – a life-or-death game, and as things stood now, I was pretty sure that we weren't going to win. We still had at least 75 miles left to walk, by my estimation, and, even if the terrain was all smooth and flat, it would be at least another week before we reached Route 11. Chances were, it would be more like two weeks, two weeks of constant exercise, a constant burning of calories, and only an occasional meal to fuel our weakening bodies.

I pushed this thought aside, and tried, for my own sake, to lighten the mood. "Maybe we'll get lucky, and stumble upon a flock of defenseless cheeseburgers."

She chuckled, showing the first signs of mirth that I had seen in hours, "You think of the strangest things... a flock of cheeseburgers...."

The thought of cheeseburgers kept us going toward the gap in the ridge, despite the fact that we both knew that no food awaited us at the end of the day.

As we closed the distance, the gap proved to be wider than I had first thought. It was at least 200 yards wide, allowing us easy passage between the two jagged sides of the otherwise unbroken ridge.

It was early evening by the time we entered the gap in the ridge. This gap proved to be a small canyon, or valley between the two ridges. It extended to the southeast for at least half a mile, which was all the further we could see, our view being blocked by a turn in the canyon wall. The rocky floor of the canyon was covered in tundra grass. There wasn't a tree to be seen, so we would have to go without a fire again tonight.

The sun had set by the time we had finished setting up our shelter, and the sky was starting to take on the greyish-blue hue of dusk. The clouds by the western horizon were painted in a majestic array of deep purple hues, touched here and there with dark orange overtones. Out toward the east, a few stars were struggling to shine through the lingering light of the sun, and the moon shone clear and bright, being already in the middle of the early night sky. Bailey and I sat looking up at the heavens, lost in our own contemplations.

After a while, I broke the silence. "Isn't it kind of ironic that something so hot can shine with so cold a light?"

"What?" she blankly replied, coming out of her trance.

"The stars. They're thousands of degrees on the surface, so hot it would instantly incinerate you or me. But to me, looking at the light right now, they seem so cold and remote."

"I've never really thought about it," she said, looking over at me for a moment, then looking back up at the heavens, as if to judge whether or not I was right.

After several moments she opened her mouth to speak, "Do you think that somewhere out there, in space, there are people looking at *their* sky, and thinking the same thing about the stars that they see?"

Reflecting, I replied, "I've often wondered that... Sometimes I think that it would be nice if there was life out there, but other times the thought scares me."

"Well, we've got enough to worry about now I guess, so there's no sense in troubling ourselves about things that we don't understand," she answered dismissively.

"Yeah, I guess you're right. Let's try to get some rest," I said, as I made my way into my sleeping bag.

A distant howl, faint and eerie, came to our ears as we settled in for the night. Somewhere out there, much nearer than the distant stars, there was life, and it was searching for other living creatures, to prey upon them.

I don't know when I actually fell asleep, but I awoke sometime before the dawn, feeling cold and tired. I had lain awake for much of the night, fretting about the rest of our journey – about food, water, fire, terrain, predators, prey, river crossings, hills to climb, valleys to descend into, and thousands of other details that weighed heavily upon me. When we started walking toward civilization, I had envisioned a hard road, but, deep down, I thought that we could do it. Now, as I lay awake, without food, without a fire, and still at least a week from civilization, the certainty of death crept over me. At times, I had envisioned myself as cut from the same cloth as the great explorers of old, but now I knew that such thoughts were vanity. William Clark had been able to walk over 20 miles in a single day, through worse terrain than this, and here we were, struggling to get further than 10 miles a day. Zebulon Pike had climbed part of Pike's Peak in waist-deep snow, having gone without food for two days, and that was just a footnote in the many adventures he had survived. Now it was pretty clear that I was no Pike or Clark, but I wasn't a weakling either. I had some grit, and a lot of determination and even some skill in the outdoors, but this situation seemed, as I thought by the pale light of the moon, to be utterly beyond my abilities.

"Don't give up," I tried to tell myself, but my words lacked power. They were empty and meaningless, wholly inadequate to strengthen my resolve. I repeated them again, in my mind at first, then whispered them aloud to myself, over and over. As I lay, whispering words of encouragement to myself, from somewhere outside of my own mind, or so it seemed, new words came to me. "Therefore, I tell you, do not worry about your life, what you will eat; or about your body, what you will wear. For life is more than food, and the body more than clothes."

But I have to eat to live! I objected.

The stream of thought continued, undeterred by my objection, "Consider the ravens: they do not sow or reap, they have no storeroom or barn; yet God feeds them. And how much more valuable you are than birds!"

But people starve all the time! I countered.

"Who of you by worrying can add a single hour to your life? Since you cannot do this very little thing, why do you worry about the rest?"

With that final statement, the words ceased.

It had been a long time since I had opened a Bible, or since I had been to a church for that matter, but I still recognized these words as the teaching of Jesus. How wise they were! Yet, they were so difficult to accept.

As I considered this message, I couldn't help but wonder what all of my fretting was accomplishing. What was my worrying doing for me? Was it filling my stomach? Would it keep me from starving? Would it make the hills and mountains level, and fill the valleys we had to walk through? Would it speed us on our way, giving strength to our weary frames?

I knew that the answer was a resounding, "No." All of my worrying was doing nothing productive. If anything, it was making my situation worse. It had kept me up all night, further adding to my weariness.

I'm not going to claim that I ceased worrying all together – I'm human, and such a thing isn't possible. But, there, in that moment, I was given a new perspective on this whole ordeal. I wasn't any less determined to find food, or to make our way to civilization; in fact, if it were possible, I was even more determined to make it home. However, I was now much more willing to accept that whatever was going to happen was going to happen, whether I wanted it to or not. All I could do was my part.

I didn't know how long this new resolve would last, but when hope had utterly abandoned me in the darkness of the night, when I had been entirely consumed with worry, it gave me a sense of peace that I desperately needed.

I was pondering this change in attitude that I had experienced, when, to my surprise, I found myself witnessing the dawn of a new day. I wanted to get as early of a start as we could, hoping to make great progress, so I decided it would probably be best if I woke Bailey.

"Bailey," I whispered, hoping not to startle her. "Bailey."

She didn't stir, so I raised my voice a little, "Bailey, time to get up." This time she stirred a little, but still didn't wake.

I moved closer and knelt beside her, placing my hand on her shoulder and shaking her lightly. "Bailey, wake up…. Bailey?"

I suddenly felt my stomach tense up. She looked pale, and her brow was dotted with little beads of perspiration. Afraid of what I might find, I reluctantly stretched out my hand toward her forehead. It was hot, very hot. She was burning up with fever. We had no thermometer; however, I didn't need a thermometer to know that this was bad.

Dismayed, I sat beside Bailey, not knowing what I should do. I was fairly certain she wouldn't be able to walk, and even if she could, I knew that would be a bad idea. I also knew that we couldn't just stay where we were either. We needed to find a source of food and water, neither of which were in this canyon, but my options were pretty limited. I couldn't carry her, at least not very far, and definitely not while carrying our guns and packs as well. Leaving her was out of the question, even for a little while, since there was no way she could protect herself if a wolf or bear found her. Leaving our gear while I carried her was also an equally bad idea. What could I do?

As I puzzled over the matter, an idea came to mind. I could build a litter, place her in it, and drag it behind me. Sure, it would be tough to do, but it seemed to be the only remotely feasible option available.

I looked down at her, shivering with fever in her sleeping bag. "Hang in there." I whispered as I got up and set about the task of building the litter.

While seemingly a good idea, actually making a litter proved to be more problematic than I had imagined. First, I had a very limited selection of materials to work with. The only wood long enough to make litter poles out of was the two tent stakes (about five feet long) and our walking sticks. However, what we really needed were two poles about seven feet long, to provide enough room to lay Bailey on the litter and allow me to stand upright while I pulled it. No matter how I tried, I couldn't figure out a way to make a full-length litter with what I had. The last wooded area I had seen was several miles to the west, and I had no idea how far to the east the next one was. So, I had to improvise.

After about 15 minutes of deliberation, I finally decided that the only thing I could do was to make a short litter; one that would allow me to strap Bailey's upper body into it, but would leave her feet trailing on the grass.

The only other option I had seriously considered was to wrap her in the tarp, and pull her behind me, trailing in the grass. However, with as rocky as the ground was, this would batter Bailey's already-weakened body. So, in the end, the litter was the only option that would work.

As much as I hated to do it, I had to sacrifice our walking sticks to cut into slats that would support her body on the litter. I used the last of the duct tape to secure these slats to the two chest-high tent posts, which would serve as the litter poles that I would grip while I dragged Bailey behind me.

Once the litter was done, I had to find a way to load Bailey onto it and ensure she didn't fall off while it was being dragged. First, I laid the litter down beside her, and, as gently as I could, I lifted her onto it. Then, using the paracord, I cut four pieces which would serve as a sort of seat, keeping her from sliding downward and off of the litter while she was being pulled. Next, I cut three more pieces of cordage and tied her down to the litter around her waist, midsection, and shoulders, being careful to leave the string loose enough to allow her to breathe easily, but tight enough to keep her from rolling off.

Despite the speed with which I worked, it was midmorning before all of this was accomplished, and I still had to figure out what to do with her pack and gun.

After several minutes of deliberation, I decided that I would hang her pack from one of the support poles, near the top, and use the sling to secure the gun across the tops of both of the support poles. I knew that this would make the litter unbalanced, but there wasn't a better way to carry her pack, at least not without it continually smacking off of my legs as I walked.

After completing these tasks, I was finally ready to press on eastward, in hopes of finding food and water, and, hopefully, some help for Bailey.

Chapter 17

The Cold, Hard Night

Progress came slowly, and with great personal effort on my part. As the day wore on, my energy, already flagging, faded into utter fatigue. The terrain in this canyon became rougher the further into it I walked, and Bailey was continually jarred around as I drug the litter over the uneven ground.

Throughout the day, I stopped frequently to check on Bailey. She had been incoherent for much of the day. She sighed and moaned often, and her eyes had a distant, glassy look whenever she opened them. I had tried to give her water several times, but she vomited almost immediately after even the smallest sip.

Earlier in the day, I had hoped that this illness was temporary, but I began to grow more worried as the afternoon wore on with no sign of improvement in her condition.

By mid-afternoon, we had made less than a mile of progress eastward and were still hemmed in between the two steep ridges, forced to continue walking in the narrow canyon. However, I was now able to see what appeared to be an opening about a half a mile away. Out on the plain, beyond this opening, there was a small wooded area. This discovery gave me new hope, and I hardened my resolved, vowing to make it to the woods before nightfall.

I was utterly spent when, a little after sunset, I set the litter down beside the edge of the small wood. I had kept my vow, but, now that we were here, I wasn't sure that I had the energy to do anything other than collapse beside the litter and rest.

Throughout the excruciating walk that afternoon, the closer I had gotten to the band of trees, the more apparent it became that these woods surrounded a small lake. This was a stroke of great fortune. We now were at least able to keep ourselves supplied with water, and we might be able to find some food as well. However, I was now too tired to go any further to investigate our surroundings.

During the rest of the day, as I trudged toward these woods, Bailey's condition had only worsened. Her teeth were constantly chattering, and her forehead was perpetually soaked with a cold sweat. This fever was sapping her energy, and the fact that she hadn't eaten anything today only served to make her weaker. She was dehydrated as well and was in desperate need of fluids, but she hadn't been able to hold down any water, despite my best efforts to keep her hydrated.

I knew that I needed to do something for her, but there wasn't anything that I could do. Our basic first aid kits didn't contain any medication that could help. And, even if they did, she wouldn't have been able to keep it in her stomach long enough to do any good anyway. I did have a couple of bouillon cubes in my first aid kit, to help with rehydration, but I wanted to save them until she could keep liquids in her stomach. I figured that they would be most effective then.

As I sat there beside her, watching her suffer, I felt utterly helpless. My mind began to fill with doubts and fears.

What if she gets sicker? What if this is something serious that won't just go away? What if she is too weak from our journey to fight off this illness? What if... what if she dies?

I stood up in horror and began pacing back and forth as I contemplated this new and terrifying thought.

"She can't die," I said aloud. "She can't die!"

My mind began to race as the light around me faded with the last, dying rays of the sun. Watching the day lose its futile struggle against the darkness of night, I hoped that this wasn't a foreshadowing of what was going to happen with Bailey.

I laid out her bedroll and got her sleeping bag set up, then, tenderly, I lifted her, and placed her onto this makeshift bed.

At this point, I knew that there was little point in continuing our journey with as sick as Bailey was. I had pushed myself to my physical breaking point, but we had only made it a mile and a half, at the most, on this day's march. I definitely couldn't keep this pace up anymore and expect to survive. So, at this rate, it would be late October or early November before we got to Route 11, and Bailey would either have gotten better long before, or we would both be dead from exposure to the brutal cold of an Alaskan winter.

Pushing aside these thoughts, I kept myself busy with the task of setting the tarp up over where I had laid Bailey. I did my best to work quickly and quietly, as, by the light of my headlamp, I constructed the shelter. However, I was so tired from the day's exertions, that setting up the tarp was a painfully slow process.

It had been dark for a couple of hours by the time I had camp made and had gotten the fire started. Once these tasks were completed, I checked on Bailey again, but her condition had not changed. Feeling the need to keep my mind distracted, lest it wander into dark and troubling thoughts, I decided to walk the short distance to the lake's shore and refill our water bottles, in case Bailey asked for a drink at any point during the night. Taking a cursory look at the lake, I promptly filled the bottles and made my way back to camp, anxious to get back to Bailey.

I don't know how long I sat there by her side, watching her for any sign of improvement and praying that she would be better soon, but at some point the sharp sound of a splash somewhere out in the lake shook me from my dark musings. For the first time in many hours, I looked around me and was astonished to realize that day had come. I had been so engrossed in keeping watch over Bailey that I had not even noticed the coming of a new day.

I tried to give Bailey another drink, but almost immediately she vomited. I tenderly brushed her hair away from her face as she laid her head back down again. Briefly, almost fleetingly, she looked up at me with recognition in her eyes, and tried to smile. Then, the moment of lucidity vanished, and she went back to whatever world the fever had her trapped in. My heart, which had momentarily lightened at what I thought was a sign of her recovery, now sank deeper into the depths of despair. I knew that unless something changed soon, she was going to die out here, and there wasn't anything I could do about it.

She had to get better. She couldn't die. I couldn't lose her. I needed her. I... I loved her.

I love her? My mind questioned as if shocked by this unforeseen revelation. *Did I love her? How could I love her? I hardly knew her.*

My mind fought to make every argument against this fact, but in matters of the heart, the mind is rarely victorious. I *did* love her. Deep down, I knew it. However, until this very moment, I hadn't known, or even suspected it before. Sure, I knew that I liked her. I thought she was intelligent and attractive, and, the more time we had spent together out here and the more I had seen her change and grow as an individual, the deeper my appreciation of her had grown. But, I didn't think that I loved her. However, now, in this moment, faced with the reality of losing her, I knew it was true. I loved her.

"What a time to fall in love," I moaned. "This is the most impossible situation, at the most impossible time, in the most impossible place, under the most impossible circumstances!"

Looking down at Bailey, my feeling of helplessness redoubled. There lay the girl that I loved, and there was nothing I could do to help her, nothing! Utterly frustrated, I stood up and walked over toward the pile of cold ash that had been our fire and anxiously paced back and forth.

Time seemed to pass in fits and starts. Sometimes it seemed like it would take ages for a second to pass as I sat by Bailey's side, hoping to see any sign of improvement. Then, at other times, I would look at the world around me and see that hours had passed while I was lost in dark and morbid contemplation.

I woke from one of my fits of despondency to realize that evening had come. In fact, the land was already growing dark around me. My good sense, which had utterly abandoned me during the course of the day suddenly returned, and I gathered wood to make a fire. As I struggled to cut small limbs and branches, I was keenly aware of how weak I had become. I hadn't eaten anything for almost three days, and hadn't slept for nearly 48 hours. Fighting against my fatigue, it took nearly an hour to do a task that, three days ago, would have taken, at most, 15 minutes. With great effort, I split the wood with my axe, and then made several feather sticks with my Model Five. Finally, nearly two hours after I had started the task, I had started a small, but steadily crackling fire.

Once the fire was established, I took my place next to Bailey, resuming my anxious watch over her. Her fever seemed to be steadily decreasing, but she still couldn't keep even the slightest bit of water down. It was now two days since she had been able to take a drink, and I was concerned that she was becoming dangerously dehydrated. Also, the infrequent moments of lucidity had all but ceased; her mind was perpetually in whatever horrid dreamland this illness had trapped her.

I had dozed sometime during the night, and was startled awake by the voice of Bailey. "No. No. No!" she muttered in a fit of delirium. She kept repeating strings of incoherent words, punctuated every now and again by an emphatic, "No."

Her fever had spiked again while I was asleep, and she was shivering violently. Seeing the deterioration of her condition, I was certain that unless there was a significant change soon, she wouldn't make it through the next 24 hours.

I tried to give her a sip of water, but she turned her head away, refusing to even attempt to drink.

Utterly dejected, I placed my head in my hands, and bitterly wept. What started as a slow trickle of tears, soon grew into an uncontrollable stream of choking sobs. I say with no shame that I cried until the tears would no longer come, and then, completely spent, I drifted into a comfortless sleep.

Day had come once again and the sun was climbing over the horizon when I woke in a panic, fearing that Bailey might have died while I was asleep. Swiftly, I bent over her, and tenderly touched her pallid brow. She was still alive. Her breathing was shallow and labored, but her fever had gone down again during the night.

Though the sun was signaling the start of a new day, the dawn had brought no hope. I was now certain that Bailey was dying. It was only a matter of time before the only woman to whom I had ever given my heart would pass forever out of this world, leaving me utterly alone.

Taking her hand, I held it in mine, determined to sit beside her until the end. Oblivious to the world around me, I caressed her brow, as I spoke to her in tender words of love. If she heard, she gave no sign. She only lay muttering and shaking her head slowly from side to side, too weak now to even utter the "no," that had been so often on her lips during her fits of delirium.

I had been sitting in this position for hours, vacillating between the feeling of loving compassion for Bailey, and dark, brooding despair for myself. No words can accurately describe the torturous hell that I experienced as I hopelessly watched the life ebb from Bailey's body. Of all of the days that I had lived through, this one was the darkest, most pitiless day I had ever experienced. The sheer weight of my despair nearly destroyed both my body and mind. I knew that when she died, I would die too. Maybe not physically, at first, but I felt that my very spirit would cease to exist, leaving my mind trapped inside of the cold and hollow shell of my body, until, inevitably, it too would die.

I was trapped in this fit of morbid thought, when my attention was aroused by a steady, droning noise that was slowly growing louder. It was very faint at first, so faint that I wasn't sure whether it was real or imagined, but moment by moment, it grew into a discernible tone. It reminded me of the annoying buzzing of a fly or mosquito, only much deeper, like a steady, baritone note played on a trombone whose slide is stuck. Frustrated by this distraction, I searched for its source, but was unable to find any clue as to where it was coming from. It almost seemed to be coming from the very air around me, carried onward by some driving wind.

A sudden light of recognition flashed in my mind. *That sounds like... no, it couldn't be. There's no way. That's impossible. I must be dreaming, or maybe even hallucinating,* I thought. But, in spite of my misgivings, the sound continued to grow louder.

In disbelief, I looked out toward the lake to see the image of a single-engine aircraft, descending toward the surface of the water, like some bird of prey swooping down for the kill. In shock, I sat, frozen with doubt and anticipation as the plane descended lower and lower, until its pontoons touched with a light splash onto the placid surface of the lake.

As if the spell that was holding me there, frozen to the ground was suddenly broken, I sprang up and sprinted toward the shore.

What this moment meant to me is impossible to explain. I was paralyzed with fear by the thought that this plane, this source of salvation for me and for Bailey, might spring away at any moment, leaving only despair in my heart, where there was now a fountain of renewed hope.

They had to see me, I thought. *I had to make them see me!*

Flailing my arms with what little strength remained in my weakened frame, I screamed as I chased the plane along the shore. Suddenly, the engine shut off, and a grizzled, bearded face poked out from the pilot's window.

"What's going on here? What do you want?" the pilot shouted, taken aback by the discovery of a man in so remote an area.

"Help!" I yelled as I gasped for breath, winded from my mad dash along the shoreline.

"What?" he asked, still in shock.

Overwhelmed with emotion, realizing that this was actually happening, that there was a plane that could bear us away from this horrible, desolate wilderness, I broke into a fit of sobbing, and collapsed into a heap on the shore. A moment later, I jumped, startled and shocked as I heard the engine throttle up again.

"Don't leave me!" I shouted in panic, as the plane started to turn around.

He was going to leave me there. That cold-hearted excuse for a human being was actually going to leave me there. I vowed in that moment that if I ever made it out of this wilderness alive, I would hunt that man down and kill him.

Almost as soon as I made this promise to myself, I realized that neither my vow nor my anger were necessary. The plane wasn't leaving after all. The pilot was maneuvering the aircraft toward me, to the very spot where I was seated on the shore, still sobbing uncontrollably.

It seemed so surreal as the plane's pontoons came to rest on the shore just feet to my left, and the pilot jumped out and ran toward me.

"What's wrong, brother?" he asked with concern. "Are you hurt? What are you doing way out here anyway? Where's your plane?"

"Can you take us home?" I pleaded. As I looked up, I saw the faces of three more men who were getting out of the plane cautiously, as if they weren't sure what to do.

"You stranded?" the pilot asked, still not grasping the situation.

Struggling to master my emotion, my voice still thick with tears, I said, "Our plane crashed. She's dying! You've got to help me! Please!"

"Who's dying?" the pilot interrupted, waving the other men over. "Where is she?"

I pointed back toward our camp. "She's over there. She's really sick. Please, take us home."

Two of the men rushed over to where I had pointed. "Bill," one of them shouted "Bill, the girl's real sick. She needs help, bad!"

The pilot yelled back to the men, "Bring her on over here, Pat!"

He looked down at me and extended his hand, "Name's Bill. Bill Parsons. I'm gonna help you and your lady friend as much as I can. Why don't you tell me what happened."

As the other men made their way back to the plane with Bailey, I gave him a very abbreviated version of our story. By the time I had finished, the men had carried Bailey over and laid her beside the plane. One of them shot a grave look in Bill's direction, then shook his head sadly. Bill nodded, and walked over to talk with the group of men he had flown out to this lake. After a brief, but hushed discussion, he walked back over to me.

"Normally, I would call an emergency crew to come out and get you, but your lady friend is in real bad shape. I'm gonna load you two in the plane and start flying back to Fairbanks, right now. The sooner we get you two in the air, the better chance your lady friend has of making it."

I nodded as I stood up, anxious to get Bailey back to Fairbanks as soon as possible. "Just let me grab my gear," I said, taking a step toward camp.

"You ain't gonna need it," he said dismissively.

"Mister," I began indignantly, "If I would have thought that on the last flight I took, I'd be dead right now. Just let me grab my gear, and then we can go."

He nodded in assent, and I quickly grabbed my pack, the shotgun, and Bailey's rifle, leaving the tarp and all of Bailey's gear behind. Two of the men were loading Bailey into the back seat as I walked up to the door of the Cessna.

"You get in the back with her, so you can keep an eye on her," Bill said as he climbed up into the cockpit.

"I'll be back to check on you guys in a day or two," he called to the men who remained behind. "You all got your emergency beacon?"

"Yup!" one of the men responded. And with that, Bill fired up the engine, taxied out into the lake, and took off, flying us back toward civilization.

Chapter 18

The Adventure of a Lifetime

The plane ride to Fairbanks was frustratingly slow. Bill tried to keep my mind off of Bailey's condition by plying me with questions from the moment we took off.

"I didn't catch your name," he said as we climbed to our cruising altitude.

"Ryan. Ryan McQuaid. And this is Bailey, Bailey Reynolds."

He keyed the microphone on his headset, and said something that I couldn't catch.

"I'm trying to get an ambulance to meet us at the airport. I'm going to get ahold of the Alaska State Troopers too, so they can let your families know that you ain't dead."

"Don't you think we should wait to do that... you know," I motioned toward Bailey, whose head was now resting in my lap. "We don't want to give her family any false hope."

"I'll make sure they know the long and short of it," Bill replied, then keyed his microphone again.

This interrupted style of conversation went on throughout the whole flight, but, as distracting as it was, it allowed me to get some of my questions answered. One particularly shocking piece of information was that Bill hadn't planned to fly out to that lake today. Bill was a guide and outfitter, and we had been in one of the remotest lakes in his region. Two of the men with him were business executives that wanted to fly to a lake that, as they put it, "nobody's fished in before." So, it was quite by chance, or rather by providence, that Bailey and I ended up being rescued. Bill also told me that he had heard about our plane crash, but that the search had been called off after three days, and we were presumed dead.

I'm sure I must have sounded like an annoying child on a long car ride, because every few minutes I asked how long it would be until we landed, and if he could make the plane go any faster. Bailey was becoming paler, if such a thing was possible, and her breathing was growing even more labored.

Despite my anxiety and the urgency of the situation, Bill assured me that the plane was going as fast as he could make it, and that we were getting to the airport as soon as possible.

"In fact, we've got an ambulance waiting to meet us at the runway," said Bill.

"That's good. Just please hurry," I implored.

After what had seemed like an eternity, Bill informed me that we were about 20 minutes from the airport. "Oh, and, take this headset. I've got a surprise for you." He handed me a spare headset with a microphone.

Putting the headset on, I heard Bill's voice in my ears saying, "Go ahead."

There was a momentary silence, then I heard a tearful, but elated voice on the other end. "Ryan? Ryan is that you?"

"Mom?"

"Ryan! It *is* you!" she sobbed. "They told us that you were dead, but I knew you weren't. I just knew. I just knew!" she repeated, crying uncontrollably.

I hadn't realized just how difficult this ordeal had been on my family. I thought about them often on my journey, but I had no way of knowing the emotional toll that this had taken on them.

"I know this has been hard on you guys. I'm sorry," I said.

"Don't be sorry. We're just glad you're OK. You are OK, aren't you?"

"I'm fine, Mom. It was hard out there, but I'm alright," I replied. I noticed that Bill gave a sidelong glance in my direction, as if he seriously doubted the truthfulness of my last statement.

"I'm going to get ahold of your dad at work, and we'll be on the next plane to Alaska!" my mother exclaimed.

"Sounds good. I'll probably be at the hospital when you guys get here," I replied, not thinking of how the words might be taken.

"The hospital? Are you hurt? You said you were fine. Were you just saying that so I wouldn't worry? You –"

"I'm fine, Mom. Honest," I interrupted. "Bailey is really sick. We're heading straight to the hospital as soon as we land. I'm... She's... It's pretty bad, mom."

"I'm sorry honey."

"It's OK... It's just hard. I've spent every minute of this ordeal with her as my only companion. We helped each other get through this, and now she might not make it..." I trailed off as a fresh stream of hot tears streamed down my cheeks.

"We'll be praying for her. I'm going to call your father now, and we'll be out there just as soon as we can."

"Thanks, Mom. See you soon."

"Love you, Ryan."

"Love you too, Mom." There was a click, and then the channel was clear again. I handed the headset back to Bill, and focused my attention back on Bailey.

Within minutes we were making our approach to the runway. As we came in for a landing, I could see a series of vehicles, all with their lights flashing, waiting for us at the end of the runway. I had a moment of near-panic as the wheels touched the runway, recalling the crash landing from nearly two weeks ago, but my anxiety was not necessary. This landing was flawless and soon we were safely stopped, next to a row of EMTs, firefighters, police officers, and emergency vehicles.

Almost as soon as the plane stopped, a couple of EMTs rushed to the door of the aircraft and opened it. One of them climbed partially inside, helping me out of the plane. Once I was out of the way, he climbed inside, gave Bailey a hurried examination, and shouted to his partner to get the gurney and a bag of saline.

People were shouting orders, asking questions, and running to and from a host of vehicles in a scene of organized chaos. Someone kept trying to lead me away from the plane, telling me I needed to be examined by one of the EMTs. Initially I refused, saying I wanted to stay with Bailey, but after I was assured that she was in good hands, and that I would be taken to the same hospital, I relented and allowed myself to be led to one of the ambulances.

As I sat on the tailgate of the ambulance, an EMT checked my vitals and listened to my heart and lungs through his stethoscope. I saw Bailey being loaded into her ambulance as several EMTs crowded around her gurney. They all wore somber expressions as they hastily loaded her into the ambulance that would rush her to the hospital.

"What happened to your arm?" the EMT asked as he rolled my sleeve up to take my blood pressure.

"Wolf."

"Seriously?" he asked in disbelief.

"Seriously," I replied curtly.

"That's hardcore," he smiled, raising an eyebrow in surprise. "You're one tough dude. Let's get you loaded up and take you on over to the hospital. I want you to be checked out by a doctor, just to make sure everything is ok."

"Is that really necessary?" I asked, not too keen on the idea of a check-up.

"I think it is. Don't worry though, we won't wheel you in on a gurney. You can walk on in like the tough guy that you are. Just sit back on the bed and rest until we get there."

"Thanks." I looked up at him and gave my best attempt at a smile.

The EMT did his best to keep my mind occupied while we rode to the hospital, but try as he would, all I could think about was Bailey. When we got to the hospital, two nurses were waiting with a wheelchair to take me into the ER. Beside them were camera crews from several news stations. The nursed advanced with the wheelchair as I got out of the ambulance.

"I can walk," I said with another attempt at a smile.

Almost immediately, the reporters started shouting questions at me. "How does it feel to be alive? What can you tell us about the accident? Can you tell America about your adventures? What can you tell us about the girl?"

I was in no mood to be interviewed, and to be frank, I was annoyed at being bothered at such an emotionally difficult time. So, I just walked past, offering them no answers and giving them no recognition. Seeing that I wasn't going to give them what they wanted, the pounced upon my EMT, assailing him with similar questions.

Better him than me, I thought as I walked through the doors of the hospital.

I was ushered into a room, given a robe, and ordered to undress. I wasn't too fond of that idea, so I decided to compromise, taking my shirt off, but leaving my pants and boots on.

Almost immediately, the nurses started an IV, took my vitals, listened to my heart and lungs, and asked me a bunch of questions. I inquired about Bailey and noticed that the nurses exchanged a quick glance. All they would tell me was that HIPPA prevented them from disclosing anything about her condition, then they continued their examination. I had a feeling that they were really just trying to keep from telling me the truth about her condition, but I was too overwhelmed to push the issue.

I was growing very impatient by the time the nurses were done with their initial exam, and made it very clear that I wanted to see Bailey immediately.

"You need to wait until the doctor has seen you," was their only reply. I didn't have long to wait before a middle-aged man in a white coat came into the room and introduced himself.

"How do you feel?" he asked as he shook my hand.

"Terrible. Look, all I want to do is to sit in Bailey's room. Can't you just tell me that I'm healthy so that I can go and be with her?"

"Well, I wish that I could, but we need to take care of *you* right now. Bailey is in good hands, and we're doing everything we can for her right now. You... you're a different story. You're dehydrated and extremely malnourished, and I hear that you were bitten by a wolf. We need to make sure that you're completely healthy before we let you go. You wouldn't want to have survived all that time in the wilderness just to die from rabies, would you?"

"Rabies?" I asked incredulously.

"Yeah, rabies," he shot back.

I knew what was coming next, and I didn't like it one bit... rabies shots. Despite their reputation, the shots weren't as bad as I thought – they were worse. And, I was given the news that this was just one of four rounds of injections that I would have to endure. However, this distraction took my mind off of Bailey for a few minutes.

Finally, after taking a bag of IV fluids, having a chest X-ray, giving a urine sample, and having more vials of blood drawn than I could count, I was told that I would be allowed to see Bailey. When I entered her room, I wasn't quite prepared for what I saw. They had admitted her into the ICU, and she was in a medically induced coma. There were tubes and machines everywhere. I could hardly recognize her. The nurse that led me to her room looked like she was on the verge of tears when she saw my reaction.

"She's been through a lot," the nurse said, "and her body is starting to shut down. Don't get your hopes up too high...."

"Is she going to die?" I asked with an expression that said I wanted the truth, whether or not it was going to be difficult to hear.

"I don't know. It doesn't look good, but I've seen people who were worse off pull through." She took a long, thoughtful look at Bailey, almost as if she was willing her to get better, then looking back at me said, "I'll be at the nurse's station if you need anything." She hastily left the room, as the tears welled up in her eyes.

I sat for nearly an hour, just staring at Bailey, hoping that she would pull through, when a knock at the door brought me back to my senses. It was a police officer from the Alaska State Troopers.

"You Ryan?" he asked as he entered the room.

"Yeah," I replied, looking at him curiously.

"I'm Sergeant Holloway. I hate to bother you at a time like this, but I need to take your statement for our investigation." He paused. "Normally, we'd have you come down to the station, but seeing as how you're not doing so hot, and your girlfriend is in pretty bad shape, I'll just go ahead and take your statement here."

"OK," I acquiesced.

"Nice Glock," he said as he took a seat across from me.

I had been wearing my sidearm for so long that I didn't even think about it anymore. I'm sure I looked out of place, and, in retrospect, I was kind of surprised that the medical staff hadn't said anything about the fact that I had been wearing a holstered gun and a fixed-blade knife the entire time I had been in the hospital. However, we were in Alaska, and they tend to take a different view on firearms than many of the other states.

"Thanks," I replied.

"Why don't you just start at the beginning, and tell me everything that happened. Don't leave anything out. I'll interrupt you if I need any clarification. Oh, and just so you know, this is being recorded," he informed me in a professional manner.

I recounted the entire story as well as I could remember. He seemed relatively unimpressed throughout my whole narrative. In fact, he only asked for clarification on three things: the details surrounding Harold's death, the shooting of the grizzly bear, and the wolf attack. I informed him that we had kept a very crude journal, which was currently in my pack. However, I realized that, at the moment, I had no idea where my pack actually was. I had been so concerned about Bailey that I had left my pack in Bill's plane. So, theoretically, it could have been anywhere by now.

"Well, that ought to do it, for now," he said as he prepared to leave. "Oh, I almost forgot. We have your guns and your pack down at the station. You'll get them back in a few days, most likely, after we've had a chance to do some more investigating."

Shortly after he left, the nurse returned with a tray of food. "We thought you might be hungry," she said as she handed it to me.

Looking down at the tray, a feeling of elation, mixed with sorrow, filled my heart. I was overjoyed at having food, real food, food I didn't have to struggle to produce, right there in front of me. However, I was filled with regret that Bailey was unable to share in my joy at so welcome a sight as this plate full of life-giving nourishment.

"Thank you," I gratefully replied. "Do you know how long it's been since I've had anything to eat?"

"No, how long?"

"As far as I can figure, it's been at least three days, possibly four." I inhaled deeply and savored the aroma of what, at any other time, I would have considered paltry fare. "It smells so good!" I smiled.

"You poor dear," she said sympathetically. "You eat as much as you want, and if you're still hungry, you let me know, and I'll get you some more." She was halfway out the door, when she stopped and asked, "Is there anything else I can get you?"

Looking up from my plate of food, which I was already doing my best to clean, I stammered, "Could I... no, I don't want to bother you..."

"You just go ahead and ask, dear."

"Could I have a cup of coffee?"

She smiled widely, and said it wouldn't be a problem. Within a couple of minutes, I was holding a steaming cup of rich, black coffee in my hands. As I looked down at the cup, I slowly drew it up toward my nose and inhaled deeply, savoring the fragrant aroma. I felt like a new man. I had a full stomach and was drinking a warm cup of coffee. I was finally back in civilization, complete with all of the comforts it provided. Yet, somehow, it just didn't feel right – it didn't feel the same. I don't know how to explain it, but the bustle of civilization seemed to grate on me in a way that it hadn't before the accident.

After my meal, I experienced a deep sense of guilt for having eaten at a time when Bailey was unable to do so. I knew that denying myself the meal wouldn't have helped her. Yet, I began to regret the fact that I had eaten so heartily while Bailey lay, fighting for her life in the bed right next to me.

Pushing the thought aside, I walked over to the bed and stroked Bailey's lovely brow. "Don't you die on me," I said, in a voice thick with emotion. "I don't know if you can hear me or not, but I need you to be OK. I need you to make it. I don't want to live without you. I... I love you." I don't know why it had been so hard to get the words to come out, but now that I had spoken them, whether she had heard me or not, I felt that, somehow, she knew.

After several minutes of standing, my weakened legs began to give out on me. I sat down, my head swimming with all that had happened, and, after a while, the rhythmic beeps of Bailey's monitors lulled me to sleep.

I must have slept for quite some time, because it was dark both inside the room and outside. Some unexpected sound had awakened me. Confused and still only half-awake, I looked around the room, which was very dimly lit by a small lamp in the corner. It took me a moment to remember where I was and how I had gotten here. I tried to coax my stiff muscles into allowing me stand up.

A voice came faintly to my ears. "Ryan?"

"Bailey?" I asked in disbelief.

"Where am I?" she asked, her voice almost too weak to hear.

"In the hospital in Fairbanks," I answered.

"How did we get here?"

"A plane. Someone found us."

"Oh," she replied, sounding like she was already getting tired from talking.

"How do you feel?"

"Tired. Weak. Dizzy. My head hurts," she explained, taking a break between each statement.

A nurse came into the room, different from the one I had talked to earlier, and interrupted our conversation. Bailey almost immediately fell back asleep as the nurse checked her vitals.

"How is she doing?" I asked as the nurse continued her examination.

"Better, but she's not out of the woods yet," she replied evasively, then went back about her work.

I could deal with "better." After all, what had our odds been in the wilderness? We managed to beat those didn't we?

The next few days went by like a blur. Bailey continued to steadily improve to the point that she was scheduled to be released soon. My parents had come, and we had a heartfelt reunion at the hospital. They wanted me to come home, or at least stay with them at a hotel, but I felt somehow that my place was beside Bailey. I had managed to shower and shave and change into the fresh clothes that my parents had brought for me, and I was beginning to look and feel like a normal person again, whatever that meant.

During Bailey's recovery, Harold's body had been recovered, and was interred in Fort Yukon, where he had lived for so long. A chaplain from the hospital came by and held a memorial service for Harold, at our request. It was an intimate and private moment for Bailey and me, the only one we managed to have since we made it back to civilization. In the quietness of that moment, I felt that I had fulfilled my promise to Harold, and that somehow he knew and was grateful.

Bailey and I had our epic feast after she was released, eating bacon cheeseburgers and french fries until we thought we'd be sick. Oddly, I found it more difficult to talk to her now that I knew how I truly felt about her.

During a lull in the conversation, I asked, "What do you plan to do now?"

"I don't know. Go home soon I guess. School starts in a few days," she said with a melancholy smile. "What about you?"

"I don't know. Go home soon too, I guess.... It just all seems so different now, doesn't it? Like we don't fit in anymore. Like most of what goes on in the world doesn't really matter. Do you know what I mean?"

"Yeah, kind of. A lot of what goes on seems pointless to me now. So, I guess I understand what you're saying. But, I'm not sure anyone else would agree, or even understand what we mean."

"Oh well, I'm sure life will feel 'normal' again after a while," I opined.

We chatted throughout the course of the evening, but each of us avoided the question that was foremost in our minds, "What was going to happen with 'us'?" During her recovery in the hospital, Bailey and I hardly had a moment to ourselves. We were plagued with reporters from all over the country. Also, being some kind of celebrities now (I'm not sure why), we were constantly getting visits from people from all over the state of Alaska. And, now that we were finally alone, much like the married couple who, making their children the sole purpose of their existence only to find that they have nothing in common once the children move out, Bailey and I found that we were unsure of how to relate to one another now that we were back in the "real world."

A couple of days later, I found myself back at the Fairbanks airport, seeing Bailey off as she boarded her flight back to California. We parted with a tender kiss, and a vow to stay in touch. However, I couldn't help but feel empty inside. I had grown so close to her in such a short period of time. She was the only companion I had in the midst of our life or death struggle, and now we were going to be a country apart. Furthermore, I hadn't been able to work up the courage to tell her how I felt about her. Here was the girl I loved, getting ready to go back to her normal life in California, and she didn't even know how I felt. I told myself that there would be time to discuss our feelings later, but I couldn't help but feel like all I was really doing was avoiding the scariest possibility of all, the finality of rejection.

Before I left Alaska and went back home, I tried to find Bill, the pilot who had flown Bailey and me back to civilization, but he was out on a chartered flight, and wouldn't be back for at least a week. I left him a note thanking him, and I gave him my cell phone number and told him to call me sometime.

The drive home (there was no way I was flying) took almost a week, and I had racked up a few thousand miles on the rental car by the time I pulled into my driveway in eastern Pennsylvania.

Throughout the course of my drive home, I had learned that it wasn't just in Alaska that I was considered a celebrity. I was a household name throughout America, with my picture plastered on every newspaper in the country. The story of our adventure had also been aired on several national and local news networks.

When I finally arrived home, I had piles of mail waiting for me. True to Bailey's predictions, I received some marriage proposals. In addition, I received accolades from many supporters and also got several death threats from the animal rights crowd, claiming that I had wantonly murdered both the bear and the wolf.

Upon my return, I also learned that my former boss, Paul, had been fired. Not only that, but I had received an offer of reemployment with my accounting firm. Apparently the news of the crash had brought national attention to my personal story, and the owner of the company began to receive some unsettling questions about why I was fired in the first place. Paul had broken several laws by firing me for taking my vacation time, and the company could have faced a very costly lawsuit. So, Paul became the scapegoat, which was fitting, since he was the cause of the problem, after all.

Try as I would, I just couldn't seem to adjust to "regular life" again. So much of what modern society consisted of seemed shallow and superfluous. I tried settling back into old routines, including going back to my old job, but everything that I did now, aside from my leisure time, seemed more empty and unfulfilling than ever. The world around me seemed bent on destroying itself in a fruitless quest for happiness and fulfilment. The more I reflected on this, the more I realized that despite the trials, some of the most formational moments I had ever experienced were out on the plains of the barren wilderness of Alaska. Out there I had no social norms to adhere to, no proverbial carrot of success being dangled in front of me, no pressure to be just like everybody else. Out there, I was just engaged in a struggle to feed myself and make it back to the very civilization that I was now learning to despise. As I reflected on this, I realized that it was almost as if the wilderness itself was in my blood now, and I wouldn't be at peace again until I went back, not for an adventure this time – no, this time it would be for good.

Initially I recoiled from such thoughts, reasoning that to do such a thing would be crazy. But was it really, or was it crazy to try to force myself into a way of life that was sucking the joy out of my very soul?

One day, several weeks after I had returned home, I found myself doing something I never thought I would do... I was standing beside Kyle's grave. Though I had hardly known him, it somehow seemed fitting, since it was his death that had started me down this road many weeks ago.

"I just wanted to thank you," I confessed beside his grave. "I know you don't know this, but your death started me on a journey that helped me find my way in life. It made me question my purpose in this world and caused me to examine my motives for being a part of this futile struggle to get more material goods, while sacrificing my true happiness. I know who I am now, and, even though you may never know it, you had a hand in helping me become the person that I am today. So, from the bottom of my heart, thank you."

Earlier in the day, I had called Jake, my outfitter for the wilderness adventure that I had planned, but never got to take. He was the only contact I had in the state of Alaska, and he was the only person I thought might actually understand what I was trying to do. After a few moments of small talk, during which he said that he had heard all about my adventure, we got down to business.

"Jake, I'm not sure if this is going to make much sense to you, or if you can even help me, but I'm thinking of moving out there... out to Alaska. I'll cut to the chase... I feel like, after all that has happened, I'm a changed man, changed for the better. But I've finally realized that I can't go back to my old life. Things are different out there. The people are genuine. They don't care about impressing each other with what they can buy. They just want to live their lives, and are willing to help their fellow man when he needs it. So, I'm leaving my old life here, and I'm moving to Alaska, because that kind of life is what I was made to be a part of. In fact, I'm all packed up and just about ready to get on the road. How would you feel about helping me learn the ropes out there?"

"Don't worry, I don't think you're crazy," he laughed. "In fact, from what I've just heard, you sound like the sanest person I've talked to in quite a while. Of course I'll help you out. That's how it is with most of us up here. The land gets ahold of you, and it won't let you rest until you return."

"That's it exactly!" I said. I couldn't believe that someone else actually understood. "I'm thinking of buying Harold's old place up in Fort Yukon, so you and I might just end up being neighbors. Hey, maybe we can even go on that wilderness adventure I missed out on," I said with a chuckle.

"Come on up. I'll be here waiting for you," he sincerely replied. With that matter settled, I ended the call.

I had one more thing to do before I drove out of the cemetery and made my way to Alaska to start my life over again. However, this was the most terrifying thing I had ever done before, more terrifying than leaving the life that I had known for so long, more terrifying than facing down a grizzly bear, and even more terrifying that the plane crash that I had survived.

Pulling out my cell phone, I dialed Bailey's number, and hit the "send" button. This was something that I had done many times since I had returned home, but this conversation wasn't going to be like any of the others.

"Hey Bailey," I said as she answered the call. "Do you have a minute? We need to talk."

"Well, I'm just getting ready to walk into class. Can it wait?"

"No. It can't wait. I've already waited way too long to do this..." My heart pounded in my chest, my palms began to tingle, and my mouth began to go dry as I continued. "Bailey, I... I love you. I've known that I loved you ever since the first night that you were sick, and I thought that I might lose you forever. I've been too afraid to tell you before, because I knew that if you don't feel the same way, it would be just as final as death – I would still lose you, or, at the very least, I would never be able to have you in the way that I want, or, rather, the way that I need."

Silence.

"I'm leaving Pennsylvania, and moving to Alaska to start life over again. You know how I've felt about not fitting into this life, and I know that in some ways you feel the same. Well... why don't you come with me? Why don't we start a new life together? Why don't... What I really mean is... I know this isn't the right way to go about all of this, and that I should be there in front of you, looking you in the eyes right now, but I've got to do this now, or I may never muster up the courage again... What I'm really asking is... Bailey, will you marry me?"

In the moments of silence that followed, I realized that I had blown it. This was absurd. I had just asked a girl that I had only known for a few weeks to marry me. She had to think I was crazy! She probably didn't even care about me in that way, let alone love me. This was it; this was the end of our relationship. I mean, how could we even go back to being friends after something like this?

"You can't be serious." She paused for a moment, then continued, "It's crazy! How would we live?" Bailey said in a voice thick with tears.

"I've got some savings, and I closed out my 401K. I figure I have enough to buy a small house and pay the bills for a while."

"And then what? What are we going to do, just sit around in a cabin somewhere?"

"No, we're going to *live*," I replied, "really live. We'll do what we want, and not get crushed by this rat race that most people consider 'life.' And as far as what we'll do to make ends meet, we'll have plenty of time to figure that out. I've got an accounting degree that I could use, maybe I'll work remotely doing people's taxes or something.... Who knows, maybe I'll even write a book about our little adventure. But, you can't tell me that you're satisfied with your life the way it is now. You can't tell me that you don't want to get away from it all. You can't tell me that the life that you're living right now isn't stealing your joy and drowning you in a flood of meaningless monotony.... You can't tell me that you don't love me, can you?"

"No.... I can't tell you that. I *do* love you. But, this just... I just... This is all happening so fast. You're asking me to leave everything I've ever known for a life of uncertainty..."

"No, I'm asking you to start a new life with me, *our* new life. There is no certainty in this world, whichever path you choose. All I'm asking is for you to share whatever uncertainties this life may bring with me."

"You really mean everything that you're saying?"

"Yes, with all of my heart."

"Then... I can't believe I'm saying this, but... yes. Yes!" she said, breaking down into a fresh flood of happy tears.

"Bailey, you've just made me the happiest man in the world!" I shouted. And I couldn't help but think that this was going to be the adventure of a lifetime.

29580472R00162

Made in the USA
Middletown, DE
25 February 2016